D1572486

# BARBICAN

A STERLING McQUEEN SPY STORY

Also by Phil Valentine

*THE GOD PLAYERS*
*THE FIRST FACE OF JANUS*

# BARBICAN

## A STERLING McQUEEN SPY STORY

A NOVEL BY
PHIL VALENTINE

Oxley Durchville Publishing

Book Cover and Interior Design by Red Raven Book Design

Oxley Durchville Publishing
118 16th Avenue South
Suite 4-387
Nashville, TN 37203

OxleyDurchville.com


For information about special discounts for bulk purchases, please contact Oxley Durchville Special Sales at business@oxleydurchville.com.

For foreign and subsidiary rights, contact rights@oxleydurchville.com.

The Library of Congress Cataloging-in-Publication Data is available upon request.

Library of Congress Control Number:  2018942972
ISBN 978-0-9968752-5-7 (hardcover)
ISBN 978-0-9968752-6-4 (ebook)
ISBN 978-0-9968752-7-1 (audiobook)


Printed in the United States of America
10 9 8 7 6 5 4 3 2 1
First Edition

# ACKNOWLEDGEMENTS

Thanks to the staff of Oxley Durchville Publishing. Also to Diogo Lando and the team at Red Raven Book Design. Additional editing was provided by Susan Byerly and Randal Delbridge. Special thanks to Ronnie Barrett and Jordan Progar at Barrett Firearms for making the sniper scene as authentic as possible.

And to all the great writers of spy fiction who have come before me. Your work has brought me many hours of pleasure and inspiration. Sterling McQueen stands on your broad shoulders.

~Phil Valentine

# Chapter One

*Brussels, Belgium*

Worry occupied a special place in Professor Franz Gerber's mind. His slender frame paced the floor like a caged tiger, stopping to ease back the heavy curtain of his hotel room and steal a quick peek out the window to the street below. He wasn't cut out for the spy business. He tried to tell them as much. A wise man once said that worry is interest paid on trouble before it's due. Trouble had just called the note.

He looked down at the cell phone in his hand as if by staring at it he could will it to ring. He ran trembling fingers through his gray hair then reached for a handkerchief and mopped his brow. Once he made his deal and delivered the information he was getting out. He had vowed to his wife. He had vowed to himself. He was going back to his peaceful, mundane life. How he longed for the excruciating boredom of the classroom.

Although it was impossible to know what he knew and not get involved, he had managed to do just that until three months ago. What Gerber knew was absolutely radioactive. It couldn't stay contained within his head, of that he was sure. It had to be told, and once he had passed it along he would try to forget it. He wished he'd never learned it. The information had ruined his life, but to the people with whom he was meeting it was espionage gold. The faces had changed over the years, but the basic goal had not. It was all about information.

"Please excuse me if I cover territory already covered by Herr Hoffman," the German man said at the debriefing 25 years prior. "You were born in Lebanon, yet you are a German citizen?"

"Yes," Gerber said. "Because my parents were German citizens. I

1

believe the legal term is jus sanguinis. It is Latin for 'right of blood.'"

Gerber had become used to being asked the same questions over and over again, but in a slightly different way. They called it cross-questioning in the spy game. He was never sure if the person across the table was an intelligence officer or a psychologist. They all looked the same. They all talked the same.

"And what was your father doing in Lebanon?" the man asked, lighting a cigarette.

"He worked for the Lebanese University, but I believe he was also working for the German government. My parents moved to Beirut with my older brother and sister. I was born shortly after they arrived."

"You say your father worked for the German government. What did he do?" The man took a drag from his cigarette.

"I do not really know. We never talked about it. *He* never talked about it."

"You have said your father was terrified of Nazi images."

"Yes, swastikas, iron crosses, old footage of Nazi parades. He would make us turn the channel if it came on the television."

"Why do you think that was?"

"I do not know." Gerber scratched his chin. "He was obsessed with this notion that Hitler had escaped the bunker and was living in Argentina and that a Fourth Reich would rise. He had nightmares about it."

The man exhaled smoke. "Interesting. Your father decided to move his family back to Germany when you were 13?"

"Yes."

"Why?"

"I am not sure. Maybe because he got another job. I know my mother had been ready to go for some time."

"But he never made it home."

"He went on ahead of us." It was a painful memory placed in a box with old photographs. "He had some things to do before we could officially move back. Papers to fill out and such things."

On the last leg of his journey, Klaus Gerber was traveling from Zurich to Munich. Out his window a powdery fresh coat of February snow blanketed the moonlit rooftops of the cozy Alpine village of

Feldkirch. In a few hours Klaus Gerber would be in Munich. His appointment was for 9:30 in the morning with an official at the immigration office. The mountains and snow were far removed from the Mediterranean refuge to which he had become accustomed.

His eyes had just closed when he first detected something was wrong. A sudden jolt forward as if the train were stopping, then the sudden sensation of acceleration. The odd tilting of the train car at first felt like a mountain turn, but it became obvious it was something much more serious. The screeching sound of metal on metal, bending and twisting as it was never meant to be contorted. The screams were in unison, much like a roller coaster ride. But the terror of this ride was real. The lights of the train car were extinguished. It rolled over on its side. The front dipped down slamming bodies into one another and against the hard ceiling then into the sides of the car. Windows smashed under body weight. The cold night air rushed in. The train car followed the ones before it down into the icy grave of the Ill River. It was the worst train accident in Austrian history.

Gerber wiped away the memory and peeked out the hotel window again. He had tried to explain to the man 25 years prior. The West had a hard time understanding the Middle East. Gerber knew one could not fully appreciate the Arab people unless one had lived among them. He understood their culture and he could see the world from their point of view. In fact, he had tried to explain that point of view yet again at the Middle Eastern symposium he was attending in Brussels that very morning.

It was all too easy for the uninformed to become prejudiced against the Arabs, he told them, never knowing the political differences. The commonality of their religion and culture did not fully reveal the innate and deep-seated incongruity which boiled beneath the surface. Gerber not only understood it, he grew up with it.

It was because of that background and knowledge that he was anxious about revealing his secret. If the world thought it understood the complexities of the Middle East, Professor Gerber's revelation was going to turn that world and its understanding completely upside down. He was eager to rid himself of his secret, to let someone else worry about the consequences. But there was more. There was the information he just discovered that caused his stomach to churn.

The three masked men worked undetected on the hotel rooftop. Two of them strung a twenty-foot span of steel cable about chest high. The other focused all of his attention on connecting wires in a box just a few feet away at the top of the elevator shaft. With the steel cable in place, one of the men pulled a black mesh net from his rucksack. The other man assisted him in spreading the thin netting underneath the cable. On each side they attached hooks into eyelets in the thick cable and pulled them taut making sure each was secure. Each man wore an earpiece, and they stopped dead in their tracks when the cell phone rang.

Professor Gerber knew he was taking a chance making an intelligence contact in Brussels. It was hard to know whom you could trust. The ring startled him even though he had been pacing in anticipation of it. He immediately engaged the phone and held it to his ear. His heart was pounding. The palms of his hands were sweating.

"Hello?"

"Professor Gerber?" the familiar German voice inquired.

"Yes."

"Are you ready?" Gustav Wagner asked.

"Yes, I am ready." Gerber shifted from foot to foot. "Let us get this over with quickly."

"Professor, there is no need to be concerned. We are taking very good care of you."

"I will feel a lot better when I have passed the information—"

"Say no more, Professor. There is a taxi waiting for you downstairs. The driver has the number nine on a sheet of paper on his passenger side window. Get into that cab and only that cab. Do you understand?"

"Yes. Number nine. I understand."

"We will talk more in a little while."

"I am on my way."

"Auf Wiedersehen."

The professor hung up the phone and returned it to his pocket. He tried to put his apprehension behind him. He had debated whether or not to reveal his knowledge to his handlers, but recent circumstances left him no choice. As uneasy as he was about the whole affair, that

ship had already sailed. There was little he could do but play it out to the end. The images of his wife and grown son filled his mind's eye. He paused a second to savor the memory.

The masked man by the elevator control box motioned for the other two men to take their places. The two men slithered down the ladder into the elevator shaft. They waited in the dark for their next orders. The lights strapped to their heads made them look like miners, the black masks like soot on their faces.

The cable television repair truck parked across the street from the hotel blended into the background of a typical busy day in Brussels. Passersby paid it no attention whatsoever. Inside, elaborate electronic equipment lined the walls. Serious looking men sat in silence listening intently to what was going on in their headphones. Gustav Wagner unwrapped a flat circular cherry sucker and popped it into his mouth. It was a nervous habit exacerbated by the fact that he was out of jurisdictional control. As the team leader on this project from German Intelligence, he had to defer to the Belgian General Information and Security Service, or GISS. Chief Inspector De Vos was in charge. Making sure all the men in the truck were ready to go, De Vos pulled the microphone which was attached to his headset down to his lips. Gustav Wagner listened in his own set of headphones. No microphone.

Although the language of commerce in Brussels was French, De Vos understood the complexity of this particular operation. He had French-speaking officers but also Dutch, and his guests from German Intelligence, of course, spoke German. For simplicity's sake, the operation would be conducted in English and he reminded his officers.

Professor Gerber had rejected the idea of an escort. He didn't want to be seen in public with anyone official. Maybe a bit paranoid, but he didn't want to take any chances. Neither did Gustav. He was intent on seeing to it that the professor made his appointment.

"Yorick, he is coming your way," De Vos informed the gentleman pretending to run cable at the end of the hallway. "Mathias, make sure you do not lose your place," he barked to the cab driver idling out front of the hotel.

"I am ready and waiting," Mathias casually talked into the microphone hidden behind the sun visor.

"Seppe, when he comes off the elevator take him."

Seppe, sitting in the hotel lobby looking over a newspaper, nodded slightly to himself.

"Make sure he gets into the right taxi."

Professor Gerber opened the door to his twelfth floor room. He first double-checked his reading glasses in the left breast pocket of his suit then the hotel key card in his right pants pocket. Satisfied, he closed the door behind him and struck out nervously for the elevators. The cable repairman whistled under his breath pretending to go about his work. Professor Gerber inspected him with suspicion then pressed the button to call the elevator. Convinced there was nothing distrustful about the repairman, he turned his attention to tracking each of the six elevators, three to either side of the hallway. After a moment, the soft bell above the elevator dinged. The doors parted and the professor rushed inside alone. He pressed the lobby key more times than was necessary.

As soon as the doors were closed the cable repairman swiveled to make sure the professor had boarded. He then said into the cuff of his shirt, "He is on the east elevator, far left."

"Got that, Seppe? East, far left," De Vos repeated from the van.

"Got it," Seppe replied almost inaudibly under his breath.

Gustav rattled the sucker from the right side of his mouth to the left with his tongue.

The two men in the elevator shaft looked at one another in the darkness, their headlights illuminating each other's masked faces. They then scurried into position. The third masked man at the top of the shaft readied himself at the makeshift control panel. Attaching clasps to the elevator cable, the two in the shaft held fast to handles at the end of the clasps and swiftly descended.

Seppe folded his newspaper and headed for the elevator. He checked the location of his subject. Tenth floor, now ninth, eighth, seventh. Seppe refocused his attention on the people hurrying into the next elevator so as not to arouse suspicion when the professor disembarked. As he glanced back up he noticed Professor Gerber's elevator appeared to have stopped on the seventh floor.

The professor reached forward and pressed the lobby key again.

Evidently there was a glitch. His pulse began to race. Why wasn't the elevator moving? What could possibly be wrong? Every muscle in his body contracted. He quickly scanned the control buttons in search of the emergency bell. Just as the terror was about to overtake him, the elevator began to move again. Anxiety flowed from his body like an opened dam. He unclenched his fists and playfully wiggled his toes which, just a moment ago, seemed to dig through the soles of his shoes. He sighed and smiled to himself at his silly overreaction. He wiped his clammy hands on his trousers.

A thud drew his attention to the ceiling of the elevator coming from just above his head. The professor had no chance to cry out. Like a bolt of lightning two men swooped down upon him. Black masks, black turtle necks, black slacks, and black gloves concealed their identities. They said nothing. They roped the professor around both arms. They duct-taped his mouth, hoisted him back through the tiny hole in the ceiling, and replaced the ceiling panel. Gerber lost consciousness from the needle that one of the men stuck into his neck.

Before Seppe became too concerned, the elevator continued on its way. Sixth floor, fifth, fourth. He pulled his paper from underneath his arm and pretended to scan the folded front page. Third floor, second, lobby. The bell and light over the far left elevator on the east side rang and lit concurrently. Seppe kept his eyes on the middle elevator, but his attention was fully focused on the doors to the left. Anticipating their opening, he turned slightly, positioning himself to head back out into the lobby after the professor.

Just before the doors below opened, the two masked men atop the elevator simultaneously hopped aboard the middle elevator in the darkness with the now very limp professor in tow. They looked back over their shoulders at the rapidly shrinking image of the elevator roof below. The cool breeze whisked through the eye holes in their masks. They gently laid the professor down and crouched beside him to steady themselves.

The east far left elevator began to open. Seppe glanced over. He did a double take. No one emerged from inside. The doors began to close. He dashed over lodging his left arm between the doors just in time. The elevator was most definitely empty. Seppe's eyes darted all over the small elevator car. The professor had vanished into thin air. He pulled his cuff to his mouth. "I thought you said east, far left," he whispered with grave concern.

"I did!" Yorick replied defensively.

"Control, we have lost him," Seppe informed the men in the van.

"What the hell is going on in there?" Gustav demanded.

De Vos ignored him. "Attention! Seal the hotel! Seal the hotel!"

Yorick dropped the cable and bolted into the stairwell heading for the roof. He scaled the steps two at a time. He drew his pistol from the holster in the small of his back underneath his work jacket. In a moment, he was at the top. He slammed through the metal door leading to the rooftop. His feet hit the gravel roof. Pop! The bullet hit him squarely in the chest. The velocity of the impact launched his body backward through the doorway he had just crossed. His feet shot out from under him. His lifeless frame tumbled like a sack of apples down the half-flight of stairs and settled in a heap against the concrete wall. The masked man by the control panel paused a moment and watched the metal door slam itself shut. He ran to the door, opened it, and aimed his gun to make sure his target didn't move. Smoke leaked from the silencer. One look down the stairs told him all he needed to know.

Seppe took off for the back hallway. He hit the rear exit, and plainclothes officers were springing from unmarked cars screeching to a halt. Seppe began barking out instructions and pointing with his drawn pistol.

The two masked men from the elevator shaft hauled the limp professor to the middle of the net. Laying him down, one of the men pulled a black nylon strap from his rucksack. He wrapped it around the professor's waist. He then fastened the strap to the net. The two masked men sat down on either side of the professor and fastened themselves to the net. The third masked man tucked away his gun and sat down with the others inside the net, fastening himself in as well.

Because of its speed, the officers didn't hear the helicopter until it was just over the roof. A huge metal hook hung from its belly. Blasting over the rooftop, the hook caught the steel cable in the middle. In an instant the three masked men and the professor were hoisted up like a school of fish. The net twisted from side to side as the chopper cruised just above the skyline of Brussels.

Two officers ran past the dead officer in the stairwell and through the door to the roof just in time to see the helicopter in the distance. The situation inside the hotel was mass confusion. Everyone was talking into their microphones at once in three different languages.

"Nous l'avons perdu," the officer yelled above the confusion informing De Vos that they had lost the professor.

Gustav didn't need a translator. He snatched the headphones from his head. Crunching down on the sucker, he yanked the stick from his mouth and threw it to the floor.

"Scheisse!" he shouted, the miniature high-pitched sound of chaos ringing from his headphones.

# Chapter Two

*Twenty-Five Years Ago*

A young boy's heritage is easily cast aside by thirteen years of shaping and molding an impressionable young mind in a foreign land. Franz Gerber was officially German, but his emotional ties were with Lebanon. The friendships he had cultivated and the roots he had planted were all Lebanese. The vision of returning to his adopted homeland had never left him. Professor Gerber's dream came to fruition when he accepted a teaching position with the Lebanese University in Beirut, the very institution that employed his father. But it was never quite the same.

Lebanon had become a battleground for the entire Muslim world. Beirut was a keg of dynamite waiting to explode. Most around him were hopelessly trapped. This hell was the only home they knew. For them, moving was unthinkable. For Gerber, it was paramount. He knew what must be done, but merely picking up and leaving was not so simple for him now. He had the responsibility of a family.

She was a beautiful young Lebanese woman with flowing black hair and large chocolate eyes. Her name was Alisashad. Gerber simply called her Lisa. She had grown up in Hadath, just south of Beirut. Her father was a carpenter and her mother took care of the home until her untimely death when Lisa was only seven years old. Her father moved to Beirut in search of work two weeks after Lisa's twenty-second birthday. She had found part-time employment in the library at the Lebanese University. That's when she met and fell in love with Professor Franz Gerber.

"She was fascinated with my stories of the West," Gerber told his German debriefer twenty-five years ago. "She longed to see these wonders of the world first hand." He looked down then back up. "I sometimes wondered if she was in love with me or if she simply found solace in my tales of another land, a land which might deliver her from that tormented country. Frankly, I did not care."

"But you did not leave with her immediately. Why?"

"Her father. The bond that forms between a father and his daughter in the absence of a mother is almost indivisible. She filled a void in his life."

"But you divided that bond."

"I did," Gerber said. "Her father never liked me very much, but it became quite clear that he had set himself up to lose. In the end, he reluctantly agreed to our union."

"And then your son, Erich, was born."

Gerber smiled. The mere mention of his name brought joy to his heart. "Yes. Just ten months after our wedding day we were blessed with a son. And something changed that day. The violence and political upheaval had been intriguing, even thrilling, for a political science professor like me, but for a husband and a father they were terrifying. There were now two lives that depended on me for their very survival."

"Why did you not leave then?"

"Her father. She would never leave Lebanon without her father and her father would never leave Lebanon." Gerber's mood turned solemn. "But, of course, that all changed on that horrible day."

As odd as it may seem to the uninitiated, construction immediately following a terrorist attack was commonplace. Like ants rebuilding their hills after a summer downpour, these Arabs diligently set about the continual task of putting their lives—and their buildings—back together. Even in times of unrest, life must go on. The dark irony was the terrorists kept Lisa's father employed. His construction team was usually the first on the scene to start the rebuilding process. Such defiance in the face of disaster bolstered the spirits of the locals.

That day two men on motor scooters weaved slowly around the stalled traffic on the crowded street. They were dressed in khaki pants and white sneakers. Their heads and faces were covered with the same white material that covered their upper bodies. They wore dark sunglasses. They stopped just meters from one another, set their kickstands, and surveyed the area.

A worker tossed bricks up to another man on a scaffolding. He stacked the new batch of bricks on the wood plank at his feet. A man mixed sand with masonry cement and water. Lisa's father pushed a load of sand in a wheelbarrow up the sidewalk toward the construction site.

The two men from the scooters pulled the coverings from their faces. The man on the scaffolding wiped his brow with a handkerchief. In that moment of rest when he looked out over the crowded street he immediately recognized the danger. He yelled a warning in Arabic. What followed was a mixture of chaos, confusion, and screams of sheer terror. The concussion blew pedestrians backwards up against buildings. The vehicle closest to the construction site was engulfed in flames. Bricks, sand, and metal rained down on the street. A large plume of smoke billowed from the construction site. Motorists far enough away from the blast bolted from their cars and ran. It was an all-too-familiar scene of gruesome savagery.

"When he did not come home for dinner we knew something was wrong," Gerber said. "We turned on the television. I remember Lisa covered her mouth in horror. She knew."

Leaving the country Gerber loved, in and of itself, would be fairly easy were he alone, but a Lebanese-born wife and son made for a different predicament altogether. It was not simply a matter of walking across the border. Mounds of paperwork had to be filled out. Miles of red tape had to be overcome.

Immigration from the Middle East in that day was difficult even if a German citizen was involved. Gerber pressed his case again and again intent on moving his family back to his native land. With each stall and delay he became more desperate. He tried to carry on as usual, but every waking moment was consumed with thoughts of removing his family from this dangerous city.

The last few students trickled out of his classroom and Professor Gerber packed his briefcase with the day's lesson. The voices trailed off down the hallway leaving behind the still silence of the room. He erased the chalkboard. The voice a few feet behind him startled him.

"Professor Gerber?" the man inquired.

"Yes?" Gerber swung around to face him.

"You have been quite busy," the German man said.

"Do I know you?" He put the eraser down.

The man smiled slightly. "You have written quite a few letters to the German authorities."

"Are you with immigration?" Gerber asked.

"Let me get right to the point, Professor." The man produced identification from his breast pocket. "I am Agent Hoffman with the BND."

Gerber recognized the insignia of Germany's Federal Intelligence Service. He closely examined the card then handed it back to Hoffman. "German police? What brings you to Beirut?"

"You do, Professor." Hoffman returned the ID to his pocket. "You have something we want."

"*I* have something?" Gerber asked in disbelief. "What could *I* possibly have that you want?"

"Knowledge, Professor." He walked slowly dragging his index finger along the top of the desk as if checking it for dust. "Insight. Perhaps even the key."

"The key? The key to what?"

"Let me back up to the beginning." The stranger rested himself on the edge of Gerber's desk. "We have become quite frustrated with the events in the Middle East. We searched for ways to resolve the conflict, but matters only seemed to worsen. Then your letters began to arrive on the desks of various dignitaries. These letters each found their way to other branches of government concerned with resolving the problems in the Middle East. The immigration authorities shared these correspondences with us in an effort to help you with your plight. We were intrigued. Your background was thoroughly checked and it was determined that you were in a unique position to help us."

"Help you? How?"

"The decision to bring a civilian into a covert operation is not taken lightly, Professor. There is the potential of leaking vital information which could prove to be detrimental to the entire operation. Many inside the organization were adamantly opposed to your involvement for that very reason. I, on the other hand," he pulled himself up to a sitting position atop the desk and drew closer to Gerber, "I thought it worth the risk. So, this is an exploratory visit."

"An exploratory visit?"

"To see if you would be willing to help us with your knowledge and experience in exchange for expediting your family's immigration to Germany."

Gerber's eyes widened. "You can do that?"

"We can and we will, Professor, but you first have to agree to help us."

"Well, of course, but I am not sure how helpful I can be."

"I suspect you can be very helpful. You know the customs of the Middle East. You know the culture. What we need is insight. Insight that only one who is of the West but has grown up in this culture can give us."

"I do not know any terrorists, Herr Hoffman."

Hoffman smiled, "I did not expect you to. If you did, this would be a visit of a very different nature. We are not asking you to spy, Professor Gerber. We are asking you to help your country."

Gerber pondered the offer.

Hoffman removed himself from the desk and stood upright. "So, we have a deal?" he asked matter-of-factly, extending his hand.

Gerber hesitated, then shook the offered hand. "I suppose we do, Herr Hoffman."

With that, Hoffman turned and walked away. Little did the professor realize, but he had just bought his family's safe passage for a price. He had traded his soul to the most private club in the world—the secret society of international espionage.

# Chapter Three

*Present Day*

With the top down Sterling McQueen could feel the heat radiating from the concrete bridge as he passed underneath. The high pitch of car tires on the drying pavement after a brief summer shower whooshed past him and the breeze blew through his hair. The setting sun sent staccato bursts of light through the treetops.

Bach's composition of *Air* from his Orchestral Suite No. 3 in D Major played on the car's speakers. *Air* had to be played at just the right tempo, for McQueen's taste. Not too fast and certainly not too slow. Some erroneously referred to the piece as *Air on the G String*, but that was a bastardization of the original that was arranged by August Wilhelmj. In the late 19th century, Wilhelmj transposed Bach's masterpiece down from its original key of D major to C major. The first violin was transposed down a full octave so that the melody could be played entirely on the violin's lowest string, the G string. McQueen thought Wilhelmj should've been hanged for butchering such a masterpiece. He knew that when it was played as Bach intended it to be played, no more beautiful piece of music had ever been composed in the history of mankind. Although it was his favorite piece of music, he wouldn't listen to it too often for fear of diminishing its impact. Hearing it as infrequently as he did nearly moved him to tears.

He down-shifted and exited the interstate, steering his car into the heart of Annapolis just as the first violin held the high note above a slow, walking bass line then melted back down into harmonic perfection. When it was performed correctly it never failed to send a chill down his spine.

His Mercedes convertible cruised down West Street. He took in the warm evening air and merged onto Church Circle around St. Anne's Church then took a right up School Street toward the State House. He entered the encircling traffic on State Circle and thought about the history contained within the confines of that old State House. The magnificent structure had once served as the nation's capitol. Within the walls of that building, Congress officially ended the American Revolution. Down in the Old Senate Chamber George Washington resigned his commission as Commander-in-Chief of the Continental Army.

Probably not a word was uttered at that ceremony about the darker side of warfare. No mention of the New Jersey Continentals. At such victory ceremonies the nasty details of how a war is actually won are often forgotten, if they were ever really known. The tale of the two leaders of the New Jersey mutiny, whom Washington ordered to be executed by firing squad at the forced hand of their own compatriots, was one of those seldom-told stories. If Washington were to jolt the rest of the army back into line and stave off a mass desertion it was something that had to be done. And Washington was not at all afraid to do it.

But it's much easier to kill a man when all you have to do is give the order. It's a different story altogether when you're forced to use your bare hands. Madrid flashed through McQueen's mind. It almost seemed a violation of protocol, an egregious breach of professional courtesy. The lamp cord appeared an inglorious ending for a worthy enemy. McQueen had hoped for a more dignified killing, if he had to kill at all, but it was not to be. They were both professionals. They both understood the ground rules. One makes do with the tools at one's disposal.

McQueen's car almost instinctively guided itself toward the waterfront. He pulled up to the guard shack at the yacht club. The guard on duty recognized McQueen and waved him through. He parked in a small single-bay garage on the property to keep his car safe from the elements. It was a classic Mercedes SL convertible with relatively low miles that McQueen had taken months to find. He wished he could enjoy it more, but work kept him on the road most of the time. The car was red with tan interior and a black top. The V-8 4.5-liter engine purred as he came to a stop. He set the hand brake, hopped out of the car, and grabbed his luggage from the trunk.

"Can I help you with that?" The voice came from behind him. It was Ransy, a young apprentice of the marina's owner, a man whom Ransy called Cap'n. McQueen continued to walk as the youngster sidled up next to him.

"How ya been, Ransy?"

"I've been great, Mr. McQueen. Just get back from somewhere exciting?"

McQueen smiled, "Just another boring business trip."

Ransy looked a bit disappointed.

"Hey, you up for making a little extra cash?"

Ransy's eyes came back to life. "You bet!"

"I hope to have a few days off. Mind helping me get the old lady cleaned up?"

"Man, I'd love to. I'll take any opportunity to board that beaut."

"If you work extra hard maybe I'll take you out on her."

"Would you?"

"If we get her cleaned up in one day."

"I'll make sure we do, Mr. McQueen. Call the marina office. I'll be helping the Cap'n."

Ransy's father had been a mechanic at the marina and a damned good one. He had died in a boating accident when Ransy was six. Ransy didn't come from the best part of town and McQueen worried that with his father gone the young boy would drift down the wrong path. McQueen saw to his mother's basic needs. Anonymously, of course. He also talked the Cap'n into giving Ransy a job as his apprentice. Ransy worked weekends and summers at the marina and was there even when he didn't have to be. He stayed occupied and out of trouble and was saving enough to buy a decent car when he turned sixteen. McQueen would match his savings so Ransy could get him something really reliable. Like that would be a problem. He could take an engine apart and put it back together in a snowstorm. McQueen had allowed him to help him on his own twin diesels.

McQueen's unconventional version of what he called home was the culmination of a dream that dated back to his days at the Naval

Academy. He longed to one day find himself on a boat at the yacht club he could see at a distance across the bay. Since the Strategic Support Branch was headquartered in Annapolis, he set out to make his Academy daydream a reality. Years of squirreling away the cash had paid off. McQueen was able to put a hefty down payment on a beautiful boat that cost a king's ransom in its heyday. The 68-foot Trumpy flush deck motor yacht of teak and mahogany with three staterooms and a separate crew quarters had been fastidiously pampered by its prior owners but none more particular than McQueen. It had been custom-built for a Hollywood mogul in 1963 and several personal photographs from those golden years were found throughout the vessel.

The main salon contained a large mahogany built-in bookshelf at one end that housed McQueen's impressive collection of first edition and signed books. At the other end of the salon was a glass-door mahogany cabinet that held fine china and crystal. The rest of the room was elegantly furnished with two antique chairs and an off-white sofa. An abundance of rich brown wood was varnished and polished to such perfection, both topside and down below, that the entire yacht seemed to sparkle.

The yacht, the car, the books, they were all extensions of McQueen's personality. He didn't much care for fads or trends. He dressed tastefully but conservatively. He was never one to jump on the latest styles. Like a fine wine, style needed an adequate amount of time to prove itself. Just because a certain vintage was old didn't necessarily mean it was good. A 1991 Chablis was mediocre at best, and a 1984 was hardly worth pouring. Silly photographs of men dressed in thin ties with tiny knots or, worse yet, wide ties with large knots looked like action shots from a circus. Loud plaids and stripes were in and out of style usually before the sun set and McQueen cringed at the thought that grown men actually ever wore Crocs.

When it came to formal wear, a proper tuxedo was always black, not blue. The shirt was always plain, possibly pleated, but, for God's sake, never ruffled. Always studs and never buttons. A turndown collar instead of wings, unless, of course, you're wearing a white tie. Speaking of which, a civilized gentleman always ties his own bow tie.

The future was the arbiter of style, McQueen believed, not fashion magazines, not runway models, and certainly not anyone who wanted to be first for first's sake. Style was proven, not manufactured. Style was good taste marinated in time.

McQueen possessed the same sense of style when it came to his yacht. Most owners preferred the low maintenance of fiberglass, but to McQueen there was nothing classic about fiberglass. Plastic boats, as he called them, had no character. Nothing could compare to a vintage wooden motor yacht. The wheel just felt finer in the hand. Knowing that it took craftsmen months to construct it rather than pulling it from a Jell-O mold gave it lasting meaning. Plastic was something you disposed of. Wood was something you kept and cherished and maintained and fussed over.

And when it came to classic wooden motor yachts nothing could compare to the elegance and refinement of a Trumpy. It was this vessel that kept his spirits high. He knew she waited for him like some secret lover content to while away the days and nights merely waiting for his return, a tangible reward for his tireless efforts if he could but hold on just a little longer. Her name was lost on most who gazed upon her varnished transom but revealed more about her owner than anyone could ever know. Her name? *Legend.*

McQueen boarded the vessel from the port side and placed his key into the door leading down below. He set his suitcase on the carpeted floor of the salon and noticed the small green light on his marine clock was lit, a signal he had a message from the Office. He locked the door then checked the windows for anyone or anything suspicious. He sat down in a chair beside a round glass-top table upon which sat a decanter of brandy and four glasses. The table top was set on a gyrostabilizer which kept the decanter and glasses upright even in rough seas. He poured himself a glass of brandy, returned the top to the decanter, then pressed down hard on the top of the glass. The entire tabletop turned upside down. On the reverse side of the tabletop was a small answering machine which now sat upright on the table. He placed his hand palm down on the glass beside the machine. A bar of white light from underneath the glass moved from his fingertips to his palm then back up again. Satisfied it was Sterling McQueen, the equipment was unlocked for his use. He hit the 'play' button then sat back on the sofa, nursing his snifter of brandy.

"McQueen," the message began, "new assignment." The voice had a gruff, no nonsense, to-the-point edge to it. The harsh quality of a drill sergeant yet refined like that of a well-to-do Kentucky horse breeder. McQueen had grown to respect that voice and the man to whom it belonged.

There were only a few people you could trust in the cloak and dagger set. Colonel Rufus Bragg was one of them. 'Colonel' was a rather disarming label. He had long ago left the military, but the title stuck.

The authoritative voice with the southern drawl resonated from the small speaker. "You leave tomorrow."

"Tomorrow?" McQueen talked back to the machine.

"Drop by the Office before you leave and pick up your orders. Oh-eight-hundred."

The line fell silent. McQueen hit the 'off' button and the message was automatically erased. He returned the tabletop to its upright position and wondered where in the world Colonel Bragg had him heading this time.

McQueen thought about his last assignment. Madrid. The man put up quite the struggle. Momentum shifted on several occasions as furniture smashed around them in that small apartment on Calle Mancebos and they fought for dominance one over the other. The chance glance at the broken lamp on the floor would be the crucial difference for McQueen. The fact that he could reach it and his adversary could not was only a matter of luck. He could feel the life oozing out of the man around whose neck he pulled the lamp cord with all his might. He could taste the desperation with every futile claw at his face, feet kicking, body convulsing, until he had literally wrung the life out of the man like wringing the last possible drop of water from a washcloth. He lingered longer than he had to. Not because he enjoyed it, but because he simply wanted to make doubly sure the job was done. And McQueen knew the roles could just as easily have been reversed had he not been a hair cleverer, a smidgen more resourceful.

Dirty work. That's how Sterling McQueen thought of it. No one in

Washington society would be raising a toast to him. Textbooks would never reveal the truth of what must be done to protect the homeland. Committee hearings, if there ever were any, would debate the wisdom of killing a man—a government agent at that—on foreign soil. It's best they didn't know, because until they ever walked in those shoes there's no way they could ever understand the indescribable conflict one feels at a time like that.

By the time McQueen had settled into his seat on the plane back home he pondered the absurdity of the question that rolled through his head. Was he the only person on that plane who had just killed a man with his bare hands? Chances were he was, which made him a member of an exclusive club. A club that held no meetings, built no clubhouses, had no rules. A club that operated with no limits, only results.

Colonel Bragg always sought to make the job more palatable. McQueen remembered the colonel once putting his arm around him in a fatherly manner after a similar mission. He spoke to him with an informality McQueen had never heard before or since. "Sterling, you have to understand somethin', son," he had said with his distinctive southern drawl. His voice lowered to an almost reverent tone. "Some folks just need killin'."

Those words stuck with him. They stripped away the mud and the road tar of politics. They dissolved a thousand hours of testimony and debriefings. It was simply an incontrovertible truth. Some folks did, indeed, need killing. He figured the man in Madrid was one of those folks.

# Chapter Four

*Nablus, The West Bank*

A woman carrying a canvas bag inspected the fresh fruit that had just been set out in a plastic crate. A young Palestinian boy dressed in a hand-me-down white jogging hoody and black jogging pants bounced a small ball on the narrow avenue while his mother shopped. Either side was brimming with wares. Several colorful umbrellas hung upside down from a clothesline that stretched across the street. A cardboard box of toothpaste and other toiletry items was stacked atop a woven basket that contained handcrafted placemats. A green two-wheeled cart with light blue trim held flowers and plants. Guitars hung by their necks and violins dangled inside cases from awnings jutting out from old buildings. The open-air market went on for as far as the eye could see. Inside the ancient structures vendors haggled with customers while keeping an eagle eye on their merchandise in the street.

No one was really sure where it came from. The bomb tore through the market place as if the people were made of paper. Tiny bits of fabric and dirt and rocks and human flesh rained down on those lucky enough to be spared. It was as gruesome a scene as anyone in Nablus could remember.

"It was this huge explosion," one survivor recounted for a reporter. "You could feel it in your chest. People were screaming and running, just trying to get out of the way. People's skin and blood were in my hair. It was just carnage, complete carnage everywhere."

The soft sobbing of the wounded was contrasted by the hysterical cries of those who came running to their aid. It was minutes before the faint sound of sirens could be heard in the distance. A thin cloud of smoke lingered on the narrow street. The burnt smell of explosives hung in the air along with the foul stench of death.

•

THE WORLD WAS an increasingly dangerous place. The CIA and the NSA had become incredibly high-tech, something that was certainly needed to keep America safe. Because of their over-reliance on technology, the lost art of human intelligence, or HUMINT, had been largely neglected. After September 11, Secretary of Defense Donald Rumsfeld took it upon himself to create an intelligence organization that would supply field operation units with the real HUMINT they needed. The secretary made a command decision in 2002 to revive their human assets through an entirely autonomous branch.

It, however, was not immune to the realities of an overly suspicious populace. The name of the new organization—the Strategic Support Branch—was somehow leaked to the press in 2005, probably by an opponent in Congress or someone inside the intelligence community. After its existence went public, the SSB was shut down by the secretary.

Years later, after being completely forgotten, the SSB was quietly resurrected, this time making it completely airtight. The reincarnated SSB was the most secretive of the secret. No congressman knew anything about it. No senator had any knowledge of it. Only the president, the secretary of defense, the head of the Joint Chiefs, and those inside the department were privy to the inner workings of the organization. It was small by design.

The CIA was famous for loathing the term "agent" for their case officers. The label "agent" was reserved for foreign spies employed by the CIA. Donovan Henry, the founder of the Strategic Support Branch, once remarked, "We're not the damned CIA. If they were doing their job there'd be no need for us. I don't give a rat's ass if they don't like the word 'agent.' If it's good enough for the Bureau (the FBI), then it's good enough for us." He scoffed at the CIA using the term 'case officer' instead, remarking, "It sounds like someone assigned to turn you down for a loan at the bank."

"Pings" were what they called the agents around the Office. It was from the acronym PNG—Persona Non Grata—which is what these agents were if anyone learned who they worked for. It was understood by each agent that in the event of their capture or death any knowledge of them or their activities would be totally and unequivocally denied by the United States government. In the highly unlikely event that an agent would turn against the section, each remaining agent would be issued an 'X-Directive.' An X-Directive was a standing order to take any means necessary to exterminate the turncoat agent. The CIA called it "dying of the measles." The pings inside SSB called it "lead poisoning," a reference to a bullet behind the ear. Whatever one called it, needless to say, there were no 'kiss-and-tell' books from this division.

The clock radio on the bedside table sounded at exactly 5:00 AM. The radio blared the sound of talk radio into McQueen's sleeping ears. A baritone announcer delivered the latest news from around the world. McQueen reached a groping hand toward the sound and slammed it down several times until it hit its target and there was silence. He pulled himself from the bed, his feet hitting the soft carpet. The boat rocked slightly as he sat on the edge and cupped his face in his hands rubbing his cheeks and struggling to open his eyes. *Not again*, he thought. Couldn't he have just a few days to catch his breath? He'd been on the road for nearly six months straight. Kazakhstan, Afghanistan, Paraguay, Italy, Spain. They all seemed to run together. As soon as he put out a fire on one side of the world another would erupt on the other.

McQueen lifted himself from the bed then fell to the floor and, as quickly as humanly possible, pumped out fifty push-ups. He grabbed his running shoes from the closet, pulled on his sweats, tied his shoes, and was out into the pre-dawn Maryland morning.

After his jog, he bought a newspaper at the marina vending box. The faint smell of fish under any other circumstances would be repulsive, but on a boat dock in a marina on a perfect summer morning it actually added to the ambience. The sun was starting another day when he boarded port, turned his key, and descended down to the salon. He took another three steps down to the companionway below and aft to the master stateroom. He allowed the hot water of the shower to massage his aching shoulders. He stepped out, dried off, and took the white robe from the hook.

In the galley he fried up three eggs, three pieces of crispy bacon, and grabbed two slices of wheat toast out of the toaster. With his breakfast and a carafe of hot coffee on a tray he headed topside.

He sat at a table of slatted teak and enjoyed the sun rising across the bay. Breakfast was his favorite meal and he insisted on enjoying it in a civilized manner, just as he preferred to face any day when he had control over it. He looked about the aft deck and admired the craftsmanship of his own vessel that true artisans of the trade had painstakingly assembled by hand decades before. A lost art that had succumbed to the demand of low maintenance and even lower tastes.

Taking another sip of his coffee, he checked the latest politics from Washington. He turned the page. Yet another hostage taken in Europe. Snatched in broad daylight. This was the twelfth such kidnapping in the past year. There had been three in Paris, two in London, one taken in Innsbruck, two in Geneva, one in Munich, two in Berlin, and the latest in Brussels. No names of the hostages were given. Muslim terrorists were suspected, but no particular group had stepped forward to take responsibility. With the Euro/Mid-East Peace Conference coming up in Vienna, diplomats had been struggling to keep the fragile peace intact, the article stated.

McQueen spread a pat of butter and a spoonful of honey on his toast. The tasty delight crunched between his teeth and he gazed out at the quiet serenity of the sailboats and the motor yachts of white hulls and weathered wood decks and polished chrome. The lines that kept them in place slowly strained and creaked then relaxed to the rhythm of the wind and the water. The gulls were the only creatures about. The humans, who enjoyed their lives of leisure, dreamt dreams of summer day-cruises to the cape and evening cocktails at the yacht club while tucked snugly in their cozy staterooms. How he longed to stay right here in this place, in this time. How he would've loved to have bottled the moment. Bottle it and uncork it when life was at its most desperate, as he knew it soon would be.

●

"YOU WANTED TO see me, Mr. Schwarzmann?"

"Shut the door, Daniel," Jacob Schwarzmann said.

Daniel shut the double doors of the large paneled library at the Hudson Valley estate and took a seat in one of the leather chairs in front of his boss. "Is this about your son? Good news, I hope."

"This is a business matter and it's a matter that can never leave this room." He pushed a sheet of paper in front of him.

"What's this?"

"A non-disclosure agreement. Once I've given you the instructions that I'd like you to carry out, you can never tell a soul about this."

Daniel took the paper and looked it over with concern. The wording was vague. The businessman's plans were not spelled out in the agreement. Only Daniel's solemn oath never to disclose a word about what he was to do. He looked up at the man whose most trusted confidante he had been for nearly 20 years. "But—"

"I know," Schwarzmann apologized. "It's lacking in detail. I will ask you to do nothing illegal. Once word starts to spread, it'll be big news all over the United States. Maybe the world. You'll be taken care of, I can assure you. You'll be able to retire in a manner you never thought possible. I just ask you to trust me."

Daniel looked at the man he had admired for so long. He looked down at the paper, picked up the pen, and signed his name at the bottom. Jacob Schwarzmann signed on the line next to his then picked up the paper, folded it, and placed it in his coat pocket.

"Now, what's this all about?" Daniel asked.

"I'm leaving this afternoon to tie up some loose ends in Philadelphia. I'll be back in two weeks. While I'm gone I want you to liquidate everything."

Daniel was stunned. "Liquidate everything? What does that mean?"

"It means just what you think it does. When I get back I want everything gone. This house, the boats, all my businesses, all my summer homes. I *would* like to enjoy the jet just one last time, so you can dispose of that when I get back."

"I can't believe this. Why?"

"Why?" Schwarzmann asked. "Because all this money, all this stuff, makes me a target. I'm tired of living with a bullseye on my back."

"But it'll take years to sell off everything," Daniel said.

"I don't want you to *sell* anything." He pushed a stack of papers across the desk to him. "I want you to give it all away. I've made a list. There are over a thousand charities on that list. Divide my assets up as you see fit. Those with a red star beside them get the businesses and the houses and any cash I have. The rest of the assets you can divide up as you see fit."

"Mr. Schwarzmann, I think you're making a big mistake. Obviously, you're upset about Brad, but I think you need to think about this."

"I've thought about it. Two weeks is all you have."

"What will you do?"

"I made my billions from scratch. I'll be fine. So will you. You'll find your fee for doing this in those papers. It's all legal. I had it all drawn up properly and witnessed in case people think I'm nuts. And they will. But when people ask you, all you have to do is say that I'm taking an early retirement. Tell them there are more important things than money. Tell them I've seen the light. It just took me a little longer than most to see it."

# Chapter Five

Sterling McQueen pulled his Mercedes into the parking garage of an Annapolis office building, parked the car, and headed for the elevator. He straightened his butter yellow tie, adjusted his cuffs, and waited for the door to open. The navy suit with mother-of-pearl buttons was custom-tailored with a feature not found in most suits. A subtle but useful slit just under the left armpit designed specifically for the easy extraction of his stainless steel Sig Sauer P232 SL .380-caliber pistol.

Colonel Bragg selected the Glock 19 for his agents. It was just like McQueen to insist on carrying something else. For the life of him, he couldn't understand why the Sig P232 was ever discontinued. No matter, he had his. Not only was the P232 highly regarded for its stopping power, the action was so smooth that jamming was virtually non-existent. It was only six-and-a-half inches long and just under 21 ounces which made it easily concealable. Its light weight and rounded shape made it fast on the draw. Each additional split second could mean the difference between life and death in the field and McQueen refused to give up that edge. Colonel Bragg didn't argue.

At a tad over six feet tall, Sterling McQueen cut an impressive figure. Suits were all the better for having clothed him. His dark hair bordered on curly and was not so neatly combed that one would think he cared. His mouth was a wry smile short of being contemptuous, his blue eyes discerning. He carried himself as if no one else were in the room, much as he lived his life. He had his hopes, his desires, his goals, though no one apart from himself was privy to them. He was as self-contained as a human was capable of being.

The doors of the elevator opened and McQueen made sure no one was aboard before entering. Where he was going was not on the menu of floors. He hit the button to close the doors then opened the emergency panel. On the keyboard he entered #-9-4-*-7-3-5-#. That locked the doors and prevented the elevator from going anywhere but its intended destination. He was never sure how far below the parking garage the Office was, but from the travel time it seemed to be four or five floors below the lowest level.

The elevator came to a stop and the doors parted. He stepped off and the officer behind the desk greeted him with a smile. "Good morning, Sterling. No worse for the wear in Madrid I see."

"Good morning, Lieutenant. Spain's lovely this time of year. Maybe the old man will send you along next time."

Lieutenant Sexton's smile was contagious. "I'm afraid he has me chained to this desk." She was an attractive young lady and, oddly enough, even more so in a uniform. A little taller than average, she was slender with black hair cut short just below her ears. "Met the new ping?" she asked.

"I didn't know we had one," McQueen said.

"While you were in Spain. The colonel hired her to replace Vinson."

"Her?"

She smiled. "I thought that would get you. She's a POW too." Lieutenant Sexton's way of calling her a piece of work. "You can keep your beer cold next to her."

"She sounds lovely," McQueen said.

A beep rang from the lieutenant's intercom followed by the booming voice of Colonel Bragg. "Lieutenant Sexton, is McQueen here?"

"Yes, sir."

"Why didn't you tell me?"

She blushed, "Sorry, sir."

"Send him in."

"Right away, sir."

McQueen walked to the end of the corridor and pushed opened the large carved-wood door made of cypress with fifteen square panels that looked more at home in a church or some English manor than a government office. It moved with amazing ease given its six-inch thickness. In fact, all of the walls in the colonel's office were of the same thickness, filled with the most effective soundproofing material available. One could set off a stick of dynamite in that office and it would scarcely be heard in the next room. The electric deadbolt lock of the door clunked behind him like a prison cell.

"Have a seat," Colonel Bragg said in his no-nonsense manner. He chomped on an unlit cigar and studied the paper in his hand.

McQueen took a seat in one of the two low-back leather captain's chairs in front of the colonel's desk. Bragg was busy initialing a document. He attentively placed it into the two-holed classification folder with the care of a public accounting actuary. He turned his attention to the next document. McQueen watched him carefully for a time then slowly reached for the Sig under the armpit of his suit coat. With his eyes glued to Bragg, he eased the pistol from its resting place. Without even a glance up, Bragg motioned with his free hand to a trivet atop his desk with a dark green felt surface. McQueen released the magazine and pulled back the action, ejecting the chambered round. He caught it in the air as if he were snatching a fly in mid-flight. He pressed the de-cocking lever which lowered the hammer from its full-cocked position. He admired the gun with the customized cocobolo wood grip for a second then placed the gun, the magazine, and the unchambered round on the green felt.

Bragg continued to examine the file on his desk. McQueen crossed his legs and took the opportunity of the lull to get a good look at his mentor, this living legend among the spooks. The colonel was a tad shorter than most. The narrow red, white, and blue lines running through his tie gave a slight hint to his undying patriotism. The heavily starched white shirt seemed so sharp it would cut you. The small Polo pony positioned where a shirt pocket would normally be was the only indication the colonel gave even a second thought to style. His short salt-and-pepper haircut was more out of habit from his military days than any edict. The matching gray coat to his pants hung on a wooden coat rack in the corner.

Once inside the confines of his office one got a better idea about the personality of the colonel. His wood-paneled walls were lined with pictures of himself in action with hunting and fishing buddies, autographed 8x10 glossies of past presidents, children's graduation pictures and family portraits with handsome young men, pretty young ladies, and snaggletoothed kids. Many awards for distinguished service were arranged inside the bookshelves including the prestigious National Intelligence Medal of Achievement.

Colonel Bragg looked up from the paper. "We got a CRITIC yesterday from BND in Berlin."

McQueen smiled to himself as he recalled the only time the colonel had skipped the acronym for the German intelligence organization and actually tried to pronounce Bundesnachrichtendienst.

"I take it you're familiar with the rash of hostages taken in Europe over the past twelve months."

"Just what I've read in the papers," McQueen said. "That's a European matter, isn't it?" He flattened a wrinkle in his pants.

"Not anymore. We've been called in at the urging of General Bushing himself. The General's never been completely comfortable with the BND. They had a dismal record of double agents during the Cold War."

"That was a long time ago," McQueen said. "My dealings with them have always been satisfactory."

"Well, the General wants to put some fresh legs in the game. And it just got worse."

"How so?"

"A bomb exploded this morning in Nablus on the West Bank. Hit a marketplace there. Dozens of casualties. The Palestinians, of course, are pointing the finger at Israel."

"Blowing up dozens of innocent people? Doesn't sound like the Israelis' style," McQueen said.

"I agree, but with nearly a dozen Jews being snatched around Europe they're thinking the Israelis would do just about anything to get even."

"You've talked with Mossad?"

"I've talked with Mossad and even Aman. They vehemently deny any involvement in the bombing. It's going to take a helluva lot more than that to convince the Palestinians. But we'll let the diplomats worry about all that. We've got a job to do." Colonel Bragg pushed a manila envelope across the desk. "We have to help the BND and the other European agencies get to the bottom of these kidnappings."

"You said nearly a dozen Jews have been kidnapped. The hostages are all Jewish?"

"All but one," Bragg said. "That guy," he pointed to McQueen's envelope.

McQueen opened it and set the stack of black and white photos in front of him. The face smiling back at McQueen was the yearbook photograph of Professor Franz Gerber.

"It seems they're very concerned about this man." Bragg pointed with his unlit cigar. "He's a professor at the University of Vienna. He was abducted yesterday in Brussels, and they don't have a clue where he is."

"And he's not Jewish?"

"No," the colonel said. "Apparently the reason for his abduction is different from the rest. They'll fill you in on what they know when you get to Brussels. I want you to cooperate fully with those guys, you hear?"

"Understood."

"This particular assignment requires your expertise. It may also require your language skills. Plus, you know the area. It's your old beat. Let's just try not to step on any toes while you're there, but we're in charge of this operation. General's orders. That may mean a few bruised egos when you get there, so take it easy. I don't need to remind you, you're an illegal, as always. Try to keep that in mind. You need to familiarize yourself with a few more of the players." He motioned again with his cigar at the pictures. "What do you know about a guy by the name of Samael Valafar?" He plucked a kitchen match from an ornate holder on the desk and struck it.

"Valafar Shipping?"

Bragg took his time lighting the Monte Cristo Epic for the third time since choosing it from its box earlier in the morning. "That's the one," he acknowledged between drags. He blew out the match with a puff of smoke.

McQueen slid the next photo to the top. The candid AP photo showed Valafar in black tie apparently arriving at what appeared to be a movie premiere waving to a crowd of onlookers. He didn't recognize the attractive redhead on his arm.

"Well, let's see. He's a German billionaire. He owns a large shipping interest," McQueen stated nonchalantly, examining the photograph.

"Primary routes are between European and former Soviet-bloc ports and the Middle East: Egypt, Syria, countries all up and down the Arabian Gulf. He's fascinated with the film industry, dabbling in it from time to time, if you can call bankrolling three films to the tune of around forty million just dabbling. If you believe the gossip columns and Spielfilm Magazine, he fancies himself a refined version of Ari Onassis. He's been known to associate with anyone and everyone from tin-horn dictators to communist bosses to neo-Nazis to heads of state. Anybody who can benefit him. Let's see, what else? He just divorced his third wife and she's in court trying to nullify their prenup which has left her without a dime."

"And he has plenty to protect too. The man has enough money to burn a wet mule."

"How does he fit in with all of this?"

"He may not fit at all. The professor had asked the BND to work up a dossier on him, but it may be totally unrelated to this case. BND just asked us for intelligence on every connection to Gerber. That one seemed a little odd to me."

McQueen shuffled the photographs to the next glossy. "Who's this?"

Bragg pushed the intercom button on his phone. "Lieutenant, is Agent Barton here yet?"

"Yes, she is, Colonel."

"Send her in." He returned his attention to McQueen. "I'll tell you in a minute. Have you met Agent Barton?"

"I don't think so," McQueen said, "but I've sure heard about her."

Bragg's face turned sour. "Lieutenant Sexton talks too much."

The great wooden door opened and McQueen rose from his seat. Bragg did not. Vivian Barton was all business. Even before McQueen clasped her outstretched hand he picked up a subtle sense of insecurity. It was as if she were ever-cognizant she was in a man's world and wore it like the pantsuit she chose from her closet that morning. McQueen guessed her hair was shoulder length, but it was only a guess because it was neatly tucked away in a bun. He recognized that her black-frame glasses were prescription-free. He figured it was either to negate her attractiveness or give her a more intellectual look so she'd be taken more seriously, or both.

"Heard a lot about you, Mr. McQueen," she said from her Carly Simon mouth. "You have quite the reputation. Impressive. A bit reckless, but impressive. Should be interesting working together."

"Working together?" McQueen turned his head toward the colonel and took his seat.

"Yes. Agent Barton will be shadowing you in Brussels."

"Hold on a second, Colonel. I don't need a chaperone."

"Agent Barton is not a chaperone, McQueen. She's backup."

"Backup? For what?"

"This case is a bit more complicated than most, Mr. McQueen," Barton interjected.

Bragg explained, "While you were in Madrid, Agent Barton was running logistics on this case. She's intimately familiar with every detail."

"Then send her," McQueen insisted.

"Believe me, Mr. McQueen, that was my first choice," she said pointedly.

Bragg said, "This is your beat, Sterling. You know the people. You know the language. You have assets there."

"And I don't need anybody getting in the way," McQueen said.

"Is that what you think women are, Mr. McQueen?" Barton asked. "In the way?"

McQueen looked at Bragg. "Oh, she's one of those."

"One of those what?" she asked.

McQueen smiled, "One of those people who's in the way."

"I'll have you know I did a great deal of legwork while you were gone."

"Sterling," Bragg warned between puffs before a crude crack could come from his mouth.

McQueen bit his tongue and said, "Well, Miss—"

"Ms.," she corrected.

"*Ms.* Barton, why don't you fill me in."

"That next photo you have there," she said, pointing to the top one in his stack, "that's Wilhelm Schmitt. He's a colleague of Gerber's. Teaches at the University of Salzburg. He was the last person, aside from the BND, to see Gerber before he was taken. He may know something, he may not. You might need to have a chat with him, so study that face."

McQueen raised an eyebrow to Bragg. "Two professors, a German shipping tycoon, and Arab terrorists with hostages? I don't get it."

"That's why we're sending you to Brussels," Bragg said through cigar-clenched teeth. "If Arab terrorists have gotten a toehold on that region, we need to know about it."

"The prime minister of Israel addresses the Euro/Mid-East Peace Conference in Vienna next week," Barton said. "In fact, he's getting some sort of award. It's my professional opinion that those kidnappings are designed to derail that. My guess is they're trying to torpedo the talks before they ever begin."

"What's this award about?" McQueen asked.

"It's a 'thank you' for not retaliating against the Muslims for all the kidnappings," she said.

Bragg said, "I don't need to remind you how volatile that situation already is. There are a lot of folks who want to throw more gasoline on the fire. It's in our country's best interest to see that these talks go off without a hitch. They seem to have the Israelis calmed down for the moment. We can't allow another kidnapping to happen. You have to find out who's behind all this so we can put a stop to it."

"Bring peace to the Middle East in just under a week," McQueen said sarcastically. "And who am I pretending to be this go-round?"

"You won't need a legend for this trip." Bragg puffed until he revived his cigar. "An old Bolshevik once said, 'Men walk easily in their own shoes.' Use your own passport. If you run into anybody from your flight crew from Spain and you're somebody else it could get complicated. Besides, you're already so far off the grid it's unlikely anyone will know your name. Your typical cover. Businessman with Peliken International. You've just been promoted to European Systems Chief. Congratulations. You're being transferred to Brussels." He handed him an envelope with his fake company's logo on the outside. "Inside you'll find your itinerary along with a company prepaid card and some spending cash. Make sure you keep your receipts for the Treasury boys. You're booked on the 4:15 out of Reagan. You'll get further instructions once you reach Brussels."

McQueen walked to the door.

"Oh, McQueen," Barton said, looking over her shoulder from her seat.

McQueen turned.

"I need a cell number," she said, "so I can contact you when I hit the ground."

McQueen smiled slightly at Bragg.

"He doesn't carry a phone," Bragg informed her.

Agent Barton paused for a moment thinking they were having a joke at her expense. "You're kidding, right?" she asked with a chuckle.

"I don't trust them," McQueen explained.

"Well, give me your e-mail address and I'll e-mail you when I'm there."

"I don't carry a computer."

"You don't have an e-mail address?"

"I don't."

"Now, hold on a minute." Barton held up her hands. "You mean to tell me you're in the espionage business and you don't have a cell phone *or* a computer?" She turned to Bragg. "How am I supposed to communicate with Mr. Flintstone over here?"

McQueen looked at Bragg, then at her. "Why don't you just tweet you're heading to Brussels? Let the entire world know you're coming." He reached for the door again then turned back to Barton. "If I need you, I'll be in touch."

# Chapter Six

*Three Months Ago*

Special Agent Gustav Wagner was not quite used to the field. As a young soldier he had moved swiftly up the ranks. After doing his time in the espionage business, he had traded in his listening devices and surveillance gear for a desk job. Then came the austerity measures. Even the spy business was not immune from the bureaucratic ax. The BND was being asked to do more with less and that meant no one would be allowed to rest on their laurels and coast to retirement. In turn, Gustav was pushed out from behind the desk and back into the field. He told himself it was a welcome change, but he was not the man he used to be. A bit heavier and a touch slower, he now spent most of his time coordinating assignments.

Agent Hoffman had taken advantage of his government's pension plan years before. His successor had no real working knowledge of the Gerber asset. The layers of time and turnover piled high. Professor Gerber was simply forgotten. Forgotten until Gustav Wagner happened upon his file. Gerber had been a treasure trove of knowledge about the Middle East, but no one was utilizing him. The job fell to Gustav to inform Professor Gerber that it was time to be reactivated.

The rain helped cool a late summer afternoon when Gustav matched the number on his phone's GPS—3405 Wiedner Haupt Strasse—with the number on the house. He parked his car across the street, turned off the engine, and stared at the home. He had read the professor's dossier. He was fully aware of the invaluable service he had provided his agency. Gerber could slam the door in his face. He had every right to. Gustav prayed he wouldn't. The stakes were much higher now than when Gerber was in action. Many more lives were on the line. Perhaps he could persuade him to help just one more time.

Gustav pulled his coat collar tightly around his neck against the rain and climbed the steps up to the stone house. After ringing the doorbell he was greeted by a lovely dark-eyed woman with long flowing black hair and handsome streaks of gray. Her radiant smile seemed to almost clear the skies. Gustav noted that even the beautiful photograph in her dossier did not do Lisa Gerber justice even though she was many years older since it was taken.

"Good afternoon. May I help you?"

The slight Lebanese accent was charming.

"I am here to see Professor Gerber. My name is Gustav Wagner. I am with the BND." He held up his identification.

The smile drained from her face as quickly as if Gustav had announced the passing of a loved one.

"Please come in where it is dry." She tried to maintain her manners. "I will tell him you are here."

"Thank you very much."

Gustav glanced around the tastefully furbished foyer. A beautiful but small Persian rug accented the marble floor. To the right was a parlor with a baby grand, a sofa, and some chairs with a fireplace on the far wall. Gustav stepped just inside the room. An antique table held cherished family photographs. He picked one up. It was the Gerbers on vacation in Paris in front of the Eiffel Tower. Professor Gerber, his wife, and their son who appeared to be about sixteen at the time the photograph was taken. He returned the picture to the table. A colorful piece of pottery sat next to the photographs. He examined it more closely and determined it to be Middle Eastern in origin. In all likelihood it was worth a small fortune.

"A gift from some friends in Lebanon," a voice announced.

Gustav turned to see Professor Franz Gerber standing in the hallway, the day's paper hanging loosely by his side. The professor didn't look the part of a college professor. He was a handsome man, a nice complement to the beautiful Lisa, Gustav thought. His skin wasn't naturally dark-complected, but he sported an attractive tan. His full gray hair was parted on the left and combed over to the right. The Tommy Hilfiger slacks and Club Monaco knit shirt were just a casual hint of his taste. Unlike Gustav, he had fought hard against the battle of the bulge and won. Gustav self-consciously glanced down at his own inferior physique while Gerber walked toward him.

"I am Franz Gerber," he said, extending his hand.

"Gustav Wagner." He took his hand. "Nice instrument." He pointed toward the baby grand. "Do you play?"

"My wife," Gerber said. "A woman of many talents."

Gustav smiled, "Is there somewhere we can talk alone?"

"Of course," he replied, leading him into a study on the other side of the foyer. Closing the double doors behind him, he turned to face Gustav. "Your phone call sounded urgent." He gestured for Gustav to take a seat.

"Yes, we have a bit of a predicament." Gustav sat down.

Gerber looked at him sternly. "You said you were with the BND. You are one of Hoffman's men, are you not?"

"Actually, Herr Hoffman retired long ago. I have taken the position he once held."

"I had hoped those days were behind me, Herr Wagner," he said, looking at nothing in particular on the rug. "I had convinced myself that your people had forgotten me. I prayed that you had anyway."

"Perhaps we would have, Professor, but any hope of that happening has evaporated."

Gerber glanced down to see what Gustav was looking at. It was the front page of his newspaper which he still held in his hand. The headlines screamed out the tragedy of another kidnapping in Germany.

Gustav said, "I do not have to tell you how volatile the state of the Middle East is at this moment. Or the world, for that matter. People want answers. Answers I cannot give them. Every side with a vested interest in peace in the Middle East has contacted NATO asking for their assistance and mediation through this latest crisis. Many lives hang in the balance. As you also know very well, the stability of the Middle East has a direct effect on the economies of the West."

"Yes. It is always about the oil," Gerber said.

Gustav nodded then paused. "We need your help again, Professor." His tone was solemn.

Actually hearing Gustav say it made Gerber's stomach tighten. "As I told your predecessor, I am no spy," Gerber said.

"We do not need spies, Professor. We need information, insight, a clue. Just as you helped us before."

Gerber rose from the sofa and walked to the window. Beads of water rolled down the panes. "What if I told you that I quit for good? A long time ago."

Gustav shrugged. "Professor, that is your decision." He looked across the room at him. "You know we will not force you to help us, but I must remind you of your promise to Herr Hoffman when he arranged your safe passage home. I read your dossier."

"Of course, of course." Gerber was agitated by the reminder.

"Professor, we cannot stop the kidnappings."

Gerber's eyes closed tight with pain as the reality of the words hit him.

"We need your help."

Gerber turned around to face him. "Can you not get someone else?"

"Oh, sure. We could get someone else, but there is no one else quite like you, Professor."

Gerber knew it wasn't idle flattery. There *was* no one else like him. No one with his particular experience.

"Believe me, Professor, if there were someone better than you, then you can be assured I would be paying a visit to them right now." He waited a moment for the words to soak in. "You know these people. You have lived among them. Surely you can give us an angle we have perhaps overlooked." Gustav was implacable.

"But it has been years since I lived in—"

"You have a better feeling for the soul of the Arab people than we could ever have. All we are asking is that you look at our data. See if it makes sense. Use your connections over there. See if they know anything that we should know."

Gerber nervously rubbed the rim of his bottom lip with his index finger.

"And what if I get too close?" he fretted. "What if someone decides to retaliate against me or, worse yet, my family?"

"We delivered your family to you, Professor," Gustav firmly reminded him. "We will do everything within our power to ensure they remain safe. But no one will know you are helping us, this I can assure you."

Gerber turned back toward the window and the pelting rain on the sidewalk.

Gustav rose from his chair. "Professor Gerber," he said softly, easing up behind him. "You must look beyond just your personal gain or loss. You are uniquely qualified to provide your country with a great service and perhaps save many lives."

Gerber cupped his chin in his hand and continued to stare out the window. Gustav waited patiently for his response.

"Give me some time," Gerber insisted, breaking the silence. He continued to stare out at the dreary day.

"Certainly, Professor." Wagner headed for the door, stopping just before he reached it. "But please do not take too long. The sooner we get your help, the more lives we can save. Auf Wiedersehen."

Wagner showed himself out and, again, pulled his collar up around his neck before slipping back out into the rain. The soft glowing image of Lisa Gerber watching anxiously shone from the second-story bedroom window. She watched Gustav return to his car and drive away.

# Chapter Seven

*Present Day*

The moist Belgian air was a welcome relief from the arid flight from Washington. McQueen caught a cab and instructed the driver to deliver him to his hotel. First he needed to make a brief cover stop en route. His cab made the turn onto Boulevard Brand Whitlock and the jet lag began to overtake his body. He never was very good at sleeping on airplanes, even in first class. Perhaps once he checked in he could get some rest.

McQueen instructed the cabbie to pull to the side of the street in front of a newsstand and asked him to wait. He approached the vendor inside who sat there smoking a cigarette and reading a magazine.

"Je voudrais un journal, s'il vous plaît," McQueen said, laying some coins on the counter.

"En anglais, monsieur?" the vendor replied, asking him if he wanted the newspaper in English.

"Oui."

The vendor placed a copy of *The Bulletin* on the counter.

"Merci," McQueen replied, unzipping his bag. "Does the moon shine on the Ixelles Ponds?"

The man looked back at him cautiously before answering. "Only when it is full, monsieur."

"And the moon is full on Monday," McQueen answered.

The vendor glanced slightly from side to side before producing a small thin package wrapped in brown paper and tied with a string. He laid it on the counter. McQueen placed it inside the fold of the newspaper then stuffed them both in his bag. He zipped the zipper and headed back to the cab.

The car pulled up to the Warwick Hotel located just a couple of blocks from Grand Place where the Duke of Wellington inspected his troops before heading into battle with Napoleon at Waterloo. McQueen paid the man across the back of the seat and exited the taxi. The driver hopped out and retrieved McQueen's suitcase from the trunk. McQueen pulled his rolling bag through the grand lobby of frescoes, handsomely detailed woodwork, and throne chairs. He approached the inlaid wood reception desk and the young lady behind it.

"Bonjour. I have a reservation. The name's Sterling McQueen."

She tapped the keyboard of her computer. "Yes, Mr. McQueen. You are a little early for check-in, I am afraid," she said with a French accent. "I can take your credit card and passport information and you are welcome to have something to eat in our restaurant while you wait. We will let you know when your room is ready. It should not be too long from now."

He pulled his bag the several paces over to the restaurant and seated himself at the bar. He ordered a croissant and a side of honey to fill in the blanks of the breakfast he had on the plane along with a glass of orange juice. The bartender walked off with his menu to the right. The voice came from his left.

"You too, huh?"

McQueen swiveled on his stool to see a young lady placing her purse on the bar and climbing up onto the stool beside him. Her shoulder-length black hair was full and lively with a touch of curl. A couple of strands on either side playfully drew the eye to her cleavage. Her olive complexion was smooth. He guessed her lineage as Syrian, perhaps Jordanian.

"Excuse me?" McQueen asked.

"I saw you checking in. Sounds like we're in the same boat." Her accent was British.

"And what boat is that?" McQueen asked.

She laughed, "They don't have a room ready for me either."

"It's an irritating little inconvenience, but, hey, what are you gonna do?"

"Yes, I suppose so." She stuck out her hand. "My name is Sabreen. Sabreen Basara."

McQueen took her hand gently. "Sterling McQueen."

"You here on business or pleasure, Mr. McQueen?"

"Business," he said. "I just got promoted and transferred here."

"Wow, very nice. Congratulations."

"Thanks."

"What line of business?"

"Computers. And you? Business or pleasure?"

"Business *and* pleasure. I have a couple of meetings, but I'm hooking up with some girlfriends for a little sightseeing, so it'll be fun."

"You're from the UK, I take it."

She smiled. "I attended school in London," she explained.

"Very familiar with that town. I usually stay at a little hotel near Albert Embankment. It has a great view of the Thames and Victoria Tower Gardens."

"Sounds like you *are* quite familiar with London."

"Yes, I've spent a lot of time there on business. You start to think of hotels like old friends. You tend to visit the same ones when you come back to town." McQueen's croissant and orange juice arrived and he unrolled the silverware from his napkin. "Care to join me?"

"Oh, no thanks," she said. "I just ate. Besides, I better check in with the office." She asked the bartender for a glass of water. "I'll leave you in peace to enjoy your meal. A pleasure meeting you, Mr. McQueen."

"The pleasure is all mine."

McQueen watched as she took her glass of water from the bar and settled into a booth with her phone. He placed his prepaid card on the bar to pay his bill and watched his new friend in the booth across the restaurant. Her hair fell across her eyes as she talked on the phone. The waiter returned his card on a tray with the bill to sign. He ignored the pen provided and pulled a Montblanc from his coat pocket. He looked over at the girl. When he thought he had a good angle he squeezed. Then again. He signed the bill.

The pronouncement that his room was ready couldn't have come too soon. He took the elevator up to the top floor. The door to his suite opened into a sitting room, the centerpiece of which was a gorgeous crystal chandelier. The room was elegantly appointed with antique furniture—a combination of Empire, Regency, and Louis XV—

beautiful paintings, lush carpeting, and a fully stocked wet bar.

McQueen never saw a hotel room as anyone else would see it. He enjoyed the luxuriousness of his surroundings as much as anyone. In fact, he appreciated the elegance more than most, but an unknown hotel room presented its own set of challenges.

He walked into the adjoining bedroom with its king size bed and a full-length inlaid painting in the wall behind it. He threw his luggage on the bed and reached inside his shoulder bag to produce what appeared to be a small digital voice recorder, the kind an executive might use to dictate a letter to a secretary. He attached the earphone plug into the device and placed the other end in his ears. He proceeded to move the device up and down the walls and slowly walked around the bedroom. In his ears all he could hear was a medium-pitched pulse. Pulling a picture away from the wall, he scanned the back of it with the device. He moved it up and down the lamp on the bedside table, then over his telephone. He did the same for the sitting room.

Satisfied, he wound up the earphone cord, tossed it back in his bag, then pulled out the brown paper package he got at the newsstand. Untying the string, he tore away the paper and opened the thin box. Inside, wrapped in tissue paper, was a Sig P232. He instantly recognized it as his own. Stainless steel, custom cocobolo wood grip. He pressed the magazine catch and released the magazine. Pulling it out, he was satisfied the magazine was full. He used subsonic .380 rounds to reduce the crack a bullet makes when it breaks the sound barrier. He placed the magazine back into the grip and snapped it into place with the heel of his palm. He chambered a round, pressed the de-cocking lever, then tucked the weapon in the waiting ready-made holster that was part of the lining of his coat.

He then retrieved a black velvet sleeve from the box that contained a sound suppressor. It was what was commonly known as a silencer although it didn't really silence anything. It merely reduced a gun shot from a loud bang to a pop, not the soft *phut* like one sees in the movies. He slid the suppressor out of the open end, examined it for a moment, and placed it in the compartment on the inner right side of his suit coat. He felt among the tissue paper and found four more magazines of seven rounds each. He stowed two in either outside pocket of his coat in areas specially designed to hold them snugly in place. He tossed the box, tissue paper, brown wrapping paper, and string in the trashcan.

He walked over and threw open the French doors which led to the balcony. The view of the city, including the 315-foot tower at Brussels Town Hall, was splendid. Before he had time to take it all in, the phone by his bed rang.

"Hello."

"Herr McQueen?" the German accent on the other end inquired.

Sterling McQueen's expression turned sour. He knew that voice well. It belonged to an old acquaintance at the BND, Gustav Wagner. "Yes, good morning, sir," he maintained the facade.

"Welcome to Brussels. How was your flight?"

"Fine. A little long, but fine."

"I am sure you would like to get some rest. How about I buy you dinner, huh?" Gustav said. "We talk a little shop."

"That would be fine," McQueen answered in his business voice.

"Very good. I will send a car for you around, say, seven o'clock?"

"Seven it is, sir."

"Bis heute Abend, mein Herr."

McQueen hung up the phone. There was not much he could do until dinner. His eyes were drawn to the comfortable bed, which he found irresistible. He assumed the yoga position, which would serve to relax his mind and allow him to get some much needed sleep. He took a deep breath, held it, then exhaled. He sat perfectly still allowing his thoughts to gently float by for 15 minutes.

His well-ordered lifestyle had saved the Office a considerable amount of time and money in training. How they now intended to use him in Brussels he hadn't a clue. Everything he needed to know would be revealed to him in good time. He had learned to be patient. For the moment, it was time to rest. He slipped between the covers, closed his eyes, and drifted off into a deep, well-deserved slumber.

●

THE WAITER BROUGHT a cup of espresso to her umbrella-covered table. She peered down the street through dark sunglasses. Her phone vibrated. She glanced at the number and ran a finger across the screen placing the phone to her ear.

"He's here," she said without being asked. She took a sip of her espresso and listened. "That's not going to be a problem," she assured the voice on the other end. "I understand."

Vivian Barton terminated the call and set the phone back on the red table, setting her eyes back on the hotel entrance a block down the street.

●

MARIE BIERMAN TOOK her seat at the head chair of the conference table. The rest of the board members were already sitting silently wondering why they'd been called in for an emergency meeting.

"I apologize for the short notice, ladies and gentlemen," she began. "I wish the circumstances could be avoided, but they cannot. I will get right to the point. I am liquidating my majority stake in this company."

A wave of shock washed across the room.

"What?" one board member asked in disbelief. "Why?"

"I assure you," Bierman said, "it has nothing to do with any of you."

"Then why?" asked another.

"I have worked very hard to build this business and my reputation here in Berlin. I feel it is time to retire."

"But you are so young," one member said. "You still have so much to offer this company."

"My mind is made up," she said.

"Please pardon the indelicate nature of my question, but does this have anything to do with your daughter?"

Marie Bierman became stoic. "I will not discuss my personal affairs here. I am simply performing my obligation of disclosure as your chief executive officer and majority shareholder."

"At what price will you be offering your shares to us?" a man asked.

"I will not be offering you my shares," she said definitively. "I will be donating my controlling interest to charity."

"What? This is outrageous. You will allow a perfect stranger to take over this company?"

She looked straight ahead avoiding direct eye contact with any member. "My mind is made up. My attorneys are preparing the paperwork as we speak. Tomorrow I will no longer be involved in this company. I am very sorry."

The room erupted in chaotic conversation. Marie Bierman sat in silence trying to conceal the devastation she felt inside.

●

THE BLUE LIGHTS reflected on the wet pavement. She tried to keep from weeping uncontrollably, taking another drag of the cigarette that had been offered by the police officer as she leaned against his car. She could see the mangled image in the street out of the corner of her eye and she turned slightly toward the officer to block the view.

"Tell me what happened," he said, poised to write on his clipboard.

It was that singular image burned into her brain that she couldn't get away from. Like the flash from a camera. A photograph she could not unsee.

"He was dead before I hit him," she insisted. She closed her eyes. She could see the snapshot just as vividly as when she first saw it. And everything leading up to it. The headlights of her car rounding the corner. The sudden awareness that there was something or some*one* lying in the street. The slamming of the brakes just a second too late. And that image. The gruesome memory of the man's blank eyes staring up at her from the pavement. The blood on the side of his face. His hair drenched. Then the horrible thump of her tires running over his body.

"You say he was already dead?"

"Yes, already dead."

"How do you know?"

She almost screamed, "I know!" She sobbed. She closed her eyes then opened them quickly to keep from seeing the image again. Another violent drag of her cigarette and she said, "I could tell. His eyes were open. But not the kind of alive open, do you know what I mean? There was no life to them."

The officer wrote on his clipboard. The woman fidgeted with her nails and exhaled smoke from her nose.

"She is right," the officer said, striding up to the squad car.

"What do you have?" The officer holding the clipboard asked.

"He has a gunshot wound to the back of the head."

# Chapter Eight

Sterling McQueen's eyes were suddenly open. Quickly his senses awakened. He pulled himself from the bed and grabbed a bathrobe from the closet. He strolled to the balcony. Tying the sash, he opened the doors to the warm early evening Belgian air that caressed his face with a delicate breeze. It was already six p.m. and he was to meet Gustav in an hour. He headed to the shower anxious as to what the evening's dinner date held for him.

He left nothing to chance. Locking the door of the bath behind him, he placed the Sig on the glass shelf just above the towels within reach of the shower. He allowed the water to cascade over his battered body. After lathering up with soap and shampoo, he rinsed then turned the nozzle to as cold as he could stand it. Satisfactorily stimulated, he cut the water and dried himself.

He then climbed into an Italian Ralph Lauren two-button charcoal suit with a blue and white striped dress shirt, a solid Charvet tie, and a pair of Brock brown calf tassel loafers he picked up at Shipton & Heneage in London. He fastened the clasp on the brown alligator-skin strap attached to his vintage Vacheron Constantin watch of 18k gold, a gift from one of Switzerland's most illustrious art collectors. A token of appreciation for McQueen thwarting a black market scheme to turn his paintings into cocaine then into cash for the Russian Bratva. Such lavish gifts were frowned upon by the Office, but his Swiss benefactor insisted and Bragg finally acquiesced after the insistence of the American ambassador in Bern. McQueen was urged to wear the timepiece as a daily complement to his wardrobe, lest he cause an international incident even though the watch cost north of twenty-five thousand American dollars.

He detested folded money. He preferred the golden brown calf leather breast wallet that kept his paper money unbent and crisp. The only other company to his cash was a Maryland driver's license and a prepaid charge card, both in his real name. In the other breast pocket he carried his passport.

He glanced at his watch coming off the elevator and at seven sharp he walked through the front door of the hotel just as a nondescript black Mercedes sedan pulled to a stop. The driver emerged and inquired over the roof, "Monsieur McQueen?"

McQueen nodded and the driver trotted around to the other side and opened the back door. He was about to sit down when, "Well, hello again," the feminine voice said.

McQueen turned around. "Sabreen, right?" He held up a hand to his driver.

"Yes." She was dressed for the evening. "Nightmare getting a cab around here." She glanced over his shoulder at his waiting vehicle.

McQueen smiled to himself. "My company sent this car for me. I'm sure they won't mind if we drop you off."

"Are you sure?"

"Quite."

McQueen led her over to the open door. She climbed into the backseat and McQueen after her. The driver closed the door and it shut with an expensive thud.

"Slight change of plans," McQueen informed the driver. "We need to drop the young lady off on our way." He turned to Sabreen. "Where are we taking you?"

She talked across the back seat to the driver. "La Bellone, please. Do you know where that is?"

"Oui, madame," the driver answered.

She turned to McQueen. "We're going to a show and we're meeting at the cafe there for dinner. I hope it's not too much trouble for you."

"Not in the least. It's right on our way, as a matter of fact. You look lovely this evening."

She smiled. "Thank you." After an awkward pause, "Sterling, right?"

"Yes."

"Did you say you were married?"

"I didn't say." He looked ahead and smiled.

She lifted his left hand and held it in hers as she examined it. "No ring. That could mean you're either not married or you tucked it in your pocket as soon as your wife dropped you at the airport."

"Which would you prefer?"

"I guess it depends," she said, locking her fingers in his. "Some women say affairs with married men are more complicated, but it depends on your definition of a complicated relationship. If you're only out for a good time, then a single guy can be more of a complication. The married man is on the same page as you. He's only out for a good time. But, of course, if you're looking for Mr. Right, then a married man is Mr. Wrong. Which one are you, the married guy out for a good time or the single man looking for a wife?"

"Why can't there be a third option? The single guy out looking for a good time with no strings attached."

"Hmm," she said, thinking about the possibility. "I guess that would be the least complicated of all."

The car pulled over to the curb.

"So, you're not going to tell me?" Her eyes twinkled at the game.

"What does it matter at this point?" McQueen asked. "I'm merely dropping you off." He opened the door, got out, and held it for her.

"Hope to see you back at the hotel," she said. "Cheers then."

McQueen enjoyed the rest of the ride to the restaurant taking in the sites of Brussels on a warm summer's evening and thinking of his flirtation with Sabreen. He periodically glanced behind them to make sure no one was tagging along. They made several left turns to smoke out a tail if they had one. There was little doubt where the driver was headed. Anytime Gustav chose the restaurant in Brussels it was always Frieda's on Wolvengracht. McQueen often wondered if the attraction was Frieda's healthy portion of her famous apple strudel with vanilla sauce or Frieda herself who served it.

McQueen paused to allow his eyes to adjust to the dimly lit tavern. He looked for the third booth on the left where he was not at all surprised to find Gustav.

"Wie gehts?" Gustav greeted with the smile of a used car salesman, struggling to extract himself from the booth and only making it to the edge of the seat.

"I'm fine," McQueen replied coolly, ignoring his outstretched hand.

Gustav looked at his own empty hand then returned it to his lap. "How long has it been?"

"Well, let's see," McQueen thought. "Last time we worked together you left me on the wrong side of a revolution with no passport and no money. Remember?"

"Oh, yes. I needed the money to buy a train ticket," he explained as if McQueen would easily understand. "I had important business to attend to. Your passport and your wallet, well, they must have been mixed up with my belongings."

"Sure, that must've been it," McQueen said.

"I am very sorry about that," Gustav explained, trying to muster an air of concern. "I sent them back as soon as I noticed the mistake. I hope that you were not too inconvenienced."

"Oh, I got 'em back. After spending three nights in a beer hall washing dishes so I'd have a place to sleep."

"I guess it is, how you say, stupid luck?"

"That's *dumb* luck and it seems to happen that way every time I work with you."

"Now, old friend, you really think I would leave you in a difficult predicament on purpose? But hey, that is ancient history. We got the job done. That is what is important. I hope you do not mind, but I took the liberty of ordering your dinner for you," Gustav informed him.

McQueen was a little perturbed, but Gustav had a way of irritating him in little ways like that. What bothered McQueen most was the fact that even with all of his annoying quirks he really did like the man as much as he tried otherwise. He was the kind of agent McQueen felt he could trust in the stickiest of situations. His practical jokes sometimes went too far, but deep down, there wasn't anyone he would rather have at his side when the odds were stacked against him.

Frieda approached the table with two orders of beef ribs and Gustav smiled a sly grin. She returned the favor and placed the meal in front of the two men then left.

"She is crazy about me. Can you tell?" Gustav grinned smugly.

McQueen ignored the comment. Gustav attacked his plate like a famished man, but he obviously wasn't going hungry. His rounded belly was a testament to his love of food. His thick caterpillar-like mustache danced over his lips to the rhythm of his chewing. His straight black hair held just a hint of gray around the temples giving Gustav a more distinguished look than he deserved. He was actually fairly attractive for a man of his size, but his table manners left much to be desired. His oversized elbows rested on the table supporting stocky arms and hands with fingers like Bratwurst that gripped a huge beef rib. He hardly looked up, his dark eyes focused on the morsels of flesh.

After a good start on the meal, Gustav began in a whisper, "Are you familiar with Professor Franz L. Gerber?"

McQueen took a more civilized approach to his meal. He delayed his answer until he had thoroughly chewed and swallowed then dabbed the edge of his mouth with a napkin. "Somewhat. He was teaching in Vienna until he disappeared just two days ago here in Brussels."

"Well, let me bring you up-to-date. There has been no contact from the kidnappers as of yet." He wiped the grease from his face with his napkin. "My theory is the PLO."

"The PLO?" McQueen was incredulous. "Come on. Brussels is a little out of their sandbox, don't you think?"

"The PLO, my friend. I assume they may not be too delighted with the deals which have been struck with the Israelis."

"You said that's *your* theory. I assume there are others,"

"Yes. It could be any number of terrorist organizations who do not want to see peace in the Middle East. Take your pick."

"The man's a college professor. Why would anyone from the Middle East want to kidnap him?" McQueen took another bite of his ribs.

"Ah, but there is more to our man Gerber than meets the eye," Gustav replied with a hint of juicier details to come. His voice became softer. McQueen moved closer across the table. The German cut his eyes to one side then back to McQueen. "The hostage situation has been a thorn in the side of the West for some time now, huh?"

McQueen nodded slightly.

"What you may not know is that off and on for the last twenty-five years we employed the services of the good professor. We either did not need him or he was forgotten for many years. Then I rediscovered him. Over the last three months he has been working very closely with me on this latest rash of abductions. He is not only very knowledgeable in the affairs and customs of the Arabs, he is also very well connected. He contacted me from Vienna last week claiming to have vital information."

"What kind of information?"

Gustav took another bite before he spoke. "He would not tell me over the telephone, only that he had a brand new light to shine on the whole affair. He seemed quite nervous when we talked. He insisted on meeting us here."

"Why here? Why not Vienna?"

"He and a colleague were already coming here to attend a symposium on Middle Eastern affairs," Gustav explained. "He did not want to arouse suspicion by canceling the meetings. So I came here to meet him."

"Well, what did you find out at the meeting?"

"Nothing," Gustav continued, tearing another shred of meat from the ribs. "Just as he was heading for our meeting, Professor Gerber disappeared from the hotel."

"What do you mean *disappeared*? Didn't you have somebody guarding him?"

"I wanted to provide him with an escort, but he refused. He was scared to death someone in his symposium would see him and start asking questions. They were all staying at the same hotel."

"Well, weren't your people at least watching him?"

"That is just it. The Belgians put GISS on the case, the very best of the best. We had six officers assigned to him. Two inside the hotel, four on the street."

"Then how the hell could kidnappers escape with the professor?"

"By helicopter from the roof. A huge—how do you say?—tailhook. It hooked a cable on top of the hotel and hoisted the professor and his captors up in a net. One of the best officers from GISS was killed on the rooftop trying to stop them. There we found tracks in the gravel. It appears there were three of them. We were coordinating the entire operation from a communications vehicle just outside the hotel. By the time we realized something was wrong, they were gone." He took a sip of beer. "Quite a professional job."

"As nervous as you say he was, how in the world did you ever persuade the professor to work for you in the first place?"

"He was stuck in Lebanon a little over twenty-five years ago. His wife and son are Lebanese. He wanted to bring them back to Germany. One of my predecessors arranged for their safe passage in return for the professor's help. We only used him for a short period after that. When the situation began to stabilize we discontinued our work with the professor. However, after the recent rash of kidnappings we deemed it necessary to involve him once again."

"So, as far as you're concerned there's only one theory. He's been snatched—by the PLO. Jeez, I can't believe I'm even saying that out loud. Any leads?"

"There is one." Gustav smiled as Frieda delivered the apple strudel.

"Oh, could I have a piece of paper, please?" McQueen asked her.

When she left, Gustav's teenage smile was once again replaced with a grimace of concern.

"What about this colleague of his?" McQueen asked.

"Very good," Gustav smiled. "I see we still think along the same lines. This is the lead to which I was referring. An Austrian by the name of Schmitt. Wilhelm Schmitt. He teaches at the university in Salzburg, but he has no idea Gerber was working for us."

"Are you sure? Have you talked with Schmitt to see what he knows?"

"No. But he knows nothing about Gerber's other life. We want to keep it that way."

"How can you be so sure he doesn't know anything?"

"Professor Gerber promised to tell no one what he was working on," Gustav said. "Not even his wife."

"His wife has no idea he's working for you? How is that even possible?"

"She knows he is working for us. She does not like it, but she knows. She just does not know *why* he is working for us. That I am sure."

"His wife and son are surely targets."

"Yes, we offered to pick her up for safe keeping. She refused. She never liked us. Now she does not trust us. We are in the process of offering protective services for his son as soon as we can locate him. He lives in Vienna too. He is grown now, of course, but that will not prevent the terrorists from getting to him."

Frieda returned and placed a blank piece of paper in front of McQueen.

"Danke." He returned his attention to Gustav. "Schmitt might know something. How can you be sure that Gerber didn't talk to him? Surely you're not going to just let him head back to Salzburg without asking him even one question."

"That is all I can tell you at this time, my friend." Gustav finished his last bite of strudel.

"Look, I don't want to feed your PLO conspiracy theory, but I had a welcoming reception at the hotel today."

"Interesting," Gustav said.

McQueen took the Montblanc pen from his coat pocket and handed it to Gustav. He pushed the blank piece of paper in front of him. "Write this name down."

Gustav took the pen from him.

"Sabreen Basara," McQueen said.

Gustav wrote it down. "Enough about work, huh? Hey, I am sure you are wanting to catch up on the world events. There is a little newsstand on Place de la Monnaie. They sell English newspapers there. They open early in the morning, say around six?" Gustav got out of the booth and looked back down at his plate. There was nothing left of the strudel. He then looked at McQueen's half-eaten meal. "You Americans. You do not know how to enjoy good food." He took the last sip of his beer. "It was a pleasure to see you again. If you are ever in my territory, do not hesitate to call. Auf Wiedersehen." Gustav folded the paper and slid both paper and pen into his coat pocket. He waved goodbye to Frieda before disappearing into the warm Belgian night.

Frieda approached the table. With an embarrassed smile she handed Sterling McQueen the check. He reached for his wallet and shook his head. Once again it was vintage Gustav.

# Chapter Nine

Professor Franz Gerber had given up trying to figure out where he was. All he knew for sure was he was in a cave. The musty smell alone could tell him that. Water slowly dripped somewhere down the hallway, but there was no other sound. Nothing else except the closing footsteps of his captor, which brought an involuntary reaction of pain. He remembered nothing of how he got there. His last recollection was pressing a button on an elevator. By the time he regained consciousness he was sitting exactly where he sat, strapped to a wooden chair in the middle of this cavernous room. His arms were fastened tightly to the back of the chair.

He wasn't sure how long he'd been sitting there. He had no sense of day or night. A dimly lit bulb hung above his head. It was the only light in the room and it was constantly illuminated, casting a shadow on the damp rock walls. They were trying to wear him down. He hadn't talked. Not yet. Not ever if he could withstand the torture. And he could withstand a lot more given the stakes.

They wanted to know what he knew. His knowledge was the only currency he had. A currency he planned to spend with Gustav Wagner to get back something that meant everything to him. If he broke and spent it with these barbarians who held him captive what he possessed would become worthless. His knowledge was a commodity only Wagner could spend. The world would survive if they broke him. His own world would surely not.

●

MCQUEEN LOOSENED HIS tie and draped his jacket over the arm of the chair. He reached for the remote control on the coffee table in the sitting room and flicked on the television. After almost a full rounding of the channels he found the BBC. Listening to the anchor, he kicked off his shoes and made himself comfortable on the sofa.

"Delegates to the Euro/Mid-East Peace Conference began arriving this morning at Hofburg Palace in Vienna," the anchor said. "They were greeted by a contingent at St. Michael's Wing from Austria's Freedom Party who protested the continued migration into their country from Muslim-majority countries. The Freedom Party were started by former Nazis in the 1950s but have worked to distance themselves from their dodgy past. The current Freedom Party is a supporter of not only Israel but the move of the Austrian embassy to Jerusalem. Riot police moved in as counter-protesters dressed in black with their faces covered violently confronted the Freedom Party members."

Video showed the black-clad protestors clashing with the Freedom Party. Riot police slugged violent offenders with batons and tried to restore order.

"This latest meeting in the rotating conference was hastily moved up from its date originally set for two months from now on the heels of the failed round of talks in Cyprus just three weeks ago. There the Israeli delegation accused the PLO, with the aid of unnamed Arab countries, of quote, 'stabbing us in the back while smiling in our faces,' alluding to the recent rash of kidnappings and the subsequent violence. The Israelis' thinly veiled rhetoric prompted the entire Arab delegation to walk out of the talks. Each Arab nation has maintained not only its innocence but complete ignorance as to the source of the recent abductions. Meanwhile, Germany has offered to mediate in an effort to bring the two sides together. Daniel Weiss has more."

The reporter was doing a stand-up in front of the Austrian Parliament Building in Vienna. "With agreement by all parties participating in the Euro/Mid-East Peace Conference, Germany has offered to play an intermediary role in an effort to keep the talks from derailing. Israel is sending a delegation as are most of the Arab nations, but the Palestinian delegation is demanding answers from Tel Aviv before continuing any dialogue. That was in reference to the bombing in the Palestinian city of Nablus. Palestinian political figure Mahmud Ibrahim is calling for a new intifada. Israel vigorously denies any involvement whatsoever.

Germany's president of the Bundestag, Heinrich Müller, who has been called in as a peace emissary by German President Sebastian Kaiser, has been meeting with all parties. He made a private and public appeal to the PLO to give the process a chance."

The reporter explained that the Bundestag was the lower house of Germany's parliament. Müller was able to avail himself at a time when the German parliament was not sitting. McQueen guessed the man to be in his late forties. His blond hair was thick and a bit too long. It had a tendency to fall down over his eyes as he spoke conveying a boyish quality. He casually brushed the locks back in place with his fingers. It reminded McQueen of old news clips of Bobby Kennedy. Müller forced a smile and addressed a multitude of microphones over the sound of dozens of camera shutters. He tried to wipe the concern from his face. His tone was conciliatory, conforming to his diplomatic position. He struck McQueen as ambitious but very likable. McQueen listened intently to Müller explaining his meeting with the Palestinians.

"I merely expressed to the Palestinian delegation that we are nearing a crucial turning point in world politics," Müller said in English with just a trace of a German accent. "What may seem in the best interest of one group could affect the entire peace process to the point of serious disrepair. I cannot emphasize enough that it is most urgent that clearer heads prevail and, in the interest of all our futures, we continue the dialogue. We each have much to contribute. We believe familiarity breeds trust. We have come too far now to abandon the peace. There may be rogue elements that want to disrupt that peace. These people know nothing else but hatred and division. We need to ignore these elements and not allow them to disrupt these talks. I urge my colleagues from each delegation to return to the table and discuss our differences instead of opting not to participate."

The gaggle of reporters screamed out their questions hoping to gain his attention. Müller cut through the confusion by pointing to a female reporter standing off to his right.

"Mr. President, how do you react to the violence on the streets at the Euro/Mid-East Peace Conference at the Hofburg?"

Müller's expression turned grave. "I condemn the presence of Nazis at this conference. I do not have to remind anyone here about the painful history of our country. We cannot allow that scourge to ever grow again."

The reporters yelled their questions, but the same female reporter was allowed a followup. "Are you saying the Freedom Party members are Nazis?"

"One should only look at their past," Müller said.

He cut through the yelling of questions once again by pointing to a reporter.

"Mr. Müller, the Americans are obviously not participating in these talks, but their ambassador to Austria condemned the violence on both sides including the anti-fascists who showed up to confront the demonstrators. Do you agree?"

"No, they are not the same. One side is racist, bigoted, Nazi. The other opposes racism and bigotry. There is only one side. Nazis have no place in this debate. 'Both sides' suggests that there's no right side or wrong side, that all are morally equal. But I reject that. It's not hard to spot the wrong side here. There is no defense or justification for evil in the form of white supremacists and Nazis. None."

The BBC reporter's face returned to the screen. "Müller termed the Palestinians' decision not to attend 'counterproductive' and urged them to reconsider what he called, 'a matter with grave global ramifications.' Müller heads the German delegation to the Euro/Mid-East Peace Conference and plans to address the next conference here in Vienna this coming week. Reporting from Vienna, Daniel Weiss."

●

THE VAN RUMBLED along the backstreets of Zurich. In the back, the wide eyes of a young lady said everything her duct-taped mouth could not. She was terrified. She sat with her back against the doors watching her captors who rode silently, their identities concealed by black ski masks. Her breathing was quick and shallow. Her heart pounded in her chest.

One of the men stood and walked toward her. He held something in his hand, but she couldn't tell what. Anxiety enveloped her. He had been the only one to speak to her since her abduction a week ago.

Or had it been two. She'd lost count of the days. How she longed to see her family again. Her college graduation trip had turned into a nightmare the night she was violently ripped from her friends off the streets of Innsbruck and taken to God knows where. Her home since she had been kidnapped was a dank cave with no light. She had been taken there blindfolded as she had been until she found herself in the back of this van.

The man began to speak. She couldn't place the accent. "I wanted this to be the last thing you knew," he said, reaching over her and unlatching the doors.

She struggled to keep her balance and not fall to the asphalt that whizzed by behind her. Then she saw what he had in his hand. He raised the gun and aimed at her. She screamed for mercy.

"Your parents have abandoned you," he said grimly. "They refused to pay the ransom."

He pulled the trigger and shot her between the eyes. The impact thrust her out of the back of the van. She was dead before she hit the street. The body rolled across the hard pavement over and over until it finally came to a grisly stop. The gunman closed the van doors and the vehicle disappeared into the night.

●

MCQUEEN HEADED FOR the bedroom, opened the door of his closet, and pulled his digital voice recorder from his bag. He brought it to the sitting room and placed it on the table while the news continued to play on the television. As before, he inserted the earpiece in his ears. He heard the familiar medium-range pulse. He moved the device to the underside of the table and the pitch became higher and louder. Kneeling down, he looked underneath the table. There it was, a mere speck on the underside. A black electronic bug.

Moving into the bedroom he ran the device over the telephone receiver and heard the high pitch of the bug indicator once again. He cut the device off and removed the earpiece then wrapped the cord around the device and returned it to his bag.

Then came a knock on the door. He zipped the bag shut. Before heading for the door he picked up the remote and clicked off the television. Cautiously he pulled the Sig from its resting place in his coat and peeked through the small hole in the door. On the other side stood a beautiful young lady with shoulder-length black hair and large expressive brown eyes. She carried a tray with a bottle of champagne and two glasses. He returned the gun to its coat holster, smiled, and opened the door.

"Sabreen," he greeted. "I thought you were at the show with your girlfriends."

She smiled and her eyes motioned toward the table by the window. "May I?"

"By all means." McQueen opened the door and stepped aside. "What happened to your big night on the town?"

"Well, we had dinner," she explained while setting down the tray. "After that, no one really wanted to go to the show. They had jet lag and wanted to go back to their hotels, so here I am."

*Jet lag?* McQueen thought. "And you got my room number how?"

"I told the front desk I was sent by your computer company to bring you a welcoming bottle of champagne."

"Very resourceful."

"I thought you might enjoy a glass with your view," she said, walking toward the balcony doors. "It's quite lovely. Don't you think?"

"Indeed it is," he said.

"You know, I probably shouldn't be here," she said with a flirty pout.

"Is that so?" McQueen smiled to himself and popped the cork. "And why not?"

"Well, I hardly even know you. And here I am fraternizing with a strange American man." She flashed a mischievous smile.

"Fraternizing?" McQueen asked as he poured a glass. "Bad choice of words. No, um—" He frowned as he searched for a suitable substitute. "I'd say 'socializing' is a better choice." He smiled and handed her a glass by its stem. "To socializing," he toasted.

"To socializing." She returned the toast and they both took a sip.

"So, why then?" he asked.

"Why what?"

"Why did you come here tonight?"

She turned away nervously. "I don't know." She fumbled for the right words. "I guess it was our conversation about London. I got a little nostalgic. Maybe I thought more conversation would do me good."

The view off the veranda was gorgeous. The magnificent tower at Town Hall lit up the night sky. McQueen pulled back the sheer curtain, opened the door, and moved aside for Sabreen to step out on the balcony.

"Isn't it romantic?" she sighed, taking in the view.

McQueen allowed the question to float by. They both leaned against the railing breathing in the atmosphere. "I'm going to guess Syria," he said.

"Excuse me?"

"Where you're from," he explained. "I'm guessing Syria."

"Close," she smiled. "Actually my parents were born in Palestine. I was born in Egypt, but we've lived all over the Middle East."

"And now?"

She took a sip of champagne. "And now I live in Paris."

"What brings you to Brussels?"

"I told you today. I have meetings, then I'm doing some sightseeing with my girlfriends."

"What kind of meetings?"

"You *are* the inquisitive one, aren't you? The dull kind."

"How did you end up in Paris? Or am I being too nosey?"

She laughed. "Not at all. After I finished school in London, I decided I didn't want to go back to the Middle East. At least not right away. There's still too much hatred there. It's getting better, I guess, but still I was not ready to return. A girlfriend and I decided to see Europe and settle where we felt most comfortable. We fell in love with Paris, and so that's where we stayed."

"And your girlfriend?"

"She was American. She returned home to the States."

"So you live in Paris all alone," McQueen fished.

"Yes, I suppose that's right," she said, looking into his eyes. "It does get a bit lonely from time to time."

She moved closer sliding her arm around McQueen's waist and leaning her head against his chest. She gazed out across the skyline of the city. After a moment, she moved even closer and, looking up, softly kissed him on the lips.

"I have a big day tomorrow," McQueen said.

"Let's not worry about tomorrow," she said softly.

"I wish I didn't have to worry about tomorrow, but unfortunately, I do. I have a very early start."

McQueen removed her arm, which was now around his neck, took a sip of his champagne, and motioned her back inside the room.

"You're going to give me a complex," she teased.

"Maybe some other time." He was serious and cold.

Her playful smile turned to a frown. She set her glass back down on the tray. He ushered her in silence to the door.

"Oh, I almost forgot," she said. "I need to return the champagne glasses to the bar."

"Don't bother. I'll handle it."

He opened the door for her and she made one last ditch effort. "Perhaps tomorrow night?"

"Sabreen means patience," McQueen said, nudging her out the door.

"How did you know that?"

"Goodnight." He closed the door and watched her through the peep hole. She paused for a moment then walked away.

McQueen picked up her champagne glass by the stem and set it on the coffee table in the sitting room. He went to the bathroom and pulled out what appeared to be a bottle of men's cologne from his toiletry bag. Walking to the bedroom closet, he retrieved the digital voice recorder. He set the recorder down on the table then gingerly picked up the empty champagne glass. Holding it by the base he slowly turned the glass and sprayed it with a thin coating. He placed the glass back down and chose 'MAGNIFY' from the menu on the digital voice recorder. The next menu gave the option of several different powers of magnification. McQueen made his choice and a clear picture of about one-fourth of a fingerprint appeared on the screen. He rotated the glass slightly until the fingerprint was centered then clicked to photograph. With his left hand he rotated the glass by turning the base until another print came into focus. With each turn he took another photograph until he had turned the glass 360 degrees.

He picked up the telephone next to the sofa and dialed the number. The red line on the phone at Lieutenant Sexton's desk rang. "Peliken International, Washington," she answered.

"Yes, Sterling McQueen here. Is Mr. Miles available?"

"I believe so, Mr. McQueen. Let me check."

She buzzed the colonel's office. "Incoming call from McQueen, sir."

"Thank you, Lieutenant." Bragg picked up the phone. "This is Miles."

"Mr. Miles, this is Sterling."

"Sterling, how's Brussels?"

"Great, sir. I've got a meeting with my new staff in the morning. Could you e-mail me the Kendall file?"

"The Kendall file? Sure. Is that all you need?"

"At the moment," McQueen said.

"Well, I'll have someone e-mail that to you immediately. We miss you around here, but Brussels is going to be a great opportunity for you."

"I learned from the best, sir. Thank you for everything."

"It's been my pleasure working with you, Sterling. Goodbye now."

"Goodbye, Mr. Miles."

Bragg slammed down the phone. "Damn it all! Who the *hell* knew he was coming?"

# Chapter Ten

The morning sun had not yet shown itself in Brussels when McQueen's eyes opened. He hit the floor for his fifty push-ups then laced up his running shoes and reached for his sweatshirt in the closet.

He ran in place at the intersection and looked up at the Royal Theater of the Mint, the opera house in the center of Brussels. He jogged into Place de la Monnaie just as the sun was rising and locked in on the outdoor newsstand.

"Good morning. Do you speak English?" he asked the man of about sixty behind the counter. His close-cropped gray hair was obscured by the blue motoring cap.

"Good morning," he replied in his Dutch accent. "Yes, what can I do for you?"

"A friend of mine told me this was a good place to buy an English newspaper."

"Who is your friend? Maybe I know him."

"Gustav," Sterling replied.

"Gustav? Sorry, I do not know anyone named Gustav." He then reached down behind the counter and produced a folded paper. "You are from the States?"

"Yes," he answered.

"You will be especially interested in how the dollar is performing."

"Thank you very much."

McQueen loved this time of the day. Getting up for an early run made him feel more alive, like he had a jump on the world. He decided to grab a bite to eat at one of the many outdoor cafes. He wanted something a little more substantial than the typical Belgian breakfast of a croissant and Gouda cheese. He ordered two fried eggs, bacon (crispy), wheat toast with honey, and coffee. He opened the newspaper and read the headline in the lower left corner. 'Berlin billionaire gives it all away.' McQueen read the story with interest.

The waiter brought his coffee. "Merci," McQueen said.

He finished reading the story on the Berlin billionaire then turned to the financial section. There taped to the page beside the currency quotations was a small portable memory chip about the size of a SIM card. McQueen discreetly removed the chip and slid it into the pocket of his sweatpants.

●

A MAN IN an olive-green suit with an open-collar shirt sat at a tiny metal-top table. His bronze forehead, in front of a prematurely receding hairline of dark brown hair, glistened in the Egyptian sun. He read the back of the folded newspaper in his left hand and sipped strong coffee from a colorful small cup in his right. Handcrafted lanterns of unpolished brass decorated with brightly colored glass hung closely together to attract the attention of souvenir-seeking tourists. The lanterns moved slightly in the gentle breeze in front of the khaki coffee house. Old men chatted and laughed at the table next to his. Around another small table sat a couple starting their day of sightseeing.

His cell phone rang inside his coat pocket and he laid the newspaper down to answer it.

"Hello." He took a sip of his coffee.

"Either he is on to us or we have the wrong man," Sabreen said as she walked through a shop-lined street.

The man set his coffee cup on the table. "We have the right man. What are his movements?" He retrieved a cigarette pack from his other breast pocket and pulled one from the pack with his teeth.

"We've been unsuccessful in following him outside his hotel."

"Then that should tell you all you need to know. This is the man the Americans have sent, but if he is evading your team, then he knows you are there. You cannot be effective if he is aware of your presence." He lit the cigarette with a silver lighter, pulled the smoke into his lungs, then out through his nose.

"Shall we move to phase two?" she asked.

The man thought for a moment, dabbed a fleck of tobacco from his tongue with his middle finger, then flicked it. "Yes. Alert your team to move to phase two. But listen to me, I want him taken alive. We must know what he knows."

"I understand."

The man terminated the call and returned the phone to his breast pocket. After a momentary reflection, he picked up the paper and continued reading.

●

MCQUEEN RETURNED FROM his morning jog and breakfast and turned on the radio in the sitting room. He grabbed the digital voice recorder from the bedroom closet and took a seat at the desk. He inserted the ear buds in his ears. He then retrieved the memory card from his sweatpants and placed it in a small slit in the side of the player. A screen appeared asking for his top secret clearance code. He entered 9194-592-526. At that point it was obliged to disclose the top secret intelligence information contained in the memory of the disc.

It was an audio/video dossier. The first image that flashed upon the screen was the college yearbook photo of Professor Franz Gerber. A computerized voice began to disclose biographical data. Instead of listening to the voice he chose to read the rest of the information. He read about the professor's involvement with the German government.

He lingered on a family photo of the Gerbers. How typical they looked. Good looking family. Both parents looked prosperous and happy and their young son was all smiles and beaming. He scrolled to another photo of the family posing on a mountain summit during a ski trip. Erich was probably seventeen or so. He had his mother's dark hair and dark eyes. Very handsome. He was all grown up now, leading his own life. And that life had been turned upside down.

The next section was a video of one of Professor Gerber's lectures at the university. McQueen studied his face. The screen switched to a still photo of Professor Wilhelm Schmitt. The computerized voice resumed. It told him that Schmitt and Gerber were close friends.

That Schmitt taught Middle Eastern Studies in Salzburg. That he was currently attending a symposium on Middle Eastern affairs in Brussels.

A videotaped lecture by the professor was next. The menu at the bottom provided many different looks at Schmitt and McQueen studied each one carefully.

At the end of every report there was an 'Action' page. This page told McQueen what his orders were. He thumbed down to the final page. 'No action at this time. Stand by for further instructions.'

McQueen smiled a frustrated smile. He figured it wasn't so much that he was untrustworthy. Bragg was a strange bird. He liked to keep these types of cases compartmentalized. Made it easier to control. The colonel just loved secrets and enjoyed the pleasure of divulging them at his leisure. Regardless, there was nothing to do now but wait.

The telephone on the desk rang and McQueen picked it up.

"Hello."

"Mr. McQueen?" the young female voice inquired.

"Yes."

"This is Sophia, the Chairman's secretary here at Peliken International, Brussels. Welcome aboard."

"Thank you," he answered.

"Are you available for brunch this morning?" she inquired.

"Yes I am."

"Good. There's a little cafe about two blocks from your hotel. Cafe Grand. Turn right on Rue du Lombard and you'll see it. Say eleven o'clock?"

"That's fine," McQueen confirmed.

He headed for the bath. It was odd, but the times McQueen felt most ill at ease were while he was in the shower. There was something about the water drowning out all other noises, the steam covering the room like a veil, and the drawn shower curtain acting as a blindfold that made him feel so vulnerable. Especially during the obligatory closing of the eyes to wash the shampoo from his hair. He found himself oftentimes ripping back the curtain just to make sure no one was there. He always kept his stainless P232 close by just in case. It's not that he was paranoid. Just cautious.

After the shower, McQueen got dressed, double-checked his Sig in its resting place in his jacket, then headed for the lobby. Exchanging greetings with the concierge, he headed out the front door of the hotel. The lead taxi looked at him inquiringly. McQueen waved him off.

He strolled along and thought about his life. It was only in the down time that he sometimes wondered if he had made the right choices. A family, even if he wanted one, would only be a liability, something used as a vehicle by his enemies to get to him. Family, in the traditional sense, meant children's birthday parties and family picnics, dance recitals and football games. He turned right at the roundabout at St. Jean Square. To the McQueen family it would mean constant suspicion of any child brought home to play and flinching each time his wife started the SUV. Family was not an option, at least not anytime soon. McQueen put the entire thought out of his mind and enjoyed the morning sun on his face. He turned right on Rue du Lombard. The walk helped him clear his head.

The screech of the tires shattered his daydream like an anvil through a plate glass window. McQueen's right hand instinctively grabbed the wooden grip of his gun and rested there awaiting further orders from his brain. The nondescript gentleman in the front passenger's seat emerged from the black sedan with heavily tinted windows and silently held open the back door. The dark glasses denied McQueen a look at his eyes. Then the voice from inside the back seat was the unmasking.

"Guten Morgen, mein Herr."

"Jeez, you scared the crap out of me," McQueen shot back angrily.

Gustav smiled his used car salesman grin and McQueen joined him in the back seat. "The boss would like a word with you," Gustav informed him.

McQueen closed the door. "Doesn't he know that it's my day off?" he asked dryly.

Gustav let out a roar and slapped his knee. "Maybe you need to start a union for spies," he joked. "My orders are to deliver you."

Gustav reached in his coat pocket and pulled out a cherry sucker. He unwrapped it, stuck the wrapper back in his pocket, and popped the sucker into his mouth.

"You still eating those things?" McQueen asked.

He pulled it from his mouth. "You know, it is funny, I first got these to help me kick my cigarette habit. Now I cannot quit the damn suckers." He popped it back in his mouth and glanced over at McQueen then back straight ahead. "Did you fall into the honey pot last evening?"

McQueen smiled without looking at him. "My ego's not that big. A girl like that falling instantly head-over-heels in love only happens in the movies."

"The pictures were not good enough to get a positive ID," he said, handing McQueen back his Montblanc pen. "Perhaps you should take a class."

"Funny. Maybe this'll help." McQueen handed Gustav a small flash drive.

Gustav deposited the drive in his coat pocket without even a glance. "I know this is a small town, but the wolves have come calling early. The potent smell of a U.S. intelligence agent is obviously a strong one. Very troubling."

McQueen glanced over at Gustav but said nothing.

"Enjoying your stay so far?" Gustav asked with a grin on his face.

McQueen looked back at him then cautiously answered, "So far."

"That is nice." Gustav smiled, looking straight ahead.

McQueen looked back at him trying to read his face then smiled a frowning smile and shook his head. Gustav loved being purposely mysterious.

The car pulled over to the side and Gustav looked out the window. "This is your stop."

McQueen got out and walked in the front door of a nondescript office building. He'd been there before. Several times, in fact. Down the hallway to the left he stopped at the last door on the right and walked in. A spotlight shone on the logo behind the receptionist's desk—Peliken International.

"Welcome back, Mr. McQueen," Sophia greeted.

"Sophia, you're like a slice of home right here in Brussels," McQueen spouted.

"Merci, Mr. McQueen. The Chairman is here. He's waiting for you in the conference room."

●

BRUNO KESSLER CALLED his core group together in the break room of a bakery in the Alsergrund section of Vienna. The proprietor sympathetic to their cause allowed them to meet and plan strategy before and after bakery hours and on Sundays when the business was closed. The handful sat around old wooden tables, exchanging light conversation, until the ominous gaze of Bruno Kessler called their attention to the front of the room.

"I do not need to remind you how important the coming week is to our cause," Kessler began. "Just as has been predicted by our forefathers, the foreign invaders have laid waste to our land. They have raped our women. They have depleted our resources. They have altered our identity. Our people have suffered deterioration in all sectors of life. We aim to eliminate the afflictions from our life which continue to foil any real recovery."

The crowd grunted in affirmation.

"How free are we, really, when we are not allowed to fly our flag in public? German-speaking leaders continue to pay lip service to our lost identity all the while acquiescing to the very forces of our destruction. There is only one solution that will save us. Anschluss! Germany and Austria will once again be one! We will fight to the death for Anschluss and this time we will be victorious!"

The group rose to its feet and cheered. "Anschluss!"

# Chapter Eleven

McQueen walked alone down a long corridor. At the end he took the elevator down six floors. Off the elevator he walked another fifty feet down another corridor. The double doors at the end opened to a large round foyer with a fountain in the middle. Four other sets of double doors opened to corridors much like spokes on a wheel. He proceeded around the fountain through the doors on the opposite side of the room.

Once through the doors he stopped in front of a marble bust on the right just a few paces from the door. The double doors closed automatically behind him. At first glance the room looked like a small but beautifully decorated study. Incredible works of art adorned the walls and bookshelves were brimming with leather-bound books. McQueen reached out and as if to push the bust from its pedestal he turned it over on end. The cap split in half and the ear of the bust came slowly to rest on the dado. A green screen lay flat on the cap and he placed his right hand on it. Not only did the computer scan for fingerprints, but it matched those prints with the size of the hand as well as any traits peculiar to the individual. Most important, it made sure there was a beating heart behind that hand. Almost as soon as his hand came to a rest on the screen a beep was heard and the bookcase in the rear of the room retracted. McQueen returned the bust to its upright position and passed through.

An armed guard stood at attention beside a small open-air tram. Another plainclothes guard stood inside the tram in front of the controls. McQueen boarded the tram and took a seat. Without a word the guard shifted the gears and the tram headed down the track. McQueen counted the guards that stood at attention at regular intervals alongside the track. There were twenty in all.

After a mile or so the track came to an end. The tram stopped and he hopped off. There were two more armed guards standing on either side of a large metal door. Another plainclothes guard stepped forward.

"Welcome, Mr. McQueen. The meeting is about to begin."

The uniformed guard on the right opened the large door. McQueen stepped inside and waited a moment in a small foyer. The large metal door closed behind him. Two large wooden doors in front of him slowly opened and a magnificent room was revealed before him. The ceiling reached more than thirty feet high. A breathtaking crystal chandelier cast slivers of light onto the marble floor as well as the solid mahogany conference table that stretched almost the full fifty-foot length of the room. Acoustically, the room was a masterpiece. Anything more than a whisper was perfectly audible anywhere else in the room. His heels clicked and echoed among the murmur of voices emanating from the conference table.

McQueen took his seat in front of his place card. A gooseneck lamp protruded from the table in front of each agent. He looked around the room smiling at old acquaintances and mentally tallying up the countries. Every nation making up the NATO Alliance Intelligence Team was present and accounted for. NAIT was the elite division of the NATO Intelligence Fusion Centre. The NIFC was headquartered in the UK. It was outside of national chains of command and fell under the operational command of SACEUR, the Supreme Allied Commander Europe. NAIT, which headquartered in Brussels, was the NIFC's elite team of agents chosen from the best that NATO members' intelligence organizations had to offer. McQueen knew any time NAIT was called together something monumental was in the offing.

The double doors at the far end of the room opened and two uniformed guards sternly entered and headed toward the table. Their steps clicked in unison. Behind them were two aides, one carrying a briefcase chained to his wrist, the other with a stack of files. Between the two aides was SACEUR himself, General Emmett Franklin Bushing. The entire room snapped to attention and it echoed across the marble expanse.

General Bushing was a large man. One got the impression that under all the medals and gray hair and considerable weight was a real fighting man. In fact, when he wore a younger man's uniform he was in peak condition. Decorated twice for single-handedly removing wounded comrades from harm's way at risk of losing his own life, he had won the respect of those who served with him and was awarded two Purple Hearts. The military was not just his employer, it was his life. An eighteen-year-old E. Franklin Bushing was down at the recruiting station signing up on his birthday. The man was hard core. His favorite quote was from United States Marine Corps General James "Mad Dog" Mattis: "Be polite, be professional, but have a plan to kill everybody you meet."

Bushing's booming voice with its precise northern accent echoed throughout the hall. "Sit," he barked and pulled his leather chair toward him settling his considerable derriere in the compressed seat.

The rest of the room followed his command. The aide with the briefcase unlocked it and placed a large file folder in front of the general.

"Ladies and gentlemen we've got ourselves a situation. As head of NATO Intelligence, it's my duty to bring it under control once and for all." The general looked down at the papers he shuffled through as he talked. He reached in his left breast pocket and pulled out a pair of white-rimmed reading glasses. The aide with the armful of files quietly distributed his load to each agent.

"The politicians and the diplomats have all had their go at it," he said, looking up over his reading glasses, "and failed."

A large projection screen slowly and quietly descended behind him. The lights dimmed and the gooseneck lamps at each seat glowed. He took one last look at the papers on the table in front of him then removed his reading glasses and rose to his full height. Turning around, he pulled a small laser pointer out of his coat's other breast pocket. A map of Europe was projected on the screen.

"As you all know, there have been twelve hostages taken over the past year." The laser pointer cast a small red dot. "One taken here in Innsbruck," he pointed, "one here in Munich, two here in Paris, one in Amsterdam, two here in London, two in Geneva, two in Berlin, and the last one right in our own damn backyard." He turned back toward those assembled at the conference table. "If you would please, ladies and gentlemen, open your files."

McQueen looked down at the file marked 'TOP SECRET.' He broke the band of paper that sealed the file and laid the stack of papers on the table in front of him looking back up at the general.

"Until now, this has been a European Union Intelligence and Situation Centre operation," General Bushing said. "EU INTCEN has been trying to break the case of the recent rash of kidnappings. They've asked for NAIT's help. Our focus is going to be this man, Franz Gerber." Each agent looked at the top photo in their packet. "You should know a little bit about the professor from your individual computer briefings. I believe he holds the key to the entire hostage puzzle. Up until last week he was a professor at the University of Vienna. Up until last week he was also a BND intelligence asset. They had him working his sources to shake loose any details on the hostage ordeal. Just when they thought he was about to bring them something big he disappeared. Next slide."

On the screen were the faces of the twelve hostages with their names and the locations of their abductions underneath. All twelve young faces smiled down on the assembled agents. General Bushing turned back toward the conference table. "Care to guess what ties all these people together?" He surveyed the table. The general looked back up at the photos.

McQueen stated casually, "Well, aside from Gerber, they all appear to be in their twenties. Their names haven't been reported in the media. They're all Jewish, or were. Except for Gerber, of course. And if my dot-connecting is accurate, at least a couple of these hostages are children of billionaires who've recently liquidated their assets."

"Yes, they're *all* children of billionaires," Bushing said. He flashed their fathers' and mothers' pictures on the screen with their purported net worth. "Of the twelve hostages taken, three have been released. Not coincidentally, the parents of these three have totally liquidated their assets. Understand, because this is important, they haven't sold anything. They've *given* everything to charity. Even the family homes. Two hostages were killed and dumped in the streets. The assumption is the families wouldn't meet the kidnappers' demands."

"Sir?" British Agent Victoria Carrington of the SIS raised her hand.

The general acknowledged her with a nod. "Carrington."

"Sir, what is the conventional wisdom as to who's behind these latest abductions?" Her accent was refined and educated. The general listened with eyes focused on the floor and hands clasped behind his back. "What I mean is the differences you've outlined might suggest we're dealing with an entirely different group of terrorists."

The general leaned forward with his palms on the edge of the table. "Different group or different tactics? In the '80s, what we had were several different fanatical groups taking hostages, each with its own agenda. What did that accomplish? Virtually nothing. The hostages became more of a liability than an asset. Then we had the ISIS hostages. They were taken for the shock value of streaming their beheadings on the Internet. My theory is these groups learned something. They learned that they could buy more with cold hard cash than with bodies. Look, these groups need money to buy weapons. They don't give a damn about trading prisoners anymore. We're close to real peace over there. It's been a peace through major compromise—on all sides. Some people have a hard time getting used to compromise. If you don't believe in what's happening you try to destroy it, and the fastest way to do that is through terrorism."

"Well, it certainly does appear it's about raising money," Carrington said.

"What these thugs need is capital to make sure the peace doesn't happen," the general said. "Where do you think they're going to find the funding they need? They may get a little cash under the table from some of the more radical Arab countries, but the eyes of the world are on these countries to make peace happen. The threat of sanctions or us kicking their asses is hanging over their heads. So these new terrorists find hostages with cash attached to them. Hostages that can really buy them what they need."

French Agent Pierre Bujot of the DST asked, "What kind of resources are we talking about, general?"

"So far, the total assets liquidated come to about $18 billion."

"Ummm," the Frenchman sighed. "That is a lot of money."

"Of course, the assets were divided up among thousands of charities. Not every charity is going to be terror-related. When you're talking about billions of dollars and thousands of charities it's easy to hide. Our people are cross-referencing those charities now."

"But what about the denial by the Palestinians?" Bujot asked.

"That's just more of what the hell I'm talking about," the general said. "Look, forget what you know about terrorist tactics. We're dealing with a new breed. A more dangerous breed. The goal is not publicity anymore. The fear generated by the abductions is just a byproduct. The primary objective is money, plain and simple. Money to support the cause. Money to buy weapons and train men. Money to keep the unrest stirred up in Gaza and the West Bank and anywhere else they can create chaos."

"So, you think it's the PLO?" McQueen asked.

"That's something we need you people to figure out. The reason we brought all of you here is because we believe whoever is behind this, their next move will be more than just another abduction."

"Meaning?" Agent Tomek Nowakowski of Poland asked.

"We don't have anything concrete yet," Bushing said. "Just some chatter. Some of you will be following up on that."

Agent Antonio de la Fuente of Spain raised his hand.

"Yes, sir," General Bushing pointed to him.

"General, I agree with Agent Carrington. It feels as though we are dealing with an entirely different group of people. The terrorists of old do not have the funding as before, but they do not have the intelligence either, yet they have been able to beat us at every turn. The abduction of Professor Gerber does not appear to be the work of some loose-knit band of radicals. It appears to have been thoroughly thought out and flawlessly executed. There is no way, in my opinion, that this act could have been carried out successfully by the caliber of terrorist with which we have become accustomed in the past. Certainly not without the intelligence needed for such an operation."

"I wouldn't disagree with that assessment," Bushing said.

"The degree of trouble to which these people went," de la Fuente continued, "indicates to me that the professor had uncovered intelligence of gargantuan proportions. No?" He looked around the room as everyone nodded. "Intelligence which would perhaps completely expose these terrorists. I believe, as the general does, that the PLO may very well be behind this latest rash of terrorism, but, if so, we are talking about a new PLO. We are not talking about the old

Arafat PLO, but a much more sophisticated faction. They have the money," he counted off on his fingers, "they have the manpower, and they have possibly the intelligence."

"Which means they possibly have someone on the inside feeding them that intelligence," Nowakowski pointed out.

The general rose slowly from his comfortable chair. "Again, anything's possible. However, let me add that our intelligence sources tell us that the PLO is more unified today than it has ever been. Are there going to be disgruntled members within that body? Sure, but do they have the means to pull off the operations we've been seeing in Europe lately? Well, that's one avenue some of you will be exploring."

Luca Bianchi from the Italian Agenzia Informazioni e Sicurezza Esterna raised his hand.

"Yes, Agent Bianchi," Bushing said.

"General, pardon me for saying so, but it seems we are chasing our own tail. We are drawing supposition from what we know of an enemy that no longer seems to apply. Without truly knowing our enemy, we are flying blind."

"Which is exactly why we're here," Bushing said. "EU INTCEN has been running into dead ends for too long. They're no closer to naming names today than they were when the first hostage was taken." He pounded his fist on the table. "We absolutely have to put a stop to these kidnappings! Stability in the entire Middle East hangs in the balance. We *have* to find Gerber," he declared as he paced. "At least find out what Gerber knew. It's hard enough trying to find these bastards as it is. Now that we possibly have someone feeding them inside information it's damn near impossible. You people are the only ones who'll have any knowledge of our plan. No elected officials, no diplomats, no presidents, no prime ministers, nobody. And nobody in this room will be given the entire plan. I'm not taking any chances with this. We find Gerber, we find out what we're dealing with, and we're in a better position to stop it. Any questions?"

There were none. The general stopped pacing and leaned across the table staring into the face of each man and woman at the table as if looking into their souls. "You're the best damn intelligence agents in the world. I'm counting on every last one of you." After a moment, the general straightened himself and relaxed his jaw. "You have dossiers on all the players on your cards enclosed in your files. Study them. You also have your orders. As usual, study, memorize, destroy. That's all."

The aide who had passed out the files quickly made his way around the table retrieving them, leaving each agent their individual memory card. General Bushing scribbled some notes then slammed his file shut and handed it to the aide chained to the briefcase. The aide slipped it into the case, locked it, and followed the general and his entourage out the double doors.

# Chapter Twelve

Leopold Hofsteiner was just the kind of man one would expect to rise up the ranks to head the BND, the German Federal Intelligence Service. He was disciplined. He was resourceful. He was connected. And he could kill you with his bare hands if he had to. His division acted as an early warning system for the German government and he took that responsibility very seriously. His title was president. He insisted on being addressed that way. He had gone apoplectic on Gustav Wagner for losing the only real chance they had of solving the kidnappings and getting a jump on the terrorists. That chance was Franz Gerber.

Hofsteiner's phone in his wood-paneled Berlin office rang. The red one. The number only a handful of government dignitaries had. He settled into his leather chair and answered curtly. "Hofsteiner."

"President Hofsteiner, this is President Heinrich Müller."

"Yes, President Müller. To what do I owe this honor?"

"This is not a courtesy call. I am in Vienna preparing for the peace conference. I want to know the status of the Gerber kidnapping."

"We have every available man on the case, Herr President. We have even enlisted the aid of our allies and their intelligence operations to help us locate him."

"And what is the progress on that front?"

"Nothing yet. They have just been called in and it will take some time."

"Let me make myself clear, President Hofsteiner, I consider the mishandling of this case the biggest failure of German intelligence since the Munich Olympics." No greater insult could be flung at a BND official. "We have a peace conference starting here in a few days and I want answers!"

Hofsteiner sat up in his chair. "Yes, Herr President." His tone was almost desperate. "I can assure you we are doing everything that is humanly possible to—"

"Then we will need superhuman results! I want to be kept in the loop with even the slightest detail. Is that understood?"

"Understood, Herr President."

The phone went dead. Hofsteiner would never tell the president of the Bundestag that he was greatly offended by the subservient role the BND was forced to play in the operation. The Gerber case had been theirs from the beginning. Gerber was *their* asset. They had utilized him off and on for decades. When he was kidnapped the big boys wanted to swoop down and take over. That call was made above his pay grade. Chancellor Armbruster had deferred to SACEUR who ran NATO's intelligence apparatus.

It was decided since so many NATO member nations were affected by the kidnappings operational control should be transferred to them. Especially since the kidnapped victims were Jewish. It created an entirely new level of sensitivity that still troubled the Germans. The 1972 Munich Olympics debacle had haunted German intelligence since that day. Israeli athletes were kidnapped by Arab terrorists and German authorities tried to rescue them, resulting in the death of every single hostage. Hofsteiner vehemently protested the transfer of authority in the Gerber case, but to no avail. The BND was forced into an ancillary role and all he could do now was make the best of it.

Still, he didn't have to like it. Truth be known, he didn't much care for the Americans. He thought their post-war treatment of Germany had been heavy-handed and condescending. They never let them forget who was in charge, or at least that's what he inferred from their actions. American military bases on their soil, acquiescing to their wishes, everything always hinging on the American dollar. It was all so demeaning, and usually it was some American general who Hofsteiner felt was inferior, intellectually, to whom he was deferring. He would help the Americans, but he would help them begrudgingly.

He went to the computer on his desk. After entering his access code, he brought up his current orders. He then clicked on the American he'd been ordered to cooperate with. McQUEEN, STERLING—

NATO—HUMAN INTELLIGENCE DIVISION—USA. He studied McQueen's mug for a lingering moment. He skimmed the highlights of his dossier. Two Golden Eagles, the highest service award given by the U.S. intelligence agencies. A French Bravado medal for his part in foiling an assassination attempt on their president.

He exited out of the file and leaned back in his seat with his arms crossed. He lightly pressed his left fist's knuckles to his lips and rocked slightly back and forth in his chair.

●

MCQUEEN RETURNED TO his room. He laid his coat on the bed and went directly to the closet. After a quick check of his luggage, it was obvious someone had been through his bags. The digital voice recorder was there. Useless, of course, to anyone who didn't have a code and didn't know what it really did. It was, however, something of value to one who knew no better and thought it was a typical piece of electronics. Yet there it was. McQueen's Cartier sterling silver cuff links worth hundreds of dollars were still there. Obviously this was not a burglary. They were looking for something. He walked to the wet bar in the sitting room and poured himself a scotch. He sipped the whisky on the sofa, gazing out the window, when the phone rang.

"Hello."

There was silence on the other end. McQueen counted in his head. Eight, nine, ten. The line went dead. McQueen placed the receiver back down on its cradle. He walked to the bedroom, grabbed his suit coat from the bed and the digital voice recorder from the closet, then headed for the lobby. Now that they—whoever *they* were—had his room under surveillance, any work would have to be done elsewhere. Once in the lobby, McQueen checked his watch. Exactly five minutes later he was paged to a courtesy phone.

"McQueen," he answered, looking around the lobby.

"The girl's name is Alena Sharabi. She is PFLP," Gustav said.

"PFLP?" McQueen was surprised. The Popular Front for the Liberation of Palestine was one of about ten factions inside the Palestine Liberation Organization. The PFLP had opposed the Camp

David Accords and called for social and political revolution in Egypt. He couldn't believe she was mixed up with a group like that.

"Nothing major, really," Gustav continued. "No terrorist acts as far as we know. Just a few arrests for protests."

McQueen said, "I still have a hard time believing they're behind all this."

"I hate to say I told you so, friend Sterling," Gustav gloated.

McQueen glanced over at the restaurant and caught the gaze of a guy in the corner with ear buds. He went back to working on his computer.

"You have not seen your orders yet?" Gustav asked with a smile in his voice.

"No."

Gustav let out a chuckle. Then the line went dead.

McQueen looked back over at the guy in the restaurant. He intently watched his computer. McQueen inspected his clothes. Most of the crowd were foreign businessmen and women. This guy didn't quite fit. He was tall and lean with dark hair and dark complexion. His coat was draped over the seat next to him. It was wrinkled in the back which indicated to McQueen that he probably spent a lot of time sitting in his car. Staking out McQueen's hotel perhaps?

McQueen headed for the restroom. He knelt down to see if anyone was in the stalls. Satisfied he was alone, he took the last stall, locked the door behind him, pulled the digital voice recorder from his pocket, plugged in the ear buds and the memory card, and waited for the device to find it.

It asked for a security code. 'TOP SECRET' appeared on the screen first followed by 'BRUSSELS OPERATION—SECTOR THREE.' McQueen pressed the arrow for further information. Next heading: 'AGENTS ASSIGNED—SECTOR THREE.' Underneath the heading, McQueen saw his own name: 'McQUEEN, STERLING—USA.' Below it was 'WAGNER, GUSTAV—GERMANY' then 'BARTON, VIVIAN—USA. MISSION: LOCATE PROFESSOR GERBER. WAIT FOR FURTHER ORDERS.'

How the hell they were supposed to accomplish that was anyone's guess. McQueen erased the memory card, pulled it from the digital voice recorder, crushed it, then flushed the remains down the toilet. He strolled back through the hotel lobby and caught the dark lean man still in the restaurant out of the corner of his eye. Time to flush the bushes. When the man saw that McQueen was heading for the front door, he was on the move. McQueen hurried out the front and hopped into the first available cab. He glanced back over his shoulder to see the lanky man dashing for his car. McQueen smiled to himself and faced forward. "Driver, do you speak English?"

"Oui, monsieur. Yes."

"There's a man in a blue sedan. He's following us."

The driver looked in his rearview mirror. "Oui, monsieur. With the dark windows. I see him pulling out. Would you like for me to lose him?"

"Oh, no," McQueen said, sitting back in his seat. "I want you to make sure you *don't* lose him. Understood?"

"Understood, monsieur."

# Chapter Thirteen

Protesters amassed outside Hofburg Palace in Vienna, the site of the Euro/Mid-East Peace Conference. They carried placards denouncing unbridled immigration from predominately Muslim countries. "Schliessen die Tür," they chanted, led by a man with a bullhorn. "Close the door," referring to the European Union's open door policy to immigrants. They were furious about the recent spate of kidnappings. Riot police with 'POLIZEI' emblazoned on their backs kept a watchful eye.

The swarm seemed to come from every direction. Young men and women dressed head to toe in black with black bandanas covering their faces descended on the protesters swinging clubs and fists. Complete mayhem broke out. Protesters tried to defend themselves, but they were no match for the self-proclaimed 'Antifaschistische' who held the element of surprise. The anti-fascists screamed and beat the protesters like people possessed. Riot police quickly jumped in to try and break up the violence but found themselves pummeled as well. Reinforcements came running from their positions around the corner to help restore order to the street in front of the stately palace.

The anti-fascists scattered in all different directions. The polizei gave chase for a few yards then fell back to their positions around the palace. They had been warned by their commander not to be lured away from their posts so that the Hofburg was left vulnerable. Their only concern was its security.

Two black-clad figures scampered down Kohlmarkt dropping their homemade clubs as they ran. A shorter one followed the lead of the taller one. Glancing over their shoulders, they turned left on Wallnerstrasse where the crowd thinned. Another peek behind and there was no sign of the polizei. They ducked down an empty alley and collapsed in a doorway. The young girl who was barely sixteen stared wide-eyed at her companion who seemed to be laughing behind his black bandana. She pulled it from his face. Her fright turned to a nervous giggle and she pulled down her own bandana. The young man, nearly ten years her senior, produced a flask from his pocket and took a shot of bravado between his chuckles. He offered her a taste. She declined.

"What is so funny?" she asked.

"That was exhilarating. What a rush." He laughed again out loud. "Did you see their faces? It felt so good to pummel that Nazi scum."

"Do you not feel the least bit guilty?"

"No," he answered incredulously. "Do you?"

"A little. We are supposed to be about peace and harmony and justice."

He reached up and held her face with his free hand. "Ingrid, listen to me. Sometimes justice is violent. You do not think those Nazis would do the same thing to you—or worse—if they ever got the chance?"

"I suppose," she said.

"They would. That is why we must make sure they never get the chance again. Do not doubt the cause. The cause is just. I know this was your first time, but you will get used to it. It is the only way to deal with these animals."

"But are we not animals when we behave as they do?"

"It is the only way. It is all they understand."

"But does that make us right?" she asked.

"You must understand something. If Hitler hated us so much we must be the good guys. You know it is true."

He waited for her smile of approval. Once he got it he lifted the flask in a silent toast and took another swig. She grabbed it from his hand and took a long swallow herself. She quickly removed the flask from her lips and almost spit the liquid all over him. Her face was contorted. She shuddered and they both laughed until they cried. Her laughter suddenly turned to longing. She gazed into the eyes of the young Austrian momentarily then thrust her face forward into his. Her lips parted and her tongue danced passionately inside his mouth.

●

MCQUEEN'S TAXI IN Brussels drove along at a leisurely pace for about a mile. The car behind them maintained a polite distance.

"Is he still there?" McQueen asked.

The cabbie looked in his rearview mirror. "Oui, monsieur."

"OK. I want you to take a right at the next light, then I want you to kick it," McQueen instructed. "Do you know what that means?"

The cabbie smiled a wide grin. "Kick it." He liked the sound of that. "Oui, monsieur. We are going to try to lose him, no?"

"Yes, we're going to try to lose him," McQueen replied.

"Hot dog," the cabbie exclaimed in his thick accent. The wheels of his taxi squealed making the right turn. "Just like American TV cop show."

McQueen smiled slightly and looked back to see if their 'tail' had made the turn. He had.

"OK, left at this next corner," McQueen ordered, looking back at his man who was staying with him about a block behind.

McQueen looked at the meter then reached in his pocket. He handed the cabbie a wad of bills over the seat.

"This should cover the cab fare and the joy ride."

The cabbie glanced down at the money, then back at the road, then back at the money, then up at McQueen in the rearview mirror. "Merci," his smile beamed. "Merci beaucoup!"

"Drop me here at this corner," McQueen instructed.

The taxi came to a screeching halt. McQueen bolted from the car. The taxi pulled away from the curb. McQueen ran up the steps of an outdoor shopping center. Just as he hit the top steps, the blue sedan was howling to a stop. The lanky man was immediately out of the car. McQueen took a right at the top of the steps and disappeared. Seconds later the lanky man was standing at the top of the steps frantically looking around. He ran to the right, but there seemed to be nowhere to run. He looked back to the left where he saw a door. Busting through it, he found it merely led back down the steps on the left side of the building. He surely would have seen McQueen running down those steps as he approached the building. He then proceeded to wade through the thick crowd of shoppers looking in every direction for a trace of his charge. There was none. After combing the entire shopping complex, he called it quits.

The lanky man returned to his car and decided to head back to the hotel and wait for McQueen's return. He couldn't face his boss with the humiliation of having lost him. He pulled away from the curb and cringed at the thought of having to admit failure. But his boss knew of Sterling McQueen. Surely he would understand.

He was preparing to switch lanes when he glanced in his rear view mirror. He saw Sterling McQueen holding his Sig, the muzzle an inch away from the base of his skull.

"Just keep driving," McQueen ordered calmly. He removed the lanky man's pistol from his breast holster. The man said nothing. "I don't know who you're working for, but I think it's about time we met him." He pressed the pistol firmly against the man's head.

"I do not understand," the lanky man confessed in a thick French accent.

"I know whoever's pulling your strings is somewhere in Brussels. I want to meet him."

"That is impossible."

McQueen tightened the gun against his head. "Did I just hear you say 'impossible?'" McQueen said through clinched teeth.

"OK, OK," the man said, trying to calm him.

McQueen kept his eyes on the road while the lanky man drove to the outskirts of town. He pulled onto a gravel road and McQueen took note of the abandoned warehouses on either side. At the third warehouse on the right the man turned in. They got out of the sedan.

"Make sure you keep your hands behind your head," McQueen said.

The two men walked up the six steps to the loading dock. McQueen had his Sig in his right hand, the lanky man's pistol in his left. Beside the two huge loading dock doors was a smaller door.

"Open it," McQueen said.

It creaked from lack of use. He pushed the lanky man inside. The vast warehouse was empty. It was hard to say what it had been used for. All the equipment was gone. The smell was musty. The summer sun streamed through the windows and the dusty air. McQueen's eyes darted continuously around the room. He scanned the dirty floor for footprints leading to doors, which might indicate the presence of someone else in the building. All footsteps led to a single door at the far end of the warehouse. Once there, the lanky man stopped in front of the door.

"Through that door," the lanky man said, motioning with his eyes.

"No, no, no," McQueen said politely. "After you."

The man opened the door and reluctantly entered first. McQueen followed and saw a single light fixture hung in the middle of the room which barely illuminated the office. Three men sat against the wall to his right, another two against the wall to his left. Each sat there expressionless. In the rear was a desk. Behind the desk was a large leather chair which was turned around facing maps on the back wall. One of the men against the wall started to reach for his waist. McQueen's head jerked in his direction. He snatched the lanky man close to his body, the Sig uncomfortably distorting the skin on the man's cheek.

"Is that a Glock?" McQueen asked the guy who had so unwisely moved his hand.

"Yeah. What about it?" he answered in his Bronx accent.

"Well, you might want to file that sight down."

"File the sight down? How come?"

"So it won't hurt so bad when I cram it up your ass," McQueen said.

The laughter coming from behind the leather chair was unmistakable. The chair slowly turned around to reveal its occupant.

"I told ya he'd take him," the man laughed through clenched teeth holding a cigar. "Now pay up."

The Bronx man rolled his eyes then continued his reach to his wallet and counted out twenty-five dollars.

McQueen's mouth was agape. "Son-of-a-bitch."

"Welcome to Brussels, McQueen," Colonel Bragg said, rising from his chair and walking around the desk. "I see you've met Agent Cassel."

Bragg took Cassel's pistol from McQueen's left hand. Agent Cassel lowered his hands and walked sheepishly over to the wall and took a seat with the others. The Bronx man laid the bills in Bragg's hand and the colonel pocketed them.

"That's pretty damn good, McQueen," Bragg said with a smile.

He popped the magazine out of Cassel's gun and engaged the action. The chambered round fell to the desk. He maneuvered the cigar from the left side of his mouth to the right and slapped the magazine back in place with his palm. Still looking at McQueen, he whipped the pistol across the room. Cassel was caught off guard and managed to awkwardly trap the gun against his upper chest just below the chin. Gaining control of the weapon, he returned it to his holster.

"He's a loaner from GISS," Bragg said. "Still got a few things to learn." He turned to the seated men. "You guys go play in the traffic or something."

When the last one filed out and shut the door McQueen asked, "Is the nanny really necessary?"

"Not if you ask me, but this one's from the general. He's not takin' any chances. He doesn't trust a damn soul, Sterling. Not even you. We've got a haint."

Friendly spies in the world of espionage were referred to as spooks. Haints were the hostile ones.

"So I hear," McQueen said. "You want me to find out who?"

"Let me worry about that. I have other plans for you. Just be damn careful who you bring into your confidence." Colonel Bragg walked back behind the desk and pointed to the map with the wet end of his cigar. "Look here. Pull up a seat." He settled back into his comfortable leather chair. McQueen grabbed a ladder-back from up against the wall and pulled it between his legs, crossing his arms over the back.

"This is the route Professor Gerber took from Vienna. We know that he left Vienna at oh-six-hundred and five hours and arrived in Salzburg at oh-nine-hundred and ten. He changed trains and caught the nine thirty to Munich arriving at eleven-hundred thirty hours. Now, here's where it gets interesting. The shorter route would've been Munich to Cologne then on to Brussels. He went from Munich to Frankfurt instead. I wanna know why. And he waited until fourteen-hundred and fifty-five hours to head for Frankfurt. That gave him about three-and-a-half hours in Munich. Not a lot of time to do much of anything, but obviously there was something in Munich."

"Well, maybe he was just waiting for the next available train," McQueen speculated.

"We checked that. He could've caught three different earlier trains, but he didn't."

"Family, maybe?" McQueen said. "He's from Munich."

"No family left in Munich since he took the teaching job in Vienna," Bragg said. "So, he took the 2:55 out of Munich. He arrived in Frankfurt at eighteen hundred and four hours and spent the night. We don't have the name of that hotel yet. He didn't use a card. I want to know if he met with anyone in Frankfurt on his overnight stay and what it was about if he did."

"Anybody in Frankfurt pick him up when he arrived?"

"No. They didn't have any reason to at the time. They can't put a tail on every asset of the BND. He'd been doing research for three months. They didn't know how crucial his intelligence was until he contacted Wagner from Brussels. He left Frankfurt the next morning for Brussels."

"Did he stop anywhere else between Frankfurt and Brussels?" McQueen asked.

"Cologne. There was a train to Brussels 11 minutes after he arrived," Bragg said. "In fact, there was a train about every hour, but he spent three hours there."

"And where do I come in?"

"You and Wagner are gonna retrace his footsteps. Pick up Gerber's trail in Munich then follow it back here. See if you can dig up anything. Talk to who he talked to. If you find out what he knew we won't have to go traipsing all over Europe tying up our best agents looking for him. I have a feeling if we find out what he knew it won't be too hard to find him."

"And the new ping?" McQueen asked.

"Agent Barton? She's here to keep an eye on you. Your cover's already blown. That's worrisome. Time to bug out. You need somebody watching your back."

"The girl from the hotel. Gustav says she's PLO, or at least an affiliated faction. I find that hard to believe."

"If she is, then we got bigger problems than I thought. If the PLO's behind these kidnappings and they've already latched onto you, then we have a hole big enough to drive a tank through."

"I'd like to work that angle."

Bragg smiled, "With the girl? I suppose you would. We'll handle that. You need to find Gerber."

"Gustav says the professor sounded like he had a bombshell to drop," McQueen said.

"Yeah, well, we wanna make sure that bombshell doesn't blow up in our faces. You better get back to your hotel and get some rest. You're catching the overnight train to Munich."

# Chapter Fourteen

In the old days, penetrating and embedding within the enemy was a much easier proposition. If you wanted the Soviets to believe you were truly willing to turn on your own country you simply stole a top-secret document as proof. It was black propaganda that would surely convince your new handlers that you meant business. Gaining their confidence was a matter of proving your worth over a period of time.

Infiltrating a terrorist organization, on the other hand, was damn near impossible. The initiation to the club was not stealing some state secret and passing it along. It was lopping off someone's head, a drastic measure no double agent was willing to take. Therefore the intelligence services of the West were flying virtually blind. Someone like Professor Franz Gerber was a rare commodity. McQueen could certainly understand why Gustav jumped at the chance at utilizing him. What was equally understandable was the terrorists' desire to silence him. That valuable asset was now gone, and it was imperative that they find either Gerber himself or the important piece of intelligence he was about to pass along in Brussels.

McQueen arrived at the platform at Brussels-South station at seven-twenty in the evening. The seven-twenty-eight to Cologne pulled in right on time. He found his seat in first class and stowed his bags above. There was an art to living in the moment. Most people are either reflecting on the past or contemplating the future. Such daydreams drop the guard of situational awareness. McQueen's mind was trained not for travel but for detecting dangers around him. He may pretend to read a newspaper or gaze out a window, but each second was spent assessing his surroundings. Heightened awareness came second nature in the field.

He looked at his watch. He had a little less than two hours before he'd have to change trains in Cologne for the sleeper to Munich. Once they were rolling, he found his way to the dining car. He took a seat at one of the booths with a white tablecloth accented with a flower in a small vase. The smartly dressed waiter in white jacket and black pants offered him a menu. He began perusing the dishes.

"Mind if I join you?" a voice from the other side of the menu began. "I figure we have a couple of hours to kill."

McQueen's jaw tightened and he slowly lowered his menu. He glanced up and down the aisle of the train car then back up at Vivian Barton. "What the *hell* are you doing here?" he whispered through clinched teeth.

"Well, I couldn't very well call you." Sarcasm dripped from her lips. She adjusted her glasses by the frame and took a seat in the booth opposite him. "Don't worry. We're in the gap."

"There is no gap out here."

"So you're not so sure of your observation skills," she said.

"I'm plenty confident of my skills. You got on three cars back. There's just no way to account for everybody on this train. You're completely out of line."

The waiter returned. "Would you like a menu, Fräulein?"

"No, thank you," Agent Barton answered. "I'll have whatever he's having."

The waiter turned to McQueen.

"I'll have the beef entrecôte, please." He closed the menu and handed it to the waiter. "Medium rare."

"Make mine medium *well*," she added.

"And to drink, Fräulein?" the waiter asked.

"Merlot, please."

"Make that a Cabernet Sauvignon," McQueen insisted. "Two"

"Very good, sir." The waiter disappeared into the galley.

"You're pretty set in your ways aren't you, McQueen?"

He snapped the cloth napkin taut and returned it to his lap. "I know what I like if that's what you mean." He was still working his jaw.

"That's *not* what I mean." She stared at him for a moment. "Is it women in general you don't like or just me in particular?" She pursed her lips slightly.

"Is there a difference?"

"We're all the same as far as you're concerned?"

"That's been my experience." There was a trace of indifference in his voice.

"What do you have against my kind?"

"Your *kind*? Aside from the fact that you talk too much?"

Barton withdrew a bit from the table just as the waiter delivered their wine. They both waited cautiously until he had poured it and excused himself. She leaned back into the table and lowered her voice. "Now, listen to me, McQueen."

"Must I?" He took a sip of his wine.

"I know you don't take me seriously."

"Tout à fait." He raised his glass.

"That means 'absolutely,'" she said. "I took four years of French."

"Congratulations."

"I don't think you quite realize what we're dealing with here."

"Then why don't you enlighten me, *Ms.* Barton."

"We're dealing with a new breed of terrorist."

"Are we? What's your theory?"

"The tactics these terrorists are using," she argued, "they're almost identical to the tactics used by the—"

"PLO," McQueen finished. "Yes, I know. Gustav has the same theory."

"It's more than a theory," Barton insisted. "Look at the motive. They don't want peace with Israel."

"Some do."

"Many don't. Not to mention the girl."

"The girl?" McQueen played dumb.

"Alena Sharabi. Sabreen. Whatever she's going by today. She's PFLP. The Popular Front has been at odds with Fatah inside the PLO for years. They certainly have motive. And then a PFLP agent just happens to show up on your doorstep."

"She *was* PFLP at one point. We have no idea how she's involved now."

"Letting a pretty face cloud your judgment?"

"Nothing clouds my judgment. I also don't jump to obvious conclusions."

"But these new terrorists—"

McQueen interrupted, "These new terrorists look an awful lot like the old terrorists, I will agree. Only this time instead of trying to change political policy, they're trying to raise money. It's as if the terrorists have decided to become capitalists. The PFLP in particular has never been known for capitalism." He raised his glass to his lips. The waiter delivered their meals. Once he was gone, McQueen continued, "I'm not sure you have a grasp on—"

"Why? Because I'm a woman?"

"Your insecurities run deep, don't they?"

She observed him for a lingering moment. "*My* insecurities? With your misogynistic attitude I would guess you satisfy your basic desires with prostitutes."

McQueen finished slicing a piece of steak. "Do I look like I have to pay for it?" He put the piece of meat in his mouth and chewed slowly. Then he spoke again, "Does buying a girl a meal qualify?"

Barton lowered her head to one side absorbing the gauche remark. She pushed her glasses back up on her nose. "You don't like me, I can tell," she said.

"Well, that makes two of us."

She frowned at the remark. "I know your kind."

"You've pretty much divided people up into 'kinds,' haven't you? What *is* my kind?"

"Cold. Calculated. You don't give a damn about anything or anyone but yourself. I read your 201 file."

"Did you now?" He smiled and cut another piece of steak.

"You love your job because you don't have to worry about anybody else. You do what you want to and you do it your way. You take what you want because you think you deserve it, like you've earned it. You think of women as disposable. You get what you want from them and then you cast them aside. In fact, you're probably looking at me right now and thinking, 'I'd like to screw her brains out.'"

"Well, apparently someone beat me to it."

Barton exhaled an angry breath from her nose. "A typical comeback from a Neanderthal. And I suppose you think you know everything about me just because I'm a woman." She shoved a slice of beef into her mouth.

McQueen finished chewing his food and swallowed. "You feel like this business is dominated by men and you think it's your duty to bust up the good ole boys club. You're a liberated woman. You don't need men."

Barton leaned back in her seat and crossed her arms.

"I'm a liberated man," he continued. "I don't need women."

Barton raised an eyebrow as if she agreed with his assessment of himself.

"You're considered enlightened, even progressive. Me? I'm called a misogynist." He cut another piece of steak, this time with anger. He put it in his mouth and pointed at Barton with his fork. "Do you know what the word for man hater is?"

Vivian Barton looked stumped.

McQueen chewed and smiled, "It's misandrist. You've probably never heard of the word. You'll never hear anyone call a woman a misandrist. Why? Because it's understood."

She looked down and cut another slice. "So, all women hate men. Is that what you're saying?"

"They tolerate us at best. But, yes, I'd say deep down you hate our guts. You'll marry us, but not because you love us. You love the person you think we can be. The person of your fairytale dreams. Then, of course, we never live up to the ridiculous expectations and you feel disappointed and betrayed."

"And then we cheat on you."

"With the golf pro or some seemingly exciting guy at the office who's already disappointed some other woman, but you think you can change him too."

"Are you finished?"

"Not quite. I don't give a damn about your petty hang-ups and your feminist mission. And I don't care if you think life is unfair or what you think of me. You're endangering this operation just by being here and you're getting off in Cologne," McQueen commanded.

"We both are. We have to change to our sleeper train to Munich."

"*I* have to change trains," he informed her. "This is the end of the line for you."

"You're not my commander, McQueen."

"Do I have to call Bragg myself?"

"And what are you going to call him *on*? Your shoe phone?"

McQueen ignored the dig.

"What is it with you and your aversion to technology anyway?" Barton asked.

"What's my aversion? You're a walking homing device." He pointed to her phone on the table. "Right now you're a blinking red light on someone's computer screen. They're no doubt listening to this conversation through that damn phone. Everything you've ever done on the Internet is known to them. They know what books you like, what movies you've seen, where you dine, who your friends are. They know everything about you."

"I'm entitled to my own life."

"You don't have your own life when you join this branch, or didn't they tell you? You can't just turn it off and go home to your own world. Everything you do online or on your phone adds to their profile of you. Profiles lead to habits. Habits get you killed. And now you've compromised me by breeching protocol and contacting me openly in the field. You've got a thing or two to learn about this business and, quite frankly, I don't have time to take on an apprentice."

Barton was fuming, but McQueen had a point and she knew it. If she had truly blown his cover, then Bragg was going to hit the ceiling. "And what am I supposed to do in Cologne?" she asked.

"I don't know. Go shopping. Get your nails done."

Her lip curled. "You bastard." She pulled herself from the booth and stormed off.

McQueen reached across the table and poured her unfinished glass of wine into his.

# Chapter Fifteen

The layover in Cologne was a little over an hour. McQueen sat patiently on the platform reading a newspaper. It was one of the more unglamorous aspects of the spy business. Waiting. He turned a page.

"So, it looks like we work together again, friend Sterling." Gustav unwrapped a sucker, stuck it in his mouth, and sat down.

"Looks like," Sterling replied dispassionately without looking up from his paper.

"Have you been briefed about our little business meeting?" Gustav asked.

McQueen took a slow look around taking inventory of the faces. He liked to relax in quiet. Gustav liked to talk. "As briefed as usual," McQueen said, "which isn't saying much."

Gustav casually looked around then lowered his head and his voice. "Once we find out who we are dealing with I would assume they will reassign the case to the Middle East sector."

McQueen folded his newspaper in his lap. "So, you really think it's the PLO."

Gustav glanced over at him. "Or a faction of it. Yes, I do. Would you like to know why?"

"Desperately."

"Aside from the obvious—that being that you have been tagged by someone from the PFLP—look at the numerical significance."

"The numerical significance?" McQueen squinted his eyes.

"Yes. How many hostages were taken?"

"Twelve."

"Not counting Gerber."

"Eleven."

"Correct. Over how many months did this take place?"

"Twelve?"

"No. Eleven."

"So?"

"Eleven means something in Islam," Gustav said, waving the sucker to accent his point.

"What does it mean?"

Gustav looked to either side. "In the Koran, the Prophet Joseph was thrown down a hole because of his vision by eleven brothers."

"So?"

"So the terrorists are very superstitious that way. The number eleven is also important to them because it is considered a bad number to the Jews. This is why there is no name having eleven letters in Hebrew."

"You're basing your theory on numerology?"

"No, I am basing my theory on *their* belief in numerology."

"Well, let's talk some real numbers. Wanna bet on it?"

"A wager?"

"Yes."

"On a predicament as serious as this?" He waved the notion aside.

"You're *not* sure," McQueen countered with a slight smile on his face.

"That is not it. I just do not think it is appropriate to place a wager on a matter of this nature. That is all."

"Gimme a break," McQueen said in disbelief. "You once bet on a tightrope artist making it to the top of Zugspitze on a cable car cable."

"Who told you about that?"

"Word gets around. Remember, I was with you in Saint-Raphael when you sat there half the night in that casino while you had me calculating odds at the roulette wheel."

Gustav laughed as he recalled.

"I gave you odds for close to two hours," McQueen said, "and not one single bet. Not one. Not until you were sure you could win."

"And I won," Gustav reminded him.

"And you won. Five thousand euros. And what did you give me?"

"I paid you for your time," Gustav insisted.

"A hundred euros?" McQueen tried not to raise his voice.

"It was a fair market price for services rendered."

"You're scared of losing your money."

"I most certainly am not."

"If you were sure the PLO was behind all this you'd bet me in a heartbeat."

Gustav looked at him, chewing on what remained of his sucker. Finally he relented. "Fine. Ten."

"Ten what?"

"Euros."

"Ten euros?" McQueen laughed out loud. He noticed Gustav wasn't laughing. "You're serious. Why not eleven?"

"Very funny."

"You have got to be the biggest skinflint I've ever met. Fifty," McQueen countered. "And make it American dollars." He offered his hand. "I want to spend it when I get back to the States."

Gustav thought for a moment then extended his own. "Fifty American dollars."

They shook on it then sat silently for a time.

"Hey, Gerber was idle for over three hours here in Cologne," McQueen said. "Should be an easy enough window to check surveillance video here at the train—"

"Sterling. Please. Do not insult me. My people are already going over surveillance video."

"He spent the night in Frankfurt," McQueen said.

"Yes, we are on it. And Munich too. We are checking everything."

"All right," McQueen said almost apologetically. "Just making sure we have all our bases covered."

"And what do you expect to find in Munich?" Gustav asked.

McQueen had been going over that very question in his mind. "The best we can hope for is to find out if the professor met with anyone there. And, if so, who? And what were they meeting about? What do *you* expect we'll find?"

Gustav looked at McQueen then back out at the empty tracks. "Not a thing. It is my belief that we are, how do you say, barking at the wrong bush?"

"That's barking up the wrong tree, and what makes you so sure?"

"I have told you. You know who I think is behind the abductions.

They have the motive and the record of terrorism. The professor was very useful in helping us track down some of the names that surfaced in our investigation of the kidnappings. Many turned out to be dead doubles."

That was a term used in the intelligence community for operatives who had assumed the identities of dead babies born close to their own birth dates. It was more elaborate than they were used to.

"Then what's your theory on why the professor took the later train from Munich to Frankfurt?" McQueen asked.

"My friend, it is a long journey from Vienna to Brussels. It can be explained as easily as stopping over for lunch. Perhaps he was picking up souvenirs for his family. There are many reasons for not taking the earlier train."

"But you said yourself he was very nervous when he contacted you from Brussels. If a man was holding information as earth-shattering as what he obviously knew, why would he dilly-dally across Europe shopping and eating? For that matter, why would he even take the train? Why didn't he fly?"

"Possibly he did not want to arouse suspicion?"

"You don't want to admit that he was meeting somebody along the way because that might blow holes in your PLO theory."

"My friend, you have already been placed under surveillance by a member of the PLO. It is your theory which is full of holes, not mine. Look, we are very much alike, you and I. We are trained to see things that no one else sees, but sometimes the obvious answer is the correct one."

McQueen couldn't argue that point. Even with the evidence that Alena Sharabi was a PLO operative it still didn't quite fit. If the PLO was involved how did they manage to hide their hostages from every intelligence organization in the world? Especially in Europe. What did they have to gain by continuing peace talks and making concessions while taking hostages that they wouldn't admit they had? And how on earth did they remove Professor Gerber undetected from a hotel in the middle of Brussels right under the nose of the BND and the Belgian secret police?

"Did you notice the Twin Towers, they looked like the number eleven?" Gustav said.

McQueen looked over at him and shook his head.

"New York City has eleven letters."

"Stop," McQueen said.

"New York was the eleventh state."

"You're embarrassing yourself."

"Flight 11 was carrying 92 passengers. Nine and two is eleven."

McQueen got up and began walking toward the track as their train pulled into the station.

Gustav spoke a little louder over the whine of the train. "George W. Bush has eleven letters."

They slogged along with the other passengers onto the train and found their places. Gustav touched McQueen's arm before he entered their side-by-side sleeping compartments. "We are being followed."

"Blond, medium height, blue suit," McQueen said.

Gustav smiled. "Very good. You have a sharp eye. How do you suppose he found us?"

McQueen shrugged as he opened the door to his compartment. His jaw tightened. *Bitch.*

# Chapter Sixteen

McQueen was jolted awake by the porter's knock. The man continued down the companionway with a quick rap on each door announcing, "Munich, one hour." McQueen hopped out of his berth and unlocked his cabin door. He stripped himself of his underwear and headed into the small shower placing his Sig within reach.

When he emerged, the porter had left him a small breakfast consisting of a couple of different kinds of breads, several slices of cheese, jam, coffee, and orange juice. He looked at his watch and figured he had about thirty minutes to enjoy it. He buttoned up his dress shirt and decided to wait until after breakfast to put on his tie. The sterile, drab buildings out his window looked more like something out of a Cold War movie. The noise barrier beside the tracks was covered in graffiti. It was not the Europe he was accustomed to nor was it the Europe one saw in travel brochures.

Munich was virtually destroyed during World War II. Post-war construction divided Munich into two cities. Many of the apartments that were built were of little imagination. Uninspired, cold concrete human warehouses, they were the product of the "modernists" who emerged at odds with the preservationists after the war. The modernists accepted Germany's responsibility for its own destruction and lobbied for a clean slate on which to rebuild a modern Munich. One need only look at the Bauhaus building in Dessau, Germany, designed by modernist Walter Gropius, to get a sense of the architecture of the time. McQueen called it "a box in a cage" when he happened upon it by accident years before.

Old Munich, however, was restored with meticulous detail. Ironically, it was the Nazis themselves, the source of all the destruction, who aided in its restoration. Although much of the art that populated

Munich's museums and private residences was removed from the city, the Nazis didn't want to create a panic in the city by removing works of art that were outside. They knew that Allied bombs were inevitable, so they painstakingly photographed every outdoor work of art and piece of unique architecture in Old Munich. After the war, and much to the protestation of the modernists, Munich was restored to its former glory as if the war had never touched it.

The train arrived at Munich station at six-thirty-two in the morning. Picking up Gerber's trail would be like looking for a black cat in a coal cellar, but it had only been a few days. Hopefully the scent was still fresh. They stuffed their luggage into overnight lockers and headed for the ticket counter. After questioning each clerk who was on duty and showing the professor's photograph they came up empty. No one remembered seeing him. They moved to the line of taxis outside the train station. Splitting up, they each showed a picture of Gerber to one cabbie after another. After about ten minutes, McQueen turned around at the sound of Gustav's whistle. He motioned for McQueen. Gustav climbed into the back of the cab. McQueen slid in beside him.

"Does he remember the professor?"

"I remember him very well," the cabbie answered in unusually good English. "I never forget a big tipper." He pulled away from the curb. "Because it helps me remember the lousy ones."

The taxi driver clipped along down Dachauer Strasse out toward the BMW museum. McQueen looked behind them to make sure their blond escort was not tagging along. A couple of miles before the museum he took a left. The taxi stopped in the middle of a slightly decaying neighborhood. The huge house the cabbie pointed to looked as though it was a splendid home many years ago. Now it was in need of more than just some basic maintenance. The bushes grew large in front, the paint was peeling, shingles were missing from the roof. An old engraved sign hung from rusty chains which read "258 Wedel Strasse" and underneath "Rooms For Rent." McQueen paid the cabbie and the two walked up the creaking steps and knocked on the front door. After a couple of minutes, an elderly lady slowly opened it.

"I am sorry, but we have no rooms." She started to close the door.

"We are not here for a room. We are looking for a friend." Gustav extended the picture of Professor Gerber. The old lady studied the photograph then looked him over carefully.

"You are with the police?"

Gustav and McQueen exchanged glances. "Well, not exactly. We just want to know who this man came to visit here last week."

"Who are you?" she snapped.

"My name is Gustav Wagner. I am with the BND." He flashed his photo identification.

"So, you *are* with the police. You are with the *secret* police? Then I was right. I tried to tell them I was right."

She opened the door wider inviting them in. Closing the door behind them, she led them into a parlor just off the main hallway. It smelled of moth balls and the morning's bacon. An intricately carved wooden cuckoo clock from the Black Forest depicting maidens hoisting beers at a biergarten hung on the wall and ticked loudly. Magazines and books were stacked all around on tables and the floor. The furniture was old and faded and the sofa springs felt uneven and uncomfortable. A dog barked in the distance. The old lady took her favorite chair.

"So, you are here about Herr Hensel," she said.

"Is that who the man in this picture came to see?" Gustav asked.

"Ja, Ja, his name was Holger Hensel."

"What do you mean *was*?" Gustav said.

"Is that not why you are here?"

McQueen and Gustav gave the old lady a quizzical look.

"Herr Hensel died yesterday," she said. "Right up there." She pointed upstairs. "A gunshot wound to the temple. Surely you knew."

"No, we did not know," Gustav said.

"Then why are you here?"

"We are looking for the man in this photograph," Gustav explained, holding up the picture again.

"Ja, he came to see Herr Hensel. Ja."

"A moment ago you said you were right," McQueen said. "Right about what?"

"About Herr Hensel," she explained. "The police say he took his own life, but I know better. It was no suicide." She looked around as if they weren't alone and lowered her voice. "Herr Hensel was murdered."

"Murdered?" McQueen suspected the bored old lady had an overactive imagination.

"Murdered," she repeated emphatically and nodded to put a period on the theory.

"Did you hear the shot?" Gustav asked.

"I did not hear anything. It was my morning to go to the market. When I returned I got worried when he did not come down for lunch. That is when I found him."

"But who would want to murder Herr Hensel?" Gustav asked, patronizing the old woman.

"Edda-Gesellschaft," she snarled.

"Edda-Gesellschaft?" McQueen repeated to make sure he heard her correctly. He looked at Gustav waiting for an explanation. None was forthcoming.

"Why would the Edda Society want him dead?" Gustav asked.

She looked Gustav deep in the eyes. "Because he knew too much."

"What did he know?" McQueen prodded further.

"I do not know. What I can tell you is he was visited recently by men who are very involved in the Society. I heard shouting coming from his room. When I asked him about it the next day he seemed very frightened. He would tell me nothing."

"Were they drinking?" McQueen asked.

"Nein, Herr Hensel did not drink."

Gustav asked, "Was one of the men he was arguing with the man in this picture?" He pointed to the photograph of Gerber.

"Nein. He came the day before the men from the Society."

"How do you know these men were from the Edda Society?"

"Herr Wagner, I am an old lady. I have seen a great deal in my years. This home has been in my family for many generations. During the war, a Jewish family hid down in the cellar," she pointed at the floor with a decrepit finger, "for six and a half months before they were able to be smuggled out of the country. The stories have been handed down." Her face turned sour as if an unimaginable stench had attacked her nostrils. "They crawl on their bellies like serpents. Evil emits its own vibration. I can feel the presence of evil. These men were evil. I know their kind. They were defeated in the war, but they are still very much alive. The people forget what horrible atrocities they committed. The people forget how easily they weaved their way into our government and how quickly they came to power. The people forget the terror of living day to day not knowing when they would force their way into your home and take you away where no one would ever find you. The people forget, but I," she pointed a thumb to her chest, "I never do."

"I know Frau…?" Gustav realized he didn't know her name.

"Hofmark," she answered. "There is no way you can know."

"My relatives were victims of the travesties of which you speak." Gustav's voice was somber. His eyes were pained. "The story has been handed down in my family of the time they suspected one of our relatives of the bravery your family exhibited during that difficult period. They came on a Sunday afternoon. All of my relatives were there. They had just finished their meal together. The lady of the house was in the kitchen washing dishes, gossiping with the other ladies. All of the men were on the back porch telling tall tales as they did every week. These animals—these, these brutal, depraved savages—stormed through the front door. They grabbed the lady of the house in the kitchen dragging her through the house and out into the front yard. She was so mortally terrified that she was actually regurgitating on herself as they pulled her out into the yard. There were so many of them the men were powerless to stop them. Her husband and the others had to stand and watch as these beasts stripped her of every stitch of clothing and held her up spread eagle for all of the neighborhood to see."

Mrs. Hofmark looked at him with horror in her eyes.

"Her husband tried to help her," Gustav continued, "but he was beaten back by the butts of their rifles. The ringleader of this band of Nazis proceeded to point at her, laughing and making degrading comments. His tone turned serious and he launched into a lecture about patriotism directed at her husband. As he spoke, he leisurely walked around her, fondling her breasts and rubbing her vagina with his pistol. Her husband and the others looked on in helpless horror. He finished his speech and slowly scanned the crowd with his steely eyes and shouted, 'Let this be a lesson.' Then he casually raised his side arm and he shot her between the eyes. The soldiers who had been holding her let go and her limp lifeless body fell to the ground. They say that the blood-curdling scream from her husband was like nothing any had ever heard before or since. The soldiers merely boarded their vehicles and drove away."

The old lady closed her eyes. Tears ran down her checks. She had heard so many similar accounts. Each story cut still deeper into her heart. "I am sorry, young man," she said, reaching over to rub his hand. "I am truly sorry."

McQueen sat in stunned silence. He had known Gustav for years, yet he had never heard that story.

"We would like to see his room if that is all right with you," Gustav said.

"That would be fine. It is the first door on the right at the top of the stairs. The police asked me to touch nothing until their investigation was complete, but I guess it is OK. You are special. Please, find these people."

Police tape X'ed the doorway of Holger Hensel's room. McQueen pushed the tape aside, opened the door, and walked into the room. He held the tape for Gustav to do the same. The noonday sun cast patterns of light on the antique wardrobe. The queen-sized pencil-point bed was covered by a duvet. The bed was still neatly made up. Everything was left just as it was when Mrs. Hofmark found him. Aside from the bed, the rest of the room was quite neat. No sign of a struggle. All of his clothes were tidily folded and tucked away in the dresser. His suits hung all in a row in his closet. The wardrobe had been converted into an entertainment center with a small television behind the doors. There was a small desk with a computer screen, keyboard, and mouse. McQueen made a mental note that the hard drive itself was missing. Probably taken by the police. On the desk was a pen, a pencil, and a pair scissors. There were two upholstered chairs on the wall opposite the TV separated by a small table. A wooden magazine rack sat beside the chair on the left. The only telltale sign of something amiss was the blood splattered on the wall beside the chair on the right.

"Apparently this is where he met his end." Gustav reached down and picked up several magazines and looked them over.

McQueen glanced over at the wall then pushed the door open to the bath and stepped inside.

"Looks like our friend Holger was into firearms," Gustav announced. "There are three different publications in here." He took a second look at the magazines. "I take that back. It looks like our friend just *recently* became interested in firearms." He walked into the bathroom holding them out for McQueen's inspection. "See? No address labels. He was not a subscriber. And all of these are recent issues."

"Interesting," McQueen said. "Look at this." He pointed to the shaving cream and razor sitting on the left side of the sink.

"So the man shaved. What does that tell us?"

"Every piece of clothing the man owned is folded and stowed away in his dresser, right?"

"Right," Gustav agreed.

McQueen peered out the door into the bedroom then looked back at the sink. "His bed is made up. His magazines are stacked in an orderly fashion. Everything is nice and neat."

"So what is your point?" Gustav failed to see the logic.

"His toothbrush and toothpaste are both in the medicine cabinet, but his shaving cream and razor are sitting out."

"So?"

"So?" McQueen said. "Why didn't he put them away when he finished?"

"He was going to kill himself," Gustav answered confidently. "Maybe he did not care about tidying up before he did so."

"I'd buy that if he hadn't taken the time to make up his bed. And why would he bother to shave? Does that sound like somebody who was distraught and preparing to kill himself?"

Gustav rubbed his chin and thought about McQueen's theory.

"I think somebody paid Holger a visit the morning Mrs. Hofmark went to the market," McQueen surmised. "Someone he knew. That would account for there being no forced entry, no struggle. A knock on the door. He's just finished shaving. He wipes his face." McQueen picked up the towel on the vanity and smelled it. "Shaving cream," he said. "He goes to the door and lets that someone in." He walked back into the bedroom and retraced the steps. "They have a seat over here."

He pointed to the twin chairs. "Obviously Holger is sitting in this chair," he said, pointing to the chair on the right. "The assailant pulls out his gun and he shoots him at close range."

"Interesting theory, but he could just as easily have shot himself."

"Not likely."

"You sound so sure."

"I am. Holger was left-handed. The shot came from the right."

"How do you know he was left-handed?" Gustav asked.

"When he hears the knock on the door he sets his razor down. It's on the left side of the sink."

"Any right-handed man could place the razor on the left side too."

"Does your right-handed man use left-handed scissors?" He pointed to the pair on the desk. "Does your right-handed man put the mouse on the left side of the keyboard? And you won't find Holger's prints on those magazines. They're plants. Leaves the subtle impression that he was into guns. Makes it much easier for the mind to accept that it's a suicide."

"So Frau Hofmark is right."

"That he was murdered? Yes. Now what's this Edda Society she's talking about?"

"It is a myth," Gustav said, "a legend. I did not have the heart to tell her that it does not exist. Since the end of the war there has been speculation and rumor that there was a top secret organization within the Nazi party with plans to become the Fourth Reich. They supposedly have these super-secret meetings periodically across Germany where they plan their strategy, plan assassinations and global takeovers, and various similar nonsense. Some believe Hitler actually escaped the bunker and was orchestrating the movement from Argentina," Gustav chuckled. "Even after enough time had passed where it would be impossible for Hitler to still be alive, the rumor surfaced that his brain had been harvested and the Edda Society was in possession of it. Their plan was to implant that brain in the body of a physically superior human and he was to carry on the work of the Führer."

"Edda? What's that mean?" McQueen asked.

"It originates in something called the Prose Edda, written by an Icelandic historian in the early thirteenth century. Apparently there are pearls of Aryan wisdom inside the writings. Legend now has it that the Edda Society never actually died but thrives to this day. It is a myth."

"The BND's found no evidence of the Edda Society existing?"

"Not a shred," Gustav said. "Do not misread what I am saying. The Neo-Nazi movement is very real and something about which we are extremely concerned. They do not brandish swastikas. The swastika and other Nazi symbols are banned by German law. So they come up with their own symbols. They form their own parties. And they run for office. There is nothing we do not know about them. They are fragmented, undisciplined, and disorganized. They are made up largely of misfits and crazies. They certainly are not the elite, secretive force permeating every major business and every level of government that the legend maintains."

"And the person who killed Hensel?"

"Thug? Yes. Nazi? Perhaps. The Edda Society? Preposterous."

Gustav's phone rang. He talked to a subordinate on the other end. McQueen checked the table beside the reading chair. A couple of health magazines, a television directory, a remote control, and a blank notepad were neatly arranged on the small table. McQueen sat down in the chair and turned on the reading lamp. Examining the pad closely, he grabbed a pencil from the desk.

"Professor Gerber made a withdrawal at an ATM at the train station in Frankfurt," Gustav said.

"Doesn't help us narrow down a hotel." McQueen lightly ran the pencil across the blank pad. "How much did he withdraw?"

"Five hundred," Gustav said. "What are you doing?"

"Saw this in a movie once," McQueen joked. After a moment, a word began to reveal itself from the impression left on the pad. A last name, and then underneath were the letters CCC. "Does the name Schneider mean anything to you?"

Gustav gave a chuckle. "Does the name Jones mean anything to you? Schneider is a very common name."

"How about CCC?" McQueen asked.

Gustav frowned and then slowly shook his head. "I cannot think of anything."

McQueen tore the piece of paper from the pad, folded it, and tucked it away in his coat pocket. "Whoever this Schneider is they might just know who killed Holger Hensel. And, more important, they might just know why."

Gustav and McQueen descended the stairs and saw Mrs. Hofmark sitting in her favorite chair watching television.

"Thank you, Frau Hofmark," Gustav said. "We will let ourselves out."

She didn't respond.

Gustav smiled at McQueen, pointed to his ears, and shrugged his shoulders. "Hard of hearing," he said. He walked into the parlor and McQueen followed. "Thank you, Frau Hofmark," he said a little louder. "We will let ourselves out."

Still no response. He walked between her and the television and her expression didn't change. McQueen walked up beside her. He gently nudged her on the shoulder. She fell forward just enough to expose the reason she hadn't responded. Between two ribs protruded a carving knife.

# Chapter Seventeen

Professor Franz Gerber trembled uncontrollably in his arm and leg restraints. His wide eyes watched the skinny pale man meticulously preparing his instruments of torture. The fact that he had so readily revealed his name indicated to Gerber that surely he would never be allowed to live. Meinhard Metzger was his name. Metzger was German for butcher. The name conjured up all manner of ugliness in Gerber's mind. The slight man with the thin, black, greasy hair turned to face him. He walked up to the professor and violently ripped his shirt open exposing his bare chest. The sound of buttons echoed across the floor.

"I'll, I'll tell you what you want to know," Gerber frantically offered.

"Of course you will," Metzger said, sucking his teeth. "Before I am done, you will tell me not only what I want to know but things you had long ago forgotten."

The sweat on Gerber's nose beaded and dripped onto his pants leg. Metzger placed two clamps on his chest, one on either nipple. He took his time walking back over to the control panel where the wires were connected. Looking back, he gave Gerber a sinister smile and delightfully pressed the button. His cold eyes peered with pleasure as Franz Gerber screamed in pain.

"Who else knew, Professor?"

Gerber moved his mouth, but he couldn't speak. Metzger cupped the professor's chin in his hand.

"A name, Professor. That is all we need and this pain will go away."

Gerber forced the words from his lips. "I sw-swear to you. No, no one else knew."

Metzger looked genuinely disappointed, like one would when one's dog doesn't perform a trick as instructed. He took a couple of steps and, with drama, pressed the red button. The jolt of electricity hit Gerber again and he screamed a long scream before his chin touched his chest. He sobbed pitifully.

"We are a very patient people, Professor." He pulled up a chair, turned it around, and sat with his arms hanging over the back. "Very patient, indeed. Listen to me when I am talking to you, Professor." He pulled his chin up and shook Gerber's face in his hand. "Your father."

Gerber struggled to open one eye.

Metzger dropped Gerber's face in order to adjust himself in his seat. "Your father, Klaus Gerber, was assigned to Lebanon because of his expertise in the Middle East. He was hand-picked because he was a trusted aide to the German diplomatic corps there, but he was one of us. A plant, if you will, inside the German government. Did you know this about your father?"

Gerber moaned in pain but was conscious enough to understand what the man was telling him.

"He was our connection to the party in Lebanon. We had common enemies: American imperialism, Zionism, capitalism. Something happened to your father after he arrived in Beirut. No one is sure what. He lost his enthusiasm for the cause. We did not know that your treacherous father was actually smuggling information about the party to the Americans." Metzger's jaw tightened. "They turned your father, the Americans." He grabbed Gerber's chin once more. "Your father was a filthy spy!" The accusation seethed from his lips. "He sensed that his party contacts were getting suspicious of him and he negotiated a transfer back to Germany. That was a mistake. He had no idea that we knew all about him. He was executed for his crimes."

Gerber struggled to make a sound. "Ev-everybody on, on that tr-train died," he finally said.

"Yes, but none more deserving than your verminous father. You see, Professor, we have a very, very long memory. And a very, very wide sphere of influence. We get what we want, even if we have to wait to get it." Metzger pushed himself up from the chair. "So I ask you once again, from the top with feeling."

Gerber dropped his head and said nothing. Metzger slowly walked over to the table. He turned to look back at Professor Gerber then pressed the red button one more time. Gerber's head jolted backwards and he screamed.

●

THE LATE AFTERNOON train pulled into the station on Düsseldorfer Strasse in Frankfurt. McQueen and Gustav walked out of the impressive entrance crowned by a sculpture of Atlas bearing the earth on his tired shoulders. McQueen could empathize. Somebody was trying to keep this secret buried and the longer they took to find it the more death that was sure to follow. Even poor Mrs. Hofmark had paid with her life just for being at the wrong place at the wrong time.

"There's not a damn thing more we could do," McQueen said, stopping in the sunshine between the main entrance and the sightseeing buses. "How much longer are you going to beat yourself up over this?"

"He had to have followed us from the train station to her house," Gustav said, referring to the blond tail they spotted on the train to Munich.

McQueen didn't have to wait for the coroner's report to know how Mrs. Hofmark met her demise. The blade angled upward between two ribs on the left side of her back punctured her heart. It's exactly how McQueen would've done it had he wanted to bring about a relatively clean and quick end. "Maybe he already knew where we were going," McQueen said.

"If that is true, then we have deep penetration, my friend."

"It also means that someone wanted Mrs. Hofmark silenced. We have to get in front of these bastards before another hostage is taken. Gerber obviously was onto something. He made contact with Holger Hensel. Hensel was murdered after they met."

"You are not suggesting Gerber could have done it," Gustav said.

"Wouldn't make sense. If he's part of this little conspiracy to take hostages, why would he become a hostage himself?" McQueen looked around as if he'd lost something.

"What?" Gustav asked.

"Based on how much he pulled out of that ATM, I'm guessing he went high dollar," McQueen said.

"High dollar?"

"Yeah, hotel or dinner."

"On a professor's salary?"

"It's not about high living. It's about information."

"What do you mean?" Gustav asked.

"I mean he left Vienna with a hunch and arrived in Brussels with proof."

"What makes you so sure?"

"Because if he had proof before he left Vienna he would've told you. He was looking for something. And he found it too." McQueen looked up and down Düsseldorfer, the street that ran in front of the train station. "Maybe he found it here."

The crosswalk light changed and McQueen headed across the street. Gustav fell in behind him. After crossing three lanes of traffic, McQueen turned left up the sidewalk.

"Where are we going?" Gustav asked, trotting up beside him.

"We're going to see what Gerber was spending his money on."

They walked into the Manhattan Hotel. Gustav showed Gerber's photograph. No one remembered seeing him. They hit the next one down, the Mercure. No luck. They turned down Mainzer Landstrasse to the Corner Hotel. "Yes," the lady behind the counter told them. She remembered Gerber.

"So much for your high-dollar hotel theory," Gustav said. The Corner was not even a hundred of the five hundred Gerber withdrew from the train station ATM.

"I said hotel *or* dinner," McQueen reminded him, turning his attention back to the desk clerk. "Excuse me, but where is the closest really nice restaurant?"

She thought a second. "Restaurant Sèvres. Just a few blocks in that direction," she pointed.

The restaurant was inside the Grandhotel Hessischer Hof. The waiters busily prepared the tables for the evening crowd. The maître d' held the telephone to his ear with his shoulder, licked his finger, then shuffled the papers on his podium. He scribbled down a reservation. A priceless collection of Jean-Pierre Feuillet porcelain plates manufactured in Sèvres, France, served as a backdrop to the white tablecloths and sterling silver dinnerware inside the dining room. The maître d' finished his phone conversation and looked up to see McQueen and Gustav standing there.

"May I help you, gentlemen?"

"I hope so." Gustav held out the professor's picture. "This man may have dined here five nights ago. Do you remember him?"

The man studied the picture for a moment. "Ja," he answered, not quite sure at first, but his memory was becoming clearer. "Yes, as a matter of fact I do."

"Was he dining alone?" McQueen asked.

"I am afraid I am not at liberty to divulge information about our guests," he smiled. "You understand."

Gustav produced his BND identification. The man's smile ran away from his face.

"Let me see," he said, flipping through his reservation book. "What is the gentleman's name?"

"Gerber," Gustav said. "Franz Gerber."

"Oh, yes. Here it is. A reservation at eight o'clock for two."

"No indication who he was dining with?" McQueen asked.

"Nein," the man said. "Just a reservation in his name." He crossed his arms and lightly tapped his lips with his forefinger. "I do believe he was in Gunther's section though. Just a moment, please." He summoned one of the waiters to his lectern. "Do you remember this man?" the maître d' asked, pointing to the picture in Gustav's hand.

"Ja," Gunther answered confidently, wiping his hands on his apron. "He was here about four or five nights ago."

"Do you have any idea who he was dining with?" the maître d' asked.

"He was with Herr Schneider."

McQueen and Gustav exchanged glances.

"Schneider?" Gustav asked with a raised eyebrow.

"Ja, Richard Schneider from Bonn," the waiter confirmed.

"Are you sure?" Gustav asked in disbelief.

"Ja. Herr Schneider is from Frankfurt, you know. He keeps a little apartment not far from here." After a pause the maître d' spoke again. "Any more questions, gentlemen?"

"No, ah, thank you both very much," Gustav answered still in a daze. He couldn't believe his ears.

McQueen and Gustav walked back through the hotel lobby and out onto the street.

"Obviously Hensel had been in contact with this Schneider," McQueen said. "Or at least there's some kind of connection between Gerber, Hensel, and Schneider. I assume by your reaction back there you know this guy."

"No, actually," Gustav answered. "I have never met him, but I surely know who he is."

"Who is he?"

"He is the top aide to the German Foreign Minister."

The apartment wasn't hard to find. Everyone seemed to know Schneider. Most thought highly of him. He was gregarious, full of life, even generous to a fault some said. The apartment was decorated in a chalet motif. The dark mahogany trim stood in stark contrast to the off-white textured concrete walls. An original oil on board painting of a ship in a harbor at dusk by Conrad Peter Bergmann hung on the far wall opposite the entrance. A staircase with open risers just to the left of the entrance led to a loft with a bedroom and a landing used as an office. The cherry Empire desk on the landing was tidy and uncluttered. The loft overlooked the living area which was beautifully decorated with a fluffy pastel-print sofa and overstuffed pillows. The living area, kitchen, and dining area downstairs were all in one huge room. On the right, as one entered the apartment, was a large stone fireplace. Above the mantel hung a colorful painting of modern abstract art by Claus Richters. To the right of the fireplace an entertainment center housed a television and stereo system with books, pictures, and vacation mementos filling in the shelves. The vaulted ceiling made the room feel even larger and the skylights at the top brightened up an already radiant living area. Dark mahogany beams began about twelve feet up and stretched the width of the room. From the beam closest to the railing on the landing hung a thick rope. At the end of the thick rope hung a very dead Richard Schneider.

# Chapter Eighteen

B y the time McQueen and Gustav arrived at the apartment the local police were finishing up their work. The body of the late Herr Schneider was on its way to the morgue. Gustav flashed his ID and the officer stationed at the door stepped aside.

"Wagner. BND," Gustav said to the man who was obviously in charge.

"Inspector Schulz," the man responded respectfully. "Frankfurt police."

"What do we have here?" Gustav asked.

"Suicide. Herr Richard Schneider, an aide to Foreign Minister Rendleman. He hanged himself. Found by his housekeeper."

McQueen began to look around while Gustav continued his line of questioning.

"Was there a note?" Gustav asked.

"Yes. On the computer screen in the office upstairs. We printed it off." He handed the note to Gustav.

Gustav read it over. Schneider blamed the act on financial pressures, a recent divorce, the inevitability of his job being taken over by someone younger and sharper. It was a page of rambling self-pity. Gustav handed it back to the policeman.

"Mind if we have a look around?" Gustav asked.

"Nein. Not at all. I think we have all we need. Our team is wrapping up. When you are finished please make sure the door is locked behind you."

Gustav climbed the stairs to where McQueen was already looking through Schneider's desk. "Find anything of interest?"

"Not yet," McQueen said. He continued to rummage through the drawers. "Seems like everybody the professor talked to on his little trip came to a sticky end."

"Seems a bit suspicious, does it not, that our friend Richard would opt to destroy himself just when we have linked him to the good professor?"

"My thoughts exactly. Maybe the good professor told him just enough to get him killed. You said Schneider was an aide to the foreign minister. Are the initials of the agency CCC by any chance?"

"No," Gustav said, "it is AA for Auswärtiges Amt, Ministry of Foreign Affairs."

McQueen went back to sifting through the desk. In the bottom drawer he found a stack of sheet music. He popped up and looked over the railing down into the living area.

"What is it?" Gustav asked.

"There's no piano," McQueen said.

"And?"

"Well, why would he have a stack of sheet music and nothing to play it on?" McQueen looked back at the sheet music. He turned a piece over. There stamped on the back was the name of a store. Stefan Rickenbacher Music.

Gustav went back downstairs. He inspected the mantle above the stone fireplace. As he did he caught the smell of soot. Puzzled, he knelt down and ran his finger across the floor of the fireplace. The residue was still fresh. Why would Schneider build a fire in July? He took the poker from the side of the fireplace and began to stir the ashes. Nothing was recognizable except the corner of a piece of paper. Gustav pulled it out of the ashes and blew it off. "Sterling," Gustav said, examining the paper.

McQueen came down the staircase and joined him at the fireplace. "Whatcha got?"

"Something has been burned recently and this is all that is left."

"What is it?"

"Looks like the corner of some kind of heavy paper. Maybe a postcard."

"That's it?" McQueen asked, examining the charred remains. There wasn't much left of the postcard. Just a corner with 'Nr. 0 - 1029' printed on it. "Do you know a good deltiologist?"

"A what?" Gustav asked.

"A deltiologist." He looked at Gustav as if he were joking. "You know, somebody who collects postcards."

Gustav looked skeptical. "I guess it is worth a shot."

McQueen continued to look around the downstairs of the impressively appointed apartment. Schneider had books on vegetarianism and how to live a vegan lifestyle. Photographs of him showed a vibrant man who was the picture of health. Hiking in the Alps. Snow skiing. He was known to be a teetotaler vehemently opposed to smoking. McQueen found it implausible that a man who went to such pains to deprive himself of life's little pleasures in order to enjoy a longer life would purposely find himself at the end of a rope.

They finished their sweep of the apartment and headed for the door. Gustav's phone rang. He held up his hand for McQueen to stop. He finally ended the conversation and placed the phone back in his pocket. "Colonel Bragg wants you on the next train to Zurich."

"What for?"

"You think they are going to tell me?"

The usual gleam in Gustav's eye was gone.

"What's wrong?" McQueen asked.

"They found video of Gerber in the Cologne train station," Gustav said. "He dined with a lady. A woman named Katharina Amstutz, a fashion editor from one of the publishing houses."

"Not likely Gerber was asking her for fashion advice."

"She was spotted recently here in Frankfurt with the late Herr Schneider," Gustav said.

"Well, that's great, right? Pick her up. Let's question her."

"Our people already paid her a visit." Gustav was somber.

McQueen waited for the other shoe to drop.

"Single gunshot wound to the head. Looks like a suicide."

●

MCQUEEN WATCHED THE sun sinking in the sky outside his first class window. As much as he scolded Gustav, he couldn't get Mrs. Hofmark out of his mind. Her fear of the Edda Society was palpable. Gustav didn't believe her, but it was hard to deny a common thread between Holger Hensel, Richard Schneider, and Katharina Amstutz. Gerber had met with them all. And now all of them were dead.

And the unfortunate Mrs. Hofmark was killed apparently just for her curiosity. If it wasn't the society, then somebody certainly wanted her dead. But why? For talking to Gustav and McQueen about Holger Hensel? She had already been interviewed by the police. Why kill her now? Was it just because she was talking to them in particular, or was it because she was talking to them about the Edda Society? If it was the latter, then the Edda Society was more plausible than Gustav cared to admit. McQueen ruminated on the possibility that Neo-Nazis were behind the kidnappings and not Islamic terrorists. It was becoming easier to make that case. If it was true, it meant the entire intelligence community had gotten it wrong. The tentacles of an operation that could pull off something like that were frightening.

The sun set on the beautiful German countryside out his window. He looked at his watch. It would be less than an hour before they crossed into Switzerland and he made his transfer in Basel. He needed a good drink. Instead of ordering at his seat, he decided to stretch his legs and treat himself to a change of scenery. He sat down at an empty booth in the dining car. A tall, slender black-haired gentleman dabbed the corners of his mouth with his napkin. The whites of his eyes almost glowed against his tanned skin. His eyes were fixed firmly on McQueen's back.

●

THE OPERATIONS ROOM located four stories below street level underneath the NATO building in Brussels was nicknamed the *Battle Room*. It was called that because of its resemblance to its more famous big brother, the War Room, in the basement of the Pentagon in Washington. The Battle Room was used as a base for small-scale clandestine operations. It was designed like a rounded pyramid with concentric circles of operation desks. There were three layers with four sets of steps equally spaced leading up to each level and ultimately Colonel Bragg's perch at the top. This allowed him to bark down commands with unobstructed line-of-sight to anyone in the room. Colonel Bragg was briefing Agent Vivian Barton on the latest developments from the field.

"This is not at all what I thought we were dealing with," Barton said.

"Caught us flatfooted as well," Bragg said. "These members are conveniently dying just before our team can reach them. I want to know who knew they were coming! Dammit!" Vivian Barton flinched as Bragg bolted up out of his chair to address the room. "If we have a haint in this room I swear to God I'm gonna kill the bastard myself!" He turned his attention to the officer positioned by his station. "I want a complete dossier on all the deceased within ten minutes!"

"Yes, sir." The officer turned to leave.

"Oh, and it goes without saying, but I'll cover our asses anyway," Bragg added, "make damn sure Hofsteiner at BND understands that nobody talks to anybody in his organization about McQueen. This is a closed-loop operation. Understood?"

"Understood, sir."

The officer scurried down the steps. Another stepped up to take his place awaiting further instructions from the colonel.

He turned to Barton. "Is Agent Wagner back from Frankfurt yet?" Bragg pronounced it like Americans pronounce Wagner instead of the German VAHG-ner, which always managed to rub Gustav the wrong way. Bragg didn't much care.

"Yes, Colonel," Barton answered.

"Get him in here."

She hurried down the steps.

"Colonel," one of the desk officers announced up to the perch, "we have dossiers on Holger Hensel and Richard Schneider. We're compiling one on Katharina Amstutz. I'm sending what we have to your screen."

Bragg returned his reading glasses to his nose and rolled his chair up to the screen. "All right, let's see." He perused the information. After a couple of minutes, he looked down and addressed the room. "Great. I get to see where they went to school and where they worked. Look, people," he raised his voice to everyone in the room, "I can get more crap than this from the DMV! I want some useful intel, all right? I want to know all known associates. I want to know where they bought their groceries, where they drank their liquor, where they did their laundry. I want to know what ties these people together. I don't care if it harelips every cow in Texas. Give me somethin', for God's sake! Dammit!"

The Battle Room door opened. Gustav and Barton walked in. "You asked to see me, Colonel?"

"Agent Wagner," Bragg began the interrogation, "before you left to meet McQueen in Cologne did you talk with anyone else about this case?"

"Well, of course I did, Colonel. Since this is a BND matter I was obliged to file a report. I did just that on the train ride there."

"And your report is filed with whom?"

"With President Hofsteiner"

"Your boss at BND?"

"That is correct, Colonel."

"I see. Anybody else?"

"I spoke with no one else."

"How about since you left Frankfurt?"

"I was preparing my report on the train, but I have not yet finished it. Why do you ask, if you do not mind my asking?"

"Looks like we've got a haint."

"Colonel, I can assure you it is not me."

"That'll be all, Wagner," Bragg said curtly. "Thank you for your help. You can return to BND headquarters. We're releasing you from this case for now. We'll contact you if we need you." He turned back to his computer screen, bringing the glasses back up on his nose.

Barton looked at Gustav then Bragg. "Colonel—"

"Not a word, Barton." His back was still turned to them.

Barton shot Gustav an apologetic glance.

"Now, wait just one minute, Colonel," Gustav said indignantly. "You cannot just open my eyes to a possible security breach inside my very own organization then simply cast me aside. I have the right to clear my name. I have the responsibility to my country to expose the guilty parties and make sure justice is served."

Bragg turned to address him. "It's not like that at all."

"You do not trust me."

Bragg stared back at him.

"Colonel, allow me to remind you of a few things. First, this was our case, our operation."

"And you blew it in Brussels and NATO asked us to take charge." Bragg's cigar anxiously shifted from one side of his mouth to the other.

"I am responsible for Professor Gerber, Colonel. I made a pledge to him and to his wife that we would take care of them. He trusted me implicitly."

"I'm gonna shoot straight with you, Wagner, because I think you deserve it. I'm not worried about you being a double. What worries me is that you're a by-the-book agent. It goes against your grain to keep your people in the dark and that's just what it's gonna take for this operation to go forward successfully."

"Colonel, you heard what I said. I will do whatever it takes. I want a chance to clear my name and cleanse my agency. I owe a debt to Franz Gerber and his family. I am obligated to see that promise through. You cannot take that away from me. Not now."

"I can." Bragg looked at Gustav for a long moment. "But I won't," he said decisively. "Not if you can understand one thing. I work at the pleasure of General Bushing who works at the pleasure of NATO. He would never ask me to do anything to betray my country and I would never ask you to do anything to betray yours. However, if you want to continue on this case you have to understand that you're no longer working for Germany. You work for me. Are you good with that?"

"I am, Colonel," Gustav said.

Bragg looked at him a moment then said, "Go back to your hotel and stand by for orders."

"Thank you, sir," Gustav said politely then excused himself.

Barton watched until Gustav left the room then turned back to Bragg. "We need him on the next operation. We're going to be in Germany and he can smooth out a lot of the wrinkles."

"I can't risk it," Bragg said. "This part is going to have to be flawless and if anyone leaked a word of it, then people will die."

"You told Gustav you weren't worried that he's a double. Did you mean it?"

Bragg let her words sink in. "McQueen needs to know the score. He needs to know somebody's compromising this operation. I'll let him make that call." He went back to reading the report.

"Well, you could call him," she said sarcastically. "Oh yeah, that's right, I forgot."

Bragg didn't bother looking up. "I get it, Barton. He's a little old school."

"A little? He's a fossil. He's living in the '60s. This is the 21st century. People are more educated."

"He graduated from the Naval Academy and he has a master's degree from MIT."

Barton stood there for a moment in disbelief. "McQueen has a master's from MIT? What in? Primitive Studies?"

Bragg looked up at her then back down at the report and smiled. "Computer science."

# Chapter Nineteen

McQueen stood up as the train pulled into Basel SBB. He never understood why people lined up in front of the doors ten minutes before the train arrived at the station. It's not like they were getting off any sooner than anyone else. The tanned man from the dining car was one of those people. He stepped off the train and checked his phone while McQueen pulled his luggage down the two steps to the platform.

McQueen looked at his watch. He had 20 minutes before his connecting train to Zurich. He found a pay station, shut the door behind him, and sat down. After inserting his prepaid card and dialing the number, the phone rang on the other end.

"Peliken International, Brussels. How may I direct your call?" Sophia asked.

"Operations," McQueen said.

"Your code, please." Even though she recognized McQueen's voice there was protocol. No one got through without a valid code.

"Bravo, six, Charlie, six, Romeo, Foxtrot, three."

"How can I help you, Mr. McQueen?"

"I'm sort of on a tight schedule. Can you patch me through to Gustav Wagner?"

"Right away," Sophia said.

Even though he was free to speak, McQueen always felt uncomfortable passing or receiving information over a telephone, even if they claimed the line was secure. No matter, he needed information from Gustav before he made his contact in Zurich.

"Wagner," Gustav answered, leaving the NATO building in Brussels.

"What did you find out at the music store?" McQueen asked.

"For someone who had no formal musical training Herr Schneider sure had a penchant for organ music."

"Organ music?"

"Yes. Herr Rickenbacher was transcribing organ music for Schneider. Schneider would bring in a thumb drive full of organ music. Got the music from some Internet site that posted it. Asked for it to be transcribed to sheet music."

"Interesting."

"And here is the *very* interesting part," Gustav added, "Katharina Amstutz's thumb drives are of the very same organ music."

"That *is* interesting. Any idea what organ?"

"Not at this point. Herr Rickenbacher thought it might be a large pipe organ."

"Anything else?"

"Yes, one more thing," Gustav said, "we have a match on the postcard number from Schneider's apartment. Kufstein."

"Kufstein? Somebody's name?" McQueen asked.

"Nein, it is a small resort town in Austria an hour or so from Salzburg by train near the German border. What do you think it means?"

"I don't know. It may mean absolutely nothing. We don't know what was written on the postcard. That may be the important part and it's gone. I'll hook up with you after my meeting in Zurich."

McQueen stored his luggage in a locker and headed out the front entrance of the station into the dark of the night. He turned left and walked for a block then turned left down a hill that led into a parking garage. The canopy lights cast a mixture of yellow hue and shadows on the oil-stained blacktop. He turned right at the bottom of the hill, quickened his pace and disappeared behind a concrete pillar. To an ordinary human being the footsteps would have been imperceptible. To McQueen's trained ear they sounded like foot falls on a gravel road.

"Remember this," McQueen's instructor in unarmed combat at Camp X had said, "the element of surprise is your best friend." He paced in front of the new recruits. "You take the high ground by getting a jump on your opponent. The last thing you want out there in the field is a fair fight. We're not concerned about Marquess of Queensberry rules." The class chuckled. "Your goal is to get out of this fight alive.

If you need to use an equalizer, use it. You know what an equalizer is?" The class members looked at one another. "A stick, a brick, a bat, anything that equalizes the situation."

The man looked like a Serbian bouncer. He was stocky with a round face, a beak nose, and a faint hint of dark hair around the outside of his skull. His massive arms were too big for his suit. The fist that came out of nowhere nearly knocked him unconscious. McQueen felt the sharp bone of the man's jaw on his knuckles. The blow completely knocked the guy off his feet. McQueen moved in close. The man popped to a standing position. McQueen struck a fighting stance. The man drew his gun. McQueen kicked it from his hand. He heard the clanging metal on asphalt just as he threw another punch at the man's jaw. This one was blocked. McQueen felt the shoe in his gut. The force propelled him backwards and slammed him hard into the concrete pillar.

The big man's eyes darted to the gun on the pavement. He dashed toward it. McQueen sprinted two steps and kicked him in the side just as he lunged for it. The man grunted in pain and staggered upright. He moved quickly toward McQueen throwing punches. The left fist. Blocked. The right. Blocked. McQueen backpedaled. Another left and it connected to McQueen's ribs. McQueen deflected the next right-handed punch with his forearm. The man tried to get close enough to grab him. McQueen stayed just beyond his grip. He knew if the man ever got his huge paws on him he was done for. He swung at the man's face. The huge head pulled back and McQueen's fist swished harmlessly by.

McQueen took an aggressive step forward and delivered a roundhouse to the man's left ear. It hardly fazed him. He kicked again, this time with the left foot. The man caught his leg. He twisted it, throwing McQueen to the pavement, then dived for him like an angry bear. McQueen scrambled aside just in time. He bounced to his feet. The man came running toward him full force. McQueen used the man's own momentum against him. He grabbed him by the lapels, fell backwards, and threw the man across the garage floor.

The big man slid to a stop. McQueen flipped over on his stomach and sprang to a standing position. That's when he realized his mistake. It was like Madrid. This time his adversary was just a tad luckier. The man leapt to his feet holding his own gun in his hand. He smiled an evil grin. In a split second his expression changed to concern. His eyes moved from McQueen to something or someone behind him. His aim moved too, but he never got a chance to pull the trigger. McQueen heard the snap behind him like the sound of a nail gun and the large man was down.

McQueen whipped around to see the lean tanned man standing there, smoke still oozing from his silencer. McQueen looked back at the lifeless body on the garage floor then turned back to face the tanned man.

"Don't worry. I'm a cop," he said with no trace of an accent.

*What kind of cop uses a suppressor?* McQueen thought. *Surely not the rail polizei. Not even undercover rail cops.* This was the exact scenario McQueen feared. He knew he couldn't rely on Colonel Bragg to bail him out. He was a NOC, an agent under non-official cover. An illegal. As far as Bragg was concerned he didn't even exist. Trying to explain who he was to the authorities was not an option. That would be a direct violation of SSB protocol. This guy was not who he thought he was when he first saw him on the train.

"Mr. McQueen," the man said with a smile.

McQueen tilted his head and frowned.

"I'm BND," he announced. "Dominik Jäger." He returned the weapon to his holster.

McQueen's eyes narrowed.

"I understand your skepticism." He reached in his coat pocket and tossed McQueen his identification. McQueen caught the ID. "I had my money on you," the man said. "That is until he came up with the gun."

McQueen looked over the BND identification. It was authentic. "I had hoped to get some information from him."

"He was going to kill you. And me."

"Yes, I suppose he was. What are you doing here?"

"Compliments of President Hofsteiner of the BND. He thought you might need an escort, especially with the stabbing death of that woman at the boarding house. He figured someone might want to kill you too. Good instincts."

"Any idea who this guy is?" McQueen turned the dead man over to reveal his face. "Or was?"

"You don't recognize him?" Jäger asked.

"No."

Jäger pulled his phone from his pocket. He called up an app, and, one by one, pressed the dead man's thick fingertips to the face of the phone. "How'd you know he was following you?"

"I spotted him on the train," McQueen said.

"How about me?"

"Yeah, I spotted you too. Thought you might be working with him. You speak damn good English for a Jerry."

The man laughed. "I went to Harvard. Undergrad and law. Grew up in Munich. Always wanted to be BND. Thought I'd broaden my horizons by schooling in the States. Make myself more attractive. Worked too." Dominik's phone vibrated and he looked down at it. "Armin Amsel was his name. Jeez! Where do I start? He was a contract killer for the German mafia," he read from the file. "And the Italian Cosa Nostra, the Albanian mafia, the Russian Tambov gang, the Serbian Zemun clan all operating out of Germany." He looked up at McQueen. "There's hardly a crime group he *hasn't* killed for. Very bad man."

McQueen looked at his watch. "I have a train to catch. The police are going to have a lot of questions."

Dominik smiled, "Mr. McQueen. I *am* the polizei."

"Yeah, but this is Switzerland."

He laughed, "I have a pretty good working relationship with these guys. Go and make your meeting in Zurich."

"Thanks," McQueen said gratefully.

"But, Mr. McQueen…"

McQueen stopped and turned back to him.

"Be careful," Dominik said. "I won't be there to save you again."

McQueen took the elevator with his luggage up to his platform and caught his train. All he knew about his destination was he would be met at the station by a man. What man he didn't know. He didn't even know what question he would be asked, but whatever it was he was to give one answer and one answer only: The commodore.

# Chapter Twenty

The rain poured most of the trip and McQueen took the opportunity to sleep. The beads of water formed on the train car window and stayed there until they became so heavy they cascaded down like teardrops. He was jolted awake by a clap of thunder and the lightning that filled the night sky. Then the rain stopped. The train was shielded from the elements pulling underneath the shed at Zurich station. It was eleven p.m. McQueen stretched and gathered his luggage from the overhead storage.

He had no idea who he was looking for nor did he have any idea where he was going. Bragg had set up this rendezvous. McQueen figured the old man knew what he was doing. He pulled his luggage behind him to the middle of the great hall of the station to make himself available. It appeared no one was expecting him until he heard a voice from behind.

"Are you looking for someone, sir?" the man with the proper British accent asked.

McQueen was thrown for a second then remembered his response. "Um, the commodore."

"Very good, sir. Follow me, please."

The man led him through the large hall of Zurich station. McQueen took note of the hideous sculpture of a guardian angel by Niki de St. Phalle hanging from the ceiling like some garish Macy's Thanksgiving Day balloon. They turned left under the sculpture and out into the elements. The man unfolded an umbrella above McQueen's head and opened the back door of the limousine. This wasn't just any limo. McQueen knew his cars. This was a 1963 Rolls-Royce Silver Cloud III. The exterior was claret, the interior beige leather. This was the way limousines were supposed to look before all the gaudy stretch models came along. It came complete with gorgeous wood fold-down tray tables. The feel of the interior was magnificent. The driver deposited McQueen's luggage in the boot then climbed into the driver's seat. They hadn't gone far before it became evident the gentleman driving was much more than an ordinary chauffeur.

"The man you're meeting is Commodore Ethan Collingwood," he said, locking eyes with McQueen in the rearview mirror. "He prefers to go by Commodore Collingwood or simply Commodore. He and Colonel Bragg worked together back when they were both stationed at the Horn of Africa running sat recon in a joint operation between America and the United Kingdom."

"Pardon my ignorance, but Bragg didn't give me a whole lot to go on. Just what am I supposed to talk with this commodore about?"

The driver looked in the mirror then back at the road then back at the mirror. The only thing breaking the awkward silence was the rhythm of the windshield wipers. "The Edda Society," he said solemnly.

The Rolls climbed the hills up to Kilchberg with ease as if it knew its own way home. The fifteen minute drive from Zurich had been delightfully luxurious and McQueen absorbed every precious second. The car pulled into a semi-circular brick drive and came to a stop in front of a tall two-story home constructed of red bricks with stone corners. The focal point of the front was the thin tower with windows all around and a dramatic conical spire on top. The windows on the tower and the rest of the house were also trimmed in stone with arched pediments using the same brick as the exterior, accented with three keystones. Lamps burned inside near the windows, which gave it a cozy feeling on a rainy summer night. Before McQueen could reach for the handle, the door was being opened by the driver and he stepped out into the refuge of his umbrella. The sound of rain on the brick driveway echoed in the night.

A butler opened the large front door just as McQueen approached it. Standing on the marble floor underneath a glittering chandelier were two people McQueen instantly took for the commodore and his wife. He was a balding gray-haired man with an over-sized gray mustache and a weathered but handsome full face. He sported a double-breasted navy blazer accented by an ascot. His white trousers, dark blue boat shoes, and crisp white shirt gave him the appearance of just having stepped off a yacht. Mrs. Collingwood was dressed in a white skirt with subtle prints, a dark blue blouse, a tasteful strand of pearls, and white summer sandals. Her hair was cut just below her ears showing off her exquisite neck and jawline. She was younger than the commodore, but not scandalously so. They looked the epitome of British society.

The commodore reached out his hand and spoke first. "We are absolutely delighted to have you here, Mr. McQueen. I'm Ethan Collingwood and this is my wife, Lillian."

McQueen shook his hand and then gently clasped the fingers of the downturned hand Mrs. Collingwood offered. "I'm delighted to *be* here." He looked around the foyer. "What a gorgeous place you have."

"Why, thank you," the commodore replied proudly.

"I am sorry to be calling so late," McQueen said.

"Nonsense," the commodore said. "It's the shank of the evening. Hamish will take your things to your room and—"

"Oh, I wouldn't dream of intruding. I'll get a hotel room down in the city."

"Don't be silly," the commodore answered with an exaggerated wave. "It's much too ghastly to be traveling about this evening. We have plenty of room. It's no trouble atall. Have you had your dinner?"

"Yes, sir. I ate on the train."

"Then you simply must have dessert," Mrs. Collingwood insisted. "Hildegard makes the most scrumptious Black Forest cake."

The commodore turned to the butler. "Markus, erzähl Hildegard, wir brauchen drei Schwarzwälder Kirschtorte." He turned back to McQueen and Mrs. Collingwood then back to the butler. "Oh, und Kaffee. Coffee, Mr. McQueen?" he asked, making sure.

"Decaf, if you have it," McQueen responded.

"Zwei regelmässige und ein entkoffeinierter Kaffee," he instructed Markus. "I'm afraid the poor chap doesn't speak a lick of English. Let's retire to the drawing room, shall we?"

The commodore led the way across the large foyer toward a couple of huge wooden doors. Lillian Collingwood locked her arm in McQueen's and pulled herself closer as they followed. "So, Ethan tells me you're a navy man," she began with an almost schoolgirl excitement.

"Yes, ma'am."

"Yes, *ma'am*," Lillian repeated in her worst American accent. "Did you hear that, Ethan? How absolutely charming. What rank were you?"

"Well, I left the navy as a Lieutenant Commander. Not nearly as successful as your husband."

"And not nearly as successful as he wants everyone to believe," she smirked.

"I heard that," came a loud but playful response from the commodore over his shoulder. He threw open the doors to a wood-paneled room, shelves brimming with books along with pictures and souvenirs from the commodore's vast travels.

"Thankfully we got the call from Colonel Bragg," Lillian said relieved. "It was cribbage night with the Silsburys. I find the both of them dreadfully boring."

"Now, now, Lillian," the commodore scolded lightly. "They're some of our closest friends." Turning to McQueen he said, "Not many ex-pats here, I'm afraid. Have a seat." He gestured toward the sofa. The commodore took the large wingback. Lillian remained attached and they awkwardly plopped down together on the sofa.

The butler arrived with a silver service. He placed a dessert on the coffee table in front of each of them then set the tray down and poured the coffee. A cup containing McQueen's decaf had already been poured in the kitchen and he placed the cup and saucer in front of him.

Mrs. Collingwood untangled her arm from McQueen's in order to reach her dessert. She stabbed her fork into the confection and quickly put a sizable chunk in her mouth slowly chewing as her eyes rolled back in her head. "Ummm," she said as drawn out as possible. "Is this not the most delectable thing you've ever put in your mouth?" She smiled at McQueen.

He took a small piece on the end of his fork. It was, indeed, incredible and he nodded with agreement.

"Let's see, I'm trying to remember the last time I saw Colonel Bragg since the Horn," the commodore said, rubbing his chin. "Oh, yes. It was 21 October, probably ten years ago. Trafalgar Day. The colonel was the guest of a group of POHMs who were part of the Commonwealth festivities."

"Ethan, please," Lillian said distastefully. "Don't refer to the Aussies as POHMs. They don't like it." She turned to McQueen. "And I don't blame them."

"POHMs?" McQueen asked.

"Yes," Lillian explained, "it's a dreadful slang term. Stands for Prisoners of His Majesty."

"Yes, dates back to when they were a penal colony," the commodore qualified. "I've known quite a few POHMs in my day. Haven't had a one take offense yet." He took a sip of his coffee. He thought he could tell what McQueen was thinking. "Oh, don't worry," he assured him. "We love yanks."

"Oh, we absolutely adore them," Lillian bubbled. "Especially ones so devastatingly handsome." She rubbed McQueen's arm lovingly. "By the by, it's Jag-yu-ar, you know."

McQueen frowned.

"Mr. McQueen, tell us," the commodore started.

"Sterling, please, sir," McQueen insisted politely.

"Jolly good, then. *Sterling*, tell us about yourself. Where do you live and such things?"

"Well, I live in Annapolis, Maryland."

"Lovely place," the commodore observed.

"Yes, quite lovely," Lillian agreed. "Isn't that where the Burghoffs were from, darling?"

"No, that was *Indi*anapolis."

"Are you sure?" She took another bite of her dessert.

"Quite."

"Annapolis is on the water on the Chesapeake Bay," McQueen explained.

"And do you yacht?" Lillian asked.

"Do you mean sailboat or cruiser?"

"Either one," she said.

"Yes, I—"

"Of course you do, ole chap," the commodore insisted. "You're a navy man. It's in your blood."

You're *so* like the Kennedys, Mr. McQueen," she said. "Isn't he like the Kennedys, Ethan?"

"Just like the Kennedys, dear."

"Were they from Annapolis or Indianapolis or wherever it is you're from?" she asked.

"No, they were from Boston."

"Ah, Boston," she said. "The tea party. You know we take our tea each afternoon on the terrace by the garden." She pointed toward nowhere in particular. "You simply must join us. The view is exquisite. We're not still sore, you know."

"About what?" McQueen asked.

"About that tea party you yanks had with our tea, of course. You threw the tea into the water instead of the other way 'round and you've been taking tea all wrong ever since. Even adding those dreadful ice cubes." She closed her eyes and shuddered.

"Well, yeah, I would say Annapolis is a good seven hours from Boston." McQueen tried to get the conversation back on track.

"Ah, yes, the Northeast Corridor," the commodore chimed in. "Some great cities up that way. Washington, Philadelphia, Boston, New York. I knew a chap from the south of Philadelphia once. Rattled on about cheesecakes or some such nonsense."

"He was probably talking about a cheese*steak*," McQueen suggested.

"Hmm?" The commodore wrinkled his face.

"Cheesesteak," McQueen said.

"Cheesesteak? What the devil is that?"

"It's al-yu-*MIN*-ee-um," Lillian said out of the blue.

McQueen looked at both of them a bit confused. "What is?"

"The word. It's pronounced al-yu-*MIN*-ee-um."

"All right, Lillian. Off you go." The commodore stood up. McQueen followed his lead. "Sterling and I have some business to discuss."

"I know when I'm not wanted," she joked and gently kissed McQueen's cheek. "Very nice to meet you, Mr. McQueen. I so wish the weather had cooperated. Would loved to have shown you the view at night." She pointed toward the side of the house. "The lights of Zurich to the left and the lights of the boats dotting Lake Zurich right in front. It's beautiful."

The commodore gently cleared his throat. "Lillian."

"I'm going, Ethan. Just being polite, you know." She left the room and closed the large doors behind her.

The commodore walked over to the bar. "Can I fix you a drink?"

"That would be great," McQueen said, sitting back down on the sofa.

"What would you like?"

"Scotch. Neat, please."

Collingwood glanced back at McQueen over his shoulder. "And I suppose you want the good stuff. I know you'd spot the difference. Could tell by the cut of your suit."

"Thank you, sir."

"Lillian's smitten with you. Did you notice the way she looked at you?" He finished pouring the drinks and began his walk back to the sitting area. "You're welcome to her, you know, but you'll have to pick up the payments," he said, handing McQueen his whisky.

McQueen smiled awkwardly.

"Now, then." He took a sip from his drink. "Bragg tells me you may have stumbled upon the Edda Society."

"I suppose you're going to tell me there's no such animal."

"Quite the contrary. They're sort of like Bigfoot. We've never seen them, but we've seen the footprints."

"But Bigfoot is a myth."

"Is it, now? Most conspiracy theories are part myth, part fact. The Society happens to be one such beast."

# Chapter Twenty-One

"**D**o we know his movements?" Alena Sharabi asked the Arab man, not quite old enough to be her father, who sat at the table in the hotel room.

"He is leaving first thing in the morning," he said. He sucked on a toothpick and watched her from behind stuffing clothing into a duffle bag.

"Then we mustn't be late. Did you bring my suit?"

"I did."

"Splendid. I want to look my best," she smiled.

"You have developed feelings for the American."

"Don't be ridiculous. I don't even know the man."

He got up from the table and walked over to the bed. "You must not let thoughts of him cloud your judgment. You have a job to do."

She spun around to face him. "I bloody well know what my job is, and I don't need any reminders from you."

He held up his hands, the toothpick hanging from the side of his mouth, "OK, OK. You are a big girl. I was just trying to keep you focused." He returned to the table and sat back down.

Her burst of anger melted and she smiled at her own overreaction. "I know you're just trying to be helpful. Are you sure you won't go in my place?"

"Alena, you flatter me. You know I am not up to the task. This is much more of your area of expertise."

"You'd be far less conspicuous."

"And far less effective, I am afraid. You are the perfect choice to take him down."

She released the magazine of her pistol, checked the rounds, then slammed it back into the grip of the gun and zipped it up in the duffle. "Let's hope you're right."

•

MCQUEEN CAME PREPARED to hear that the Edda Society was a complete fabrication. Instead, a legend of the spy business was telling him they were part myth, part fact.

"How so?" McQueen asked the commodore.

"What's the easiest way to stay completely under the radar whilst striking fear in the hearts of men?"

McQueen shrugged.

"The story has to be so fantastical that it cannot possibly be true but so terrifying that if it is you make sure you stay out of their way. Hitler's brain being preserved and transferred to another body like some Nazi Frankenstein? Pure rubbish. Men—and some women, mind you—who want to return Germany to its glory days? Absolutely true."

"Well, who are these people?"

"That's precisely the problem. No one knows. You chaps found more in the last few days than we've ever seen before."

"Yeah, but they're all dead."

The commodore rubbed down his considerable mustache. "True, but a dead Bigfoot is still a Bigfoot, now isn't it?"

McQueen hadn't thought about it that way. "How do we know these three people were part of the Edda Society?"

"There's no way to know for sure, but they have all the hallmarks." The commodore adjusted himself in his chair. "They're all health nuts. They all detest smoking. They're all teetotalers. My dear departed Pappy once told me never trust a man who won't take a drink." The commodore took a large swig of his own.

"I'm not following you. I saw the health food books in Schneider's and Hensel's apartments, but what does clean living have to do with Nazis?"

"Hitler was bonkers over it. Did you know that he never allowed smoking in his presence? In fact, he didn't allow smoking in any room he was likely to enter. Guess you could say he was the original cigarette Nazi. Not only that, he was a teetotaler and a vegetarian. He was an animal rights kook as well. He forbade vivisection of animals for research. Ironic, don't you think? The bloody bastard ordered medical experiments on people, caused untold misery for hundreds of millions of humans, outright murdered millions of them, then fretted over some damned dog or some such nonsense."

"So, you think this new incarnation of Nazis, the Edda Society, is emulating Hitler instead of the Nazis in general."

"It certainly would appear so, but the Edda Society are not new. Are you familiar with the Thule Society?"

"Vaguely."

"The Thule Society was started in Munich just after the first World War. It was named for this mythical country in Greek legend. This organization sponsored the German Workers' Party, which was later reorganized by Hitler into the National Socialist German Workers' Party."

"The Nazis," McQueen said.

Collingwood nodded. "Rudolf Gorsleben was a member of the Thule Society during the Bavarian Soviet Republic in 1919. That's when they tried to have their own little socialist government in the German state of Bavaria. Didn't last long. It was put down by the Weimar Republic. Anyway, this Gorsleben narrowly escaped being executed by the communists. In 1925, he founded the Edda Society. This was a mystic study group. Gorsleben formed his own religion based on the Armanism of Guido von List. Are you familiar with List or his cockamamy theories?"

"No," McQueen said.

"Do some research on this List chap some time. You shan't believe some of the wild theories he supposedly came into possession of through clairvoyant illumination. Armanism is wisdom in regards to the Aryans. You are familiar with the Aryans, aren't you?"

"Of course."

"In other words, the Eddas didn't just believe the Aryan race was superior. They elevated their belief to a religion. You're no doubt familiar with Hermann Goering?"

McQueen said, "He was Hitler's right-hand man. Vice-Chancellor of Germany, as I recall."

"Correct. Hitler made him deputy in all of his offices. As a matter of fact, Hitler was the godfather to Goering's only child. A daughter. Do you know what her name was?"

"No."

"Edda."

"Interesting."

The commodore cleared his throat. "Yes, well, it tells you how high this little society goes. You see, this group considers itself the purest form of Nazis. They don't go in for the skinhead set. Unless, of course, they can use them to rally support. They believe the reason the movement failed was because too many Nazis were, themselves, inferior. Their healthy lifestyle is their form of worship in this, this religion, if you can call it that. Hitler had the right idea, they believe. It's just that his followers were flawed. Had his followers not been defective, then the Third Reich would've lasted for a thousand years." He took a drink.

"But you're not suggesting that people who watch their health are Nazis, are you?"

The commodore let out a laugh. "Of course not, my dear boy. I envy them. Had I known I was going to live this long I would've taken better care of myself. No, what I'm saying is if you suspect one of being tied up in this organization, then it's a sure bet they're going to be nutter over their health."

"If you don't mind my asking, how do you know so much about this group?"

"You'd almost think I was one of them with all I know about them. Mind you, I had a nice juicy steak for dinner, I'm enjoying this scotch with you, and if the missis is asleep when we're done here I'm liable to sneak out on the terrace for an evening smoke. But, to your point, this may sound odd, but it's become a bit of a hobby for me. Like you, I was in the spook business for years. Can't say that I've gotten the birdwatcher out of my blood. I heard about the Edda Society from a friend of mine down at the yacht club. I dare say, I was intrigued. Warmed up some old connections of mine in the spy game and before you know it I had assembled quite a profile. The only thing I was missing was an actual sighting. Then an interesting thing happened. I was contacted by a Swiss banker down in the city. He was concerned about some money that was being moved about by some shady characters. A chap by the name of Samael Valafar was one of them."

"The shipping tycoon," McQueen said.

The commodore nodded, "The Swiss are very edgy about the whole Nazi thing ever since the war. Don't want to be seen as facilitators and what have you. These bankers are notoriously tight-lipped, but he told me more than he should have. And, of course, spies are the worst keepers of secrets. So one thing led to another and my fascination with the subject got back to my old friend, the colonel. Once bodies started turning up in Germany he called me, and Bob's your uncle." He took a satisfied sip of his whisky.

"They found a file on Valafar in Professor Gerber's office."

"What kind of file?" the commodore asked.

"Just biographical."

"Valafar has Middle Eastern ties, you know. Shipping investments there. Terrorism is bad for business. He's been more than willing to lend his vast resources to Western intelligence to hunt the bastards down. He'll play any angle that serves his interest."

"So you don't think he's part of this Edda Society?"

"Unlikely. Doesn't mean he's above being a hired gun."

"Did Colonel Bragg tell you about the organ music?" McQueen asked.

The commodore nodded as he savored the scotch in his mouth before swallowing it. "Damndest thing, that music. Two of the victims had a copy. Is that right?"

"In some form," McQueen confirmed. "Either an audio copy or sheet music."

"And this Hensel character," Collingwood said, "he was a Hanns Eisler man, I understand?"

"Hanns Eisler, the composer?"

"Hanns Eisler, the music school," the commodore clarified.

"In Berlin?"

"Yes, that's what Bragg tells me."

McQueen smiled to himself.

"Did he not tell you?" Collingwood asked.

"The colonel loves to keep secrets," McQueen said.

"Perhaps I've spoken out of turn, but Hensel was a graduate of the school."

"Which gives him a common link of music with Schneider and Amstutz. Schneider was obviously no musical scholar. He was having his audio copies transcribed into sheet music. A lot of trouble to go to for someone who couldn't play an instrument."

The commodore retrieved an envelope from a drawer of the table beside his chair and placed it in front of McQueen. "This is the sheet music from Schneider's flat. I've looked it over. There's nothing particularly unusual. It's sheet music for organ standards, for the most part. *Fantasy* by Bach. *Sonata Number One* by Mendelssohn. *Mass for Parishes* by Couperin. Pieces like that. Some pieces I don't recognize. Maybe you will."

McQueen pulled the sheet music from the envelope and looked it over.

The commodore continued, "I guess a logical question would be, what kind of organ? That might get you closer to the source. I understand these selections were designed for very large pipe organs."

"Interesting," McQueen said. "No telling how many of those there are in Europe."

"Oh, there are plenty, to be sure, but it would make sense that if we're talking about Nazis we're probably talking about somewhere in a German-speaking country. That narrows it down considerably. There's the Cathedral Organ of Saint Steven in Passau. That's in Germany. There's the Marienbasilika or St. Mary's Church in Kevelaer. Germany as well. Splendid organ, by the way. If you're looking for the largest *outdoor* organ, well then, that would be the Heldenorgel or Heroes' Organ at the fortress in Kufstein, a little town in Austria."

McQueen's head tilted toward the commodore. "Did you say Kufstein?"

"You know the town, do you?"

"Never been there, but a postcard that was burned in Schneider's fireplace had the markings of Kufstein."

"Quite interesting. Speaking of that Schneider chap, his assassination in particular tells me he had become a security risk with the Society."

"How so?" McQueen asked.

"Are you familiar with Reinhard Heydrich?"

"Other than he was a high-ranking Nazi during World War II, no."

"Oh, he wasn't just any Nazi. Reinhard Heydrich was one of the primary architects of the Holocaust. His nickname was 'The Hangman.' There's an assassin for the Society who goes by the same nickname."

"Who is he?"

He shrugged. "No one knows. He's apparently very professional. Stays in the shadows. Usually a gunshot wound to make it look like a suicide, but with high profile players he makes a point of staging a suicide by hanging, thus the nickname. He is the terrifying force that adds cohesion to the movement. Once you're in, you don't want to do anything that would invite a visit from the Hangman. It would be certain death."

McQueen nodded slightly as he absorbed the information.

The commodore slapped both thighs and hoisted himself to a standing position. "Well then, I've told you about everything I know. Care to join me for a cigarette?"

"No, thank you, Commodore," McQueen answered, rising and offering his hand. "You've been very helpful and more than generous. I really appreciate your putting me up for the night."

"Glad to," the commodore said.

"I'll see you and Mrs. Collingwood in the morning."

McQueen lay awake in the opulence of one of the Collingwoods' four guest rooms. The walnut blades of the ceiling fan gently cut the air above him. The fan was rotating just slowly enough that he could fixate on an individual blade and follow it round and round, which he did for a time as he lay there processing all the information he had accumulated. Slowly, his eyelids became heavy from the hypnotic turn of the blades and he drifted off to sleep.

He had only been asleep for what seemed to be moments when he opened one eye and then the other to find a rope held by black gloved hands moving toward his head. He commanded his arms to grab the hands. They disobeyed and lay still at his side. He was frustrated in his panic. The rope moved ever closer. He was powerless to stop it. He couldn't make out a face. In fact, he could see virtually nothing beyond the black gloves.

It was the decaf. It must've been. Did Markus, the butler, drug him on his own or did the commodore give the order? McQueen tried to scream out, but nothing would come from his mouth. He felt the noose wrap up over his head. It tightened around his neck. The face looking down on him from beyond the gloves was a blur. One hand held the knot while the other pulled with all its might on the other end of the rope. McQueen felt himself losing consciousness. He tried to reach for the rope or the gloves or the arms of his assailant. Anything. All he could do was suffocate. The image of the gloved figure slowly melted away.

# Chapter Twenty-Two

Instinctively, McQueen grabbed for his throat and bolted upright in the bed. His heart beat severely and his breath was short. It took him a moment to gather his surroundings in his mind and make sense of them. The Collingwoods' guest room. The ceiling fan slowly turning above him. The glimmer of sunlight that shone through the curtains. The chirp of the birds just outside his window. The sweat-soaked sheets below him.

He rolled out of bed and observed his face for a moment in the bathroom mirror. He touched the tender bruise on his stomach that approximated the size of a man's shoe. He splashed hot water on his face to prepare for a shave. After shaving, he took a quick shower then chose the Caraceni mid-gray fresco suit from his garment bag. The shirt was an all-cotton medium weight white luxury basketweave. Classic collar. The tie was a navy repp silk. The belt, calf leather, as were the shoes he retrieved from his suitcase. The Italian pocket square was white linen.

Satisfied with the size and position of his knot in the mirror by the door and nervous not to draw it too tightly he headed down the grand staircase where he was greeted at the bottom by the butler. Markus informed him in German that the commodore was taking his morning coffee on the terrace and that Mrs. Collingwood had not yet risen. McQueen followed the hallway to the far right rear of the residence where he found the French doors that opened to the terrace.

Mrs. Collingwood had been right about the view. The evening's rain had washed the sky clean to a brilliant blue. It was accented with the remaining few clouds that the rising sun had turned amber. The city of Zurich was waking up below to the left. To the right a handful of sailboats with white sails left small wakes in the otherwise glassy surface of Lake Zurich. The sun was barely visible above the mountains on the other side of the lake and it sent shafts of light down upon the water.

"Good morning, Sterling," Commodore Collingwood greeted after turning to see who had emerged from the house. "I was going to wake you, but then Markus said you were stirring already. Got a ring from Colonel Bragg this morning. He wants you on the seven o'clock to Frankfurt. You'll be briefed once you're there. 'Tis a pity, though. I'd hoped to welcome the day with you here on the terrace. Afraid there won't be time for that. Your train leaves within the hour."

"I appreciate the gesture."

"Hamish is waiting for you out front. Markus should have fetched your things and put them in the boot by now." The commodore rose to shake his hand.

"Please send my regards to Mrs. Collingwood," McQueen said.

"I shall, indeed. I so enjoyed getting to know you. My best to your colonel when you see him next."

McQueen strode out the front door where he found Markus holding his door and Hamish behind the wheel of the elegant Silver Cloud.

"Danke, Markus." Even the closing of the door sounded snobbishly rich. "Morning, Hamish."

"Morning, sir. Jolly good day it is. Certainly beats the evening."

"It does." McQueen ran his hand across the soft leather that surrounded him.

Hamish started the Rolls and pulled gently out of the driveway. McQueen took in the panoramic view of the lake through the window. They drove down the hill from Kilchberg toward the city. The streets were still wet from last night's rain. A refreshed feeling rose with the sun over the mountains. Early risers walked their dogs or jogged down the sidewalks leading to the lake. McQueen took in his luxurious surroundings and savored the morning, his favorite time of day.

The seagulls lined the railing by the Limmat River that was fed by the lake instead of the other way around. They crossed the river and dodged trams and pedestrians with the Rolls. Hamish deposited him at the entrance to the grand train station. He found his platform and his train. The interior of the train, first class as it was, was a decided let-down from the Rolls. He ordered breakfast at his seat and watched beautiful Zurich with its spires and clock towers and Romanesque architecture disappear out his window.

He spent the bulk of the three-hour trip reading the newspaper in German. The story of Richard Schneider was front page news. The headline claimed suicide. McQueen had his doubts. There was no mention of his Nazi affiliation or the Edda Society.

Katharina Amstutz's death was on page three, in the people and lifestyle column. They listed her numerous contributions. The file photograph was flattering. A middle-aged stylish woman with great features. The fashion world was shocked by her suicide. McQueen wondered how much more shocked they'd be to find out she was a Nazi. He arrived in Frankfurt just past eleven.

"I am afraid we do not have a great deal of time," Gustav said, trotting up beside him, foregoing his usual greetings.

"What's up?"

"Much, my friend. Much. Follow me."

●

MCQUEEN UNBUTTONED HIS dress shirt to reveal a white t-shirt. He began pulling his arm out of the left sleeve.

"You cut it mighty close back there on the way to Zurich," Colonel Bragg said. He sat behind a small desk in a nondescript office that obviously wasn't his own.

"Yeah, well, good thing I had a nursemaid from the BND," McQueen said sarcastically. He finished pulling his arm from the other sleeve and grabbed a fresh shirt from its hanger.

"You joke, but apparently the man saved your life."

McQueen looked down as he began to button his shirt from the bottom up. "Your idea?"

"Hofsteiner offered. I accepted. Obviously somebody was on to you. That was some serious muscle. Whoever hired him knew you'd have a chore taking him down."

"Have you traced him back to the Edda Society?"

"No," Bragg said, "and I don't expect to."

"You don't think they exist?"

"It's not that. I think they've made themselves impossible to find."

"Like Bigfoot?"

"What?"

"Nothing," McQueen said. "But we have found them. They're just dead."

"And dead men don't talk. We can link them together with that organ music, but until we find that link among the living it does us no good."

"And you think offering me as bait will do that."

"Barton's on her way from Brussels. She says we have two hunters on the quarry right now." Bragg gave McQueen a serious stare. "I know about her blowing your cover on the train."

McQueen looked up a bit surprised. He paused briefly then resumed his task. "I don't think that had anything to do with this incident," he countered. "We have a haint somewhere and we need to find out who that is. Whoever's trying to disrupt my investigation knew I was going to be on that train before I even boarded it. They apparently know everything."

"Can you trust her?" Bragg asked. "I don't mean like she's some double or anything like that. Do you think she's up to the job?"

McQueen pondered the question for a moment. "That's your call, Colonel. You know more about what she's capable of than I do. She just needs to be more careful." McQueen continued to change clothes then looked back up at Bragg and asked, "Just curious. Who told you about Agent Barton blowing my cover?"

Bragg looked at him for a moment then answered, "She did."

●

THERE WAS ONE player close to Professor Gerber who had remained untouched. That was his close friend and colleague Wilhelm Schmitt. The conference in Brussels was over and he was taking the train back home to Salzburg, albeit reluctantly. Professor Schmitt was gravely concerned about his colleague. He resisted leaving Brussels without him, but pressing matters back at the university demanded his attention. Besides, the case had the full attention of the authorities.

There was nothing he could personally do to gain Gerber's release.

Bragg was betting that whoever nabbed Professor Gerber had no intention of allowing Schmitt to make the trip undistracted. They would be watching the professor's every move, waiting for the perfect opportunity to pounce. Bragg calculated the most logical point would be somewhere between the time he got off the train in Frankfurt to when he boarded his connecting train to Salzburg.

Professor Wilhelm Schmitt looked the part of a college professor. Rather unruly gray hair, a bit too long for his age. Round horn-rimmed glasses. A soft wool tweed jacket with brown patches on the sleeves. His salt-and-pepper beard was neatly trimmed, a contrast to his tousled tuft. Schmitt's thoughts were with his friend as he walked from the platform into the cavernous Frankfurt station. His shoes clicked against the gray tiled floor along with all the other travelers. Announcements echoed from the PA system. Every sound came back like a boomerang. The recognition of his own name over the loud speaker penetrated his distracted thoughts.

"Wilhelm Schmitt, bitte kommen Sie zum informationsstand," the woman's voice reverberated through the station. "Wilhelm Schmitt, please come to the information booth."

His heart raced at the anticipation of news about Gerber. He prayed it was good.

"My name is Wilhelm Schmitt," he informed the young man behind the counter.

"Yes, Herr Schmitt. You have a call from your university. You can take it through that door," he said, pointing to an 'Employees Only' door behind the counter.

"Danke," he answered nervously and headed through the door.

Gustav eyed the station making sure the two tails Vivian Barton spotted on the train from Brussels were waiting for the professor to emerge from his telephone call. A short black-haired man with a blue business suit pretended to peruse a newspaper while leaning against a coffee kiosk. The other, a taller blond man with a gray trench coat, was less obvious. He glanced back at the information booth every few seconds. He purchased a hot dog from a vendor. Gustav recognized the gentleman and made a mental note of special caution.

Wilhelm Schmitt walked through the employees' entrance and two men stepped forward from a back room. One locked the door behind the professor.

"Was ist das?" Schmitt asked suspiciously.

"Professor Schmitt." One of the men raised his identification. "I am with the polizei."

"Is this about Professor Gerber?"

"Well, yes. In a way."

Schmitt looked queerly at the man who emerged from the back room. Standing in the doorway was Sterling McQueen. Down to the salt-and-pepper beard he looked exactly like Professor Schmitt.

# Chapter Twenty-Three

"**E**yes on the shadows?" Bragg asked into the microphone.

"Affirmative," Agent Barton answered from a newsstand further down the concourse.

"Ja," Gustav said softly to no one in particular as travelers hustled by.

"Very good," Bragg said. "Release the rabbit."

The door behind the information booth opened and McQueen stepped out from behind the counter. He wore Professor Schmitt's tweed jacket with brown patches on the elbows. He glanced at Gustav across the station floor and was on his way, the spitting image of Wilhelm Schmitt. The short man was right behind. The blond in the trench coat stuffed the remainder of the hot dog into his mouth and quickened his pace to keep up. The hunters had fallen for the decoy.

As Professor Schmitt, McQueen made it to the platform with plenty of time to spare before his train to Salzburg began boarding. Nearly a quarter-mile of glimmering white cars with red stripes down their sides awaited their passengers. Cleaning crews busily readied them for another journey. He bided his time before the boarding call with a newspaper. Gustav sat several yards behind keeping an eagle eye on his old friend and his two new ones. He thought it unlikely that anyone would make their move in broad daylight, but again he wasn't sure with whom they were dealing. An umbrella with a poison tip casually stuck in the leg. An undetectable addition to his coffee or his soft drink. Anything could happen. Gustav's job was to make sure neither stalker got too close. He had been embarrassed in Brussels. He made a vow to himself to never let it happen again.

Gustav concentrated on the man sitting closest, several yards beyond McQueen, facing them both. He looked barely 5'4" and maybe 120 pounds. He was a darker-skinned gentleman, possibly Arab. He had black hair and a black beard.

"He definitely has eyes on you," Gustav informed McQueen.

McQueen gently rubbed his lip enabling him a brief response. "I see him," McQueen said.

"Do not worry, my friend. I will not allow him close enough to do you harm."

Barton's voice packed a trace of panic. "Anybody have the eyeball on the blond?"

"He was yours," Bragg said.

She whispered, "I looked down for one second and he was gone."

"Come on, people," Bragg grunted in their ears.

"Do not worry," Gustav said. "They only need one man to kill the professor and he is sitting right in front of me."

Barton continued to look around for the blond man.

Once the Salzburg boarding announcement was made Gustav gave instructions to McQueen. "Sterling, go ahead and make a deliberate move to the train. Almost a run. If our shadow follows, that is all I need to know. We do not need to play this charade on a five-and-a-half-hour trip to Salzburg or risk him killing you before the train leaves. I will take him before you board the train."

McQueen quickly stood up and began a trot toward the train. The short shadow in the blue suit popped up and quickened his pace to keep up.

Gustav made his move. "I am going in," he informed the team.

Passengers crowded around the various entrances to the train and Gustav moved up close to the diminutive hit man. The barrel of his pistol concealed by his raincoat pressed into his back.

"Do not make a move, my friend. I would have no problem killing you right here," Gustav said in almost a whisper.

He escorted the man back to the main hallway of the train station and through service doors beside a newsstand. Looking around, he made sure they were alone. He forcefully spun the man around and pushed him up against the wall.

"Who sent you here?"

The small man was silent.

"I said who sent you here?" Gustav backhanded him across the face.

The man screamed out a high-pitched scream. It was not the scream of a man at all. Gustav looked closer then removed the wig and ripped the beard from his face. It was a woman.

McQueen looked around for Gustav or the shadow. Seeing neither, he started back toward the main terminal. He felt the hand tighten on his left arm and the pistol press into his back. He wondered where in the hell Gustav could be.

"Keep walking," the blond man instructed, casually looking around. "Let us not make a big fuss."

McQueen said nothing but followed his orders. The blond man led him down a ramp and onto an unused section of track behind the station. McQueen looked around, but Gustav was nowhere to be found.

"The Mukhabarat el-Aam?" Gustav asked in disbelief. "You work for Egyptian Intelligence? Why do you want the professor dead?"

"We don't want him dead," she said angrily. "We want to find Professor Gerber. He knows who's behind the terrorism."

"It is the PLO," Gustav insisted.

"No, no. It's *not* the PLO," she refuted adamantly.

"Hamas?"

"No!"

"ISIS?"

"No, no. None of them!"

"Well, who then?" Gustav yelled in disgust.

"I don't know!" she yelled back. "That's why we're looking for Gerber."

"If you shoot me here," McQueen said in Professor Schmitt's voice, "the police will surely find you before you leave the station."

"You people got ears on this?" Bragg asked.

The girl continued the argument. "If you're so set on finding Gerber yourselves why—"

"Sh-h-h," Gustav ordered. He held his finger to his ear.

"Your boss would surely not be happy if I passed along the information and you killed the only man who knew to whom," McQueen said.

"Stall him, Sterling," Gustav said. "Tell me where you are." He darted back out the service doors and into the main terminal. The girl followed close behind.

"You mean you led me all the way down here behind this train station just to kill me?"

The blond man said nothing. He aimed the gun at the base of McQueen's skull.

McQueen was getting nervous. Where the hell was Gustav? "Do you think I have taken the information given to me by Herr Gerber and simply kept it to myself?"

Still the man said nothing. He took a step away from McQueen's back, his grip still firm on his arm. The man steadied himself, lengthened his arm, and prepared to shoot. He eyed his surroundings looking for a quick exit once the deed was done.

"Eyeball on the decoy anybody?" Bragg asked.

"Ears only," Gustav answered. His voice was labored. "Working on a visual."

"Barton?"

No answer.

The commotion of the footsteps rounding the other end of the train car diverted the blond man's attention. He pulled the gun from McQueen's head and shot. McQueen heard the pop of the suppressor and the shattering of the window in the train car. Before the blond man could fire off another round, the snap of the silencer hit home in his chest. He fell dead between the tracks.

"Where the hell have you been?" McQueen yelled.

"A simple 'thank you' would suffice," Agent Barton shot back. She holstered her weapon and walked over to make sure the gunman was dead. "Decoy secure," she informed Bragg.

"Status report," he answered.

"One hostile dead," she said.

Out of breath, Gustav came running around the back of the train car.

"Perfect timing," McQueen said.

"I was pursuing another stalker," Gustav admitted sheepishly.

The girl timidly walked from behind the train car and stood at Gustav's side. "I'm afraid that was my fault, Professor."

McQueen did a double take. He hardly recognized her in a man's suit. "Sabreen?"

Gustav looked at the girl. "The girl from the hotel?"

She walked up for a closer inspection of McQueen. She hesitated before she uttered the name. "Sterling?"

"Wait a minute. This is Alena Sharabi?" Vivian Barton asked. "The PLO operative?"

"Time to clear out, people," Bragg said in their ears.

McQueen looked at Alena, then at Barton. "Take her to the rendezvous point."

Gustav pointed to the corpse on the ground. "Does this gentleman look familiar?"

McQueen turned around. It was his first opportunity to see the man's face since he stuck a gun in his back in the train station. It was the man who followed them to Frankfurt, the man who almost certainly murdered Mrs. Hofmark.

●

THE INFORMATION ON Gustav's phone filled four pages. The database revealed the dead man's criminal record and Gustav read each page eagerly. "Uh-huh. Yes. This is just what we suspected."

"Talk to me," McQueen said. He splashed water from the basin on his face and removed the last remnants of makeup. He watched Gustav in the mirror.

"The prints match a Rudolf Schiller. Your basic thug. Arrested for kidnapping, armed robbery, extortion, and numerous petty crimes. Suspected in three hits but never arrested. Never spent one day in jail," he announced, looking up at McQueen. "Never even went to trial on the more serious charges."

"Well, that is interesting," McQueen observed caustically. He wiped his face with the hotel towel. "Either Rudolf was completely innocent of everything they ever accused him of," he blotted his mouth with the towel then threw it on the counter, "or he's got some mighty influential friends. Who'd he work for?"

"You mean legitimately?" Gustav queried.

"Yes."

Gustav checked the screen. "SonneProgressiv."

"What's that?"

"It is a solar company."

"Who owns it?" McQueen asked.

"Good question. I will find out." Gustav switched screens on his phone and dialed up the NATO headquarters in Brussels. Relying on his own BND for even a mere background check at this point was too risky.

"I guess this Neo-Nazi thing sorta blows your PLO theory out of the water," McQueen said.

"The game is not over, friend Sterling," Gustav said, covering the mouthpiece with his hand. "There is still the girl. Even though she says she is Mukhabarat el-Aam, we know for certain of her membership in the PLO. Perhaps she is lying."

"Let me know when you have something. I'll be down at Barton's room."

Gustav nodded and continued to wait on the phone.

The hotel was decorated in a fifteenth-century Bavarian motif with large wooden beams and castle-like doors. McQueen walked the twenty feet or so to the room where Agent Barton was keeping an eye on Alena Sharabi.

"How did you end up in the GIA?" McQueen was curious. The General Intelligence Agency, the English translation of Egypt's Mukhabarat el-Aam, was not famous for hiring women.

"I hate to admit it, but I am a legacy," she explained. "I had a relative who served under President Sadat. He worked hard to purge the organization of the pseudo-intelligence officers who spread terrorism during the Nasser years. He was head of the same intelligence agency I work for."

"Wait a minute." McQueen stopped her to confirm his revelation. "The head of the GIA back in those days was Akeem Nakham?"

"Yes."

"Who's Akeem Nakham?" Vivian Barton asked.

"Akeem Nakham was instrumental in Sadat even being present for the Camp David Accords," McQueen explained.

"That is correct," Alena confirmed. "As head of GIA he assured

President Sadat that his intelligence sources could supply enough data to confirm Israel's compliance with the Accords."

"He died with Sadat on that reviewing stand during the assassination in October of '81," McQueen said reverently.

"Never realizing his dream of seeing Egypt's role on the world stage as more than just a stooge for the Soviet Union," she added, "an arm of their insatiable greed for real estate. It is ironic that he died by the very act of terrorism he had tried to stop, inflicted by the very people he had tried so hard to help."

McQueen paused a respectable amount of time before asking his next question. "And the PLO demonstrations you participated in?"

"I was a plant," she explained. "What better person to infiltrate the PLO than a naive little college girl who just happened to be from the family of one of the most legendary spies in Egyptian history?"

"So, what were your plans for Professor Schmitt?" Agent Barton asked.

"My orders were to stay with him and keep him safe until our operatives could question him about what Gerber knows."

"And how much does Schmitt know about Gerber's intelligence?" Barton asked.

Alena looked at her with a sarcastic smile. "You tell me. You have him now." She turned to McQueen. "Sterling, we had something beautiful together."

"I don't think I need to hear this," Barton said, getting up and walking across the room.

"We had nothing. You were trying to play me."

"But our kiss meant nothing to you?"

"OK." Barton held up her hands. "You know what? I'm gonna excuse myself."

There was a knock on the door. McQueen checked the peep hole then opened it.

"The girl checks out," Gustav said walking in. "Bragg says to let her go."

"Let her go?" Barton said. "Just like that?"

Gustav shrugged.

Alena rose from the chair with a satisfied smile. "Well, I guess this is goodbye." She brushed past McQueen then stopped and looked back at him over her shoulder. "Pity."

Barton watched her leave then raised an eyebrow to McQueen.

"We'll need to check orders." McQueen opened the door and allowed Gustav to exit first. He looked back at Barton. "You earned your keep out there today."

Barton frowned for a second. "You're welcome, McQueen."

McQueen turned and walked out the door.

"Quite interesting," Gustav said, walking back to their room.

"What is?"

"Where this thug worked, SonneProgressiv.

"Who owns it?"

"It is owned by none other than Herr Samael Valafar."

# Chapter Twenty-Four

McQueen walked the six blocks from the hotel to a corner electronics store that sold all grades of phones, chargers, and accessories.

"That one," McQueen said, pointing to a clean burner phone in the display case.

He handed the man some bills, took the change, and declined the receipt. Stepping out of the store he opened the phone and deposited the box in a nearby trashcan. He dialed the number.

"Peliken International, Brussels. How may I direct your call?" Sophia asked on the other end.

He told her 'Operations,' gave her his code, and moments later Colonel Bragg was on the line.

"Permission to explore the Zurich lead," McQueen said, referring to Kufstein.

"Permission granted. First, you're to investigate the place of employment of the person of interest." That would be the university where Schmitt worked in Salzburg. "Transportation will be waiting," Bragg added. "Ask the man at the newsstand for the name of the clockmaker."

"The clockmaker," McQueen repeated.

"The answer is Hans."

"Hans."

"And like you, Hans is always on time. Your colleagues will set up in the next location. Rendezvous at twelve-hundred hours tomorrow. Understood?"

"Understood."

The line went dead. McQueen removed the SIM card from the phone and dropped it in his coat pocket. He wiped the phone with his coat sleeve and casually dropped it in the next trashcan.

He caught a train to Munich then changed trains for Salzburg. Ninety minutes after leaving Munich McQueen was standing and stretching while his train pulled into Salzburg station. This was one of his favorite cities in the world. Luck had placed him there during the most festive time of the year, the annual Salzburg Festival. McQueen dodged musicians with violin and cello cases with his eye on a newsstand where he purchased a magazine.

"Wie heisst der Uhrmacher?" McQueen asked the man for the name of the clockmaker.

"Sein Name ist Hans," the man said.

That was correct. His name *was* Hans. Now for the confirmation that Hans was always on time. "Hans ist immer auf Zeit."

The man reached down and handed McQueen a small manila envelope. He walked to a trash receptacle where he ditched the magazine and unsealed the envelope. Inside was a ticket like one might use to exit a parking garage with a barcode on one end. McQueen looked around. Over by the escalator to platform 5 he saw the entrance to the storage lockers. He found locker number 09-20 that corresponded with the number on the ticket. It was a small locker about eye level. He inserted the card in the vending machine. The door opened and inside the locker was another envelope. This one was the small padded variety. He unsealed it and removed a key fob.

He found the black BMW coupe he was told would be waiting for him in the train station parking lot and headed to his hotel. He used the hotel computer to check Schmitt's summer school class schedule. He had a class at nine then the next not until two, both taught by an associate during his absence. McQueen would slip in after the first class for a little snooping. He then brought up the city of Kufstein and pored over the pages.

The next morning after breakfast at the hotel he made the walk over to the university. The city was alive with music. Street musicians entertained passing crowds for a few coins dropped in their baskets. Old men played a life-size game of chess on a huge chessboard. An actor, who was dressed and painted as a statue of Mozart, clasped a lamp post with one hand and appeared to miraculously hover in mid-air as he gestured dramatically to the crowd with his free hand.

McQueen entered the main building from University Square. He walked down the huge hallway that felt more like the Louvre than a university. After making several turns, he cautiously entered the large lecture room. About ten different levels were filled with rows of chairs with small writing desks attached. Behind the top row was a metal railing. The focal point in the front of the classroom was a large wooden desk with huge drawers. Posters representing each country studied in the Middle Eastern Cultures class lined the wall above the chalkboard. The soles of McQueen's shoes echoed down each step toward the desk.

Double checking the entrances, he tried the first drawer. Locked. Reaching into his breast pocket he produced his wallet. Opening it fully then running a fingernail down the lining in the back he peeled back the inside to reveal a lock pick. He maneuvered it around until he unlocked the middle drawer, which unlocked the entire desk. Rummaging through he found what one might expect to find in a professor's desk. Books, blank pads, extra chalk, pens, pencils, file folders. In the back of the third drawer he found something a little more unusual. A small envelope containing a thumb drive with a note that read, "Listen and give me your opinion. FG." McQueen pocketed the envelope in his breast coat pocket and continued searching. He had just finished inspecting the last drawer when he was startled by a booming voice.

"May I help you?" the voice echoed through the classroom.

McQueen looked up to see a very serious man leaning over the metal railing at the top of the auditorium. "Oh, hi," McQueen began awkwardly. "I'm Warren Schmitt, Professor Schmitt's nephew." The solemn man silently made his way down the steps toward the desk. McQueen continued his explanation. "I'm spending the summer here with my uncle. Well, actually, he's not *here* here at the moment. He's in Brussels. He phoned me this morning. Says he's staying in Frankfurt, I believe, a few days."

The large man was standing in front of the desk, looking down at him suspiciously. He said nothing; instead he listened to McQueen's explanation.

"He wanted me to e-mail him the syllabus for his fall course so he could make some edits, but I've looked all through his desk and I can't find it. Do you know where I might find it, Mr., um?"

"*Professor* Kohl," the man spoke at last. "You're American?"

"Yes, sir," McQueen answered. "Professor Schmitt's sister is my mother. She lives, well, *we* live in New Hampshire. That's in the northeastern section of the United States." Fortunately, McQueen had studied Schmitt's dossier.

"When did you say you talked with your uncle?" the man inquired.

"Well, just this morning," McQueen answered. "So, Professor uh, I'm sorry, I'm terrible with names."

"Kohl," the stranger reminded him.

"That's right, Professor Kohl. You teach here with Uncle Wilhelm?"

"Yes, I do." The stranger was starting to loosen up a bit. "If you would tell me where I can contact him I would be happy to e-mail him the syllabus myself. Where is he staying in Frankfurt?"

"Well, I would tell you if I knew," McQueen hedged, "but he phoned me from Frankfurt and said he would call me back later today."

"I see," the professor replied. "I would very much like to talk with him to make sure he is doing fine."

"He sounded fine to me." It was time for McQueen to make his exit. He started up the steps. "I'll tell him about your offer when I speak with him. Have a good day."

"Guten Tag," Kohl replied. He watched suspiciously as McQueen scaled the levels and left the classroom.

On his way out of the building McQueen dropped by the information desk.

"Excuse me, but do you have a Professor Kohl employed here?"

"Ja, we do. He is a professor of Middle Eastern Culture," the receptionist informed him.

McQueen was disappointed. He was sure something wasn't quite right with the man he just met.

"And he's teaching this summer?" McQueen asked.

"Oh no, Professor Kohl is off for the summer. He usually spends his holiday hiking in Switzerland."

McQueen looked over his shoulder. "Thank you very much."

He turned the BMW loose on the A1 West Autobahn toward

Kufstein. He reached inside the envelope from Schmitt's desk and retrieved the thumb drive. He inserted it into his digital voice recorder and brought the player up on the car's Bluetooth then adjusted the volume. Organ music. It was Mozart's Adagio Und Allegro in the key of F for a barrel-organ, Part 2. It was stirring. McQueen was lost in the beauty of the piece.

Somewhere in his detachment he realized there was a flashing blue light in his rearview mirror. Odd. It was a dashboard light, the kind you plug into a cigarette lighter for an unmarked car. He couldn't remember the last time he saw one of those. He hit the pause button on the player and slowed down to allow the car to pass. Instead of passing, the unmarked police car slowed with him. McQueen pulled down an off-ramp to get away from the high-speed traffic of the autobahn and came to a stop.

A plainclothes cop, his gun drawn, approached the car. "Step out of the automobile very slowly."

McQueen looked over his shoulder into the barrel of his gun. "This must be some sort of a misunderstanding. What was I doing—"

"It is no misunderstanding. Get out of the car!"

# Chapter Twenty-Five

McQueen remained seated in the car. Something wasn't right.

"Move!" the officer shouted.

McQueen unbuckled the seatbelt, opened the door, and slowly rose from the seat. With the gun still aimed at him, he raised his hands.

"Get into the car," the man insisted.

"I'm going to have to see some ID, if you don't mind."

The man tightened his jaw in agitation. His well-defined philtrum led to flared nostrils. His lips became thin. "I said get into the car," he growled.

McQueen moved slowly toward the car. As he came abreast of the man, the man held out his free hand. "Stop."

McQueen obeyed.

The man gingerly reached inside McQueen's coat to remove his Sig.

McQueen could see his instructor back at Camp X vividly in his mind. It was drilled into his head as a recruit. Clear, control, disarm. He went over the sequence in his mind as he had done in hours of training. Clear, control, disarm. He played the role of the gunman in front of the small class. The instructor, in slow motion, used his arm to push the gun away from his body. If the gun fired, the instructor pointed out, it would do no harm. The instructor then grabbed the gun and twisted it to the side. The dummy gun in class had the trigger removed so it wouldn't take off a student's index finger. Almost in a blink of an eye the instructor was holding the gun on him. He turned the gun on McQueen and told him to take it from him. He tried and failed. Again. And again he failed. Again! He found the gun in his own hand.

The man was off to McQueen's left side. He was reaching across his own body with his left hand to take McQueen's gun from the left side of his coat. That gave McQueen a slight advantage. He wouldn't have to shift his entire body to clear himself from the line of fire. The man went to grab the butt of his gun and McQueen shoved the man's right arm with his own left hand shifting his entire body to the right. The gun fired harmlessly into a berm. Almost simultaneously McQueen's right hand grabbed the gun hand and turned the weapon on him nearly taking the man's index finger off in the process. The man was stunned. He was standing there, holding his wounded right index finger in his left hand, and looking at the business end of his own gun.

"Hands behind your head," McQueen ordered. The man wasn't moving fast enough to suit him. "I said hands behind your head!"

The man slowly raised his hands behind his head.

"Lock your fingers."

The man locked his fingers together.

"Now, turn around and get on your knees."

The man was frozen.

"On your knees!"

The man's face was filled with terror. His eyes were frantic. He slowly dropped to his left knee, then his right.

"I'm sorry to have to do this," McQueen said softly. "You left me no choice."

The man closed his eyes. The gun shot was loud. The man jumped then fell back on his folded legs. He heard the car door slam. The tires of the BMW threw gravel then squealed on the pavement. The man looked to his left and saw the flat front tire of his car.

McQueen put some road between himself and whoever he left beside the disabled car. If he was a cop there would be an armada bearing down on him within minutes. He pulled into one of the gas stations that were peppered along the autobahn at approximately thirty-mile intervals. He picked up the pay phone outside and dialed the number. After two rings it picked up.

The familiar voice of Sophia smiled through the line. "Peliken International, Brussels. How may I direct your call?"

"Operations."

McQueen gave his code and waited for Colonel Bragg to come on the line.

"Bragg."

"Colonel, I need you to run a check with the Austrian Highway Patrol. See if an Autobahnpolizei pulled me over in the last half-hour." McQueen waited as Bragg relayed the message to a subordinate.

"Where the hell are you, son?"

"Austria. About 30 miles from the German border. A man tried to take me for a ride."

"What's his status?" Bragg asked.

"Temporarily neutralized, probably in need of some clean shorts. I also paid a visit to Professor Schmitt's classroom and was confronted by someone posing as a colleague, a Professor Kohl. Checked it out. Kohl's on vacation in Switzerland."

"We'll take a look at it," Bragg assured him. "Just a second." Bragg leaned back as an aide fed him the information he wanted. "That's a negative from the Austrian Highway Patrol."

"I don't know who we're dealing with, Colonel, but they have mighty long arms."

"Keep at it, McQueen. We have to find out what Gerber knew."

"On the way to the rendezvous point now."

"Keep me posted."

McQueen surveyed the parking lot, got back in his car, and back onto the autobahn. He hit the play button on the player and finished listening to the Mozart piece. Mozart was followed by Chopin then a piece he didn't recognize at all. It was pleasant if not disjointed. Obviously not one of the masters. Perhaps a modern interpretation of baroque. It was followed by a piece by Handel, then Johann Ludwig Krebs. What was the significance of the organ music? Was it meant to stir, to inspire?

He exited the Autobahn onto Munchner Strasse and pulled alongside a train station. Turning left, he slowed to take in the scenery. In front of him and across the Inn River lay the small town of Kufstein. It looked like a Monet painting. A wood-frame bridge spanned the swiftly running, icy cold Inn which was fed by the snow of the Swiss Alps and meandered on through Bavaria to meet the Danube. Freshly planted flowers in flower boxes lined either side of the bridge splashing the length of it in a rainbow of colors. On the banks across the river stretched rows of quaint buildings in bright pastels of pink, sky blue, and yellow. A cobblestone street wound up the heart of town with specialty shops spilling out onto the sidewalk with their wares. Looming high above the town as if keeping watch was an eleventh-century fortress which served present-day Kufstein as a monastery.

McQueen pulled the BMW down a side street and parked. Setting the brake he hopped out and breathed in the fresh mountain air. He walked around the corner where Gustav Wagner and Vivian Barton sat underneath an umbrella at an outdoor cafe. Gustav sipped a beer while Agent Barton nursed an espresso.

"I would've been here earlier, but I had company along the way," McQueen informed them, taking a seat.

"Interesting," Gustav responded.

"What kind of company?" Barton asked.

"The kind that only shows up if whoever we're getting close to is very well connected."

"How connected are we talking?" asked Gustav

Barton listened to the conversation but watched a monk from the monastery buying some bread from the vendor next door. He paid with cash and stowed his purchase away in a canvas bag.

"I checked with Bragg," McQueen said. "No report of the Autobahnpolizei pulling me over. Had to have something to do with the guy posing as Professor Kohl."

"Professor Kohl?" Gustav asked.

"He's a colleague of Professor Schmitt, or at least the real Professor Kohl is. I ran into this guy while looking through Schmitt's desk drawer. Turns out the real Professor Kohl is out of the country."

"Anything of interest in the drawer?" Gustav asked.

"Another flash drive with organ music. And a note from Gerber asking Schmitt to take a listen and give him his thoughts."

"So, that tells us that Gerber was aware of the organ music and thought it meant something."

"Yeah," McQueen said, "but it doesn't tell us what it meant."

"Hey, I hate to interrupt," Barton said, "but are either of you aware of any monastic rule that allows the wearing of jewelry?"

"I am not," Gustav responded.

McQueen shook his head. "Why do you ask?"

"Because that monk who just bought some bread next door has a tan line where his watch usually goes."

The monk, his face lost in the shadow of his hood, slowly walked up the cobblestone street back toward the fortress.

McQueen looked down at his own wristwatch, then back up at Gustav and Barton. He held a hand to the sky. The air filled with organ music. Barton and Gustav looked at each other.

"Nice trick," Barton said.

"Toccata and Fugue in D Minor by Bach," McQueen announced.

Barton had a distasteful look on her face. "That's downright creepy."

"It's the classic horror movie track," McQueen said. "They used it in *Dr. Jekyll and Mr. Hyde* in 1931. It was in *Fantasia* in 1940 and countless other films, probably most famously in *Phantom of the Opera* in 1962."

"And how did you know the organ music was coming?" Gustav asked.

"That's part of the reason we're here."

"Where's it coming from?" Barton asked.

"The fortress," McQueen informed them, pointing up. "It's the Heldenorgel. Heroes' Organ," he translated for Barton. "Almost 5,000 pipes. The monks play it twice a day this time of year. Beautiful, isn't it?"

"It's ghoulish," Barton said.

McQueen called the waiter over. "Can we take a tour of the fortress?"

"The monks used to be very good about allowing limited tours, but they shut the tours down sometime back," he said.

"Why?" McQueen asked.

"Not sure why or when they are going to reopen. We really miss that. We get lots of business in the summer off-season from tourists who want to see the fortress. Gets us through to the next ski season."

"Danke."

The waiter went about his business.

Gustav explained to Barton, "In the possession of two of the people Gerber went to see we found recordings of organ music."

"And Professor Schmitt had a thumb drive of it in his desk," McQueen added, "compliments of Franz Gerber. I listened on the way up here. It's that organ."

"Those recordings could be any organ," Gustav said.

"Come on, Gustav. The unburned piece of postcard depicting Kufstein in Schneider's fireplace?" He held up both hands. "The organ music that sounds just like this organ? Monks with wristwatches? We've *got* to see that fortress."

"And how do you propose we see the inside of that fortress?" Gustav asked. "You heard the gentleman. No tours."

"I'm working on an idea."

Barton held up a finger as if she had just remembered something. "Oh." She pulled a small piece of paper out of her purse. "Bragg wanted me to give you this."

McQueen unrolled it then unfolded it. It was a hand-written note. The words *Known Associates* were at the top.

"They found it hidden among Gerber's things at the hotel," Barton explained. "Old school. Hidden in a hollow space in the handle of his shaving brush."

"Shaving brush," McQueen repeated with a smile. "I like his style."

Underneath *Known Associates* was a list of names.

*Holger Hensel - Munich*

*Katharina Amstutz - Cologne*

*Richard Schneider - Frankfurt*

*It was more like a hit list*, McQueen thought. Surely Gerber had no idea his meeting with each person would turn out to be so lethal. Whatever Gerber knew was too important to risk getting out. Somebody was making sure it didn't.

"Interesting list," Gustav said.

"Yeah, it is," McQueen said. "For some reason meeting with Franz Gerber is tantamount to the kiss of death."

The final note of Bach's Toccata and Fugue in D Minor ended dramatically and echoed into the mountain air.

# Chapter Twenty-Six

"This is suicide," Barton insisted.

Dressed in black cycling pants, a black long-sleeve men's training shirt, and black climbing shoes, McQueen ignored the comment and continued applying camouflage makeup in front of a mirror.

"How high is that cliff?" Barton asked.

"It is ninety meters," Gustav answered from across the room.

"That's about what, twenty-five stories up?" she speculated.

"More like twenty-seven," McQueen corrected, "but what does it matter? I'm road kill after about ten meters anyway."

Barton was in no mood for jokes. The thought of watching a colleague plunge to his death right before her eyes terrified her even if it was Sterling McQueen.

"How many times have you free soloed a cliff like this?" Barton asked.

"I've always wanted to," McQueen said, looking in the mirror and smudging more black camo on his nose.

Barton was stunned. "You have *got* to be kidding me! You've *never* climbed a cliff before?"

"Oh, I've climbed plenty of cliffs. Just never one without ropes. But we can't take the chance of doing it the sane way. The clanking of all that equipment would be too loud. Besides, it would take too long." He stopped and looked at her in the mirror. "Climbing with my bare hands. It's only fitting for a Neanderthal like me, don't you think?" McQueen smiled.

"You're crazy," she said.

"Maybe. Ask Gustav. I'm sure he's already run the odds."

Gustav didn't laugh.

McQueen rose from his seat and double-checked the small rucksack he had Colonel Bragg send him via express delivery. McQueen had vetoed the idea of a two-way in his ear. He didn't want to risk those at the top picking up their signal. He also didn't want the distraction. Every ounce of his attention had to be on each grasp and footing. One false move and he was a dead man.

"Sterling, look here," Gustav said, spreading a schematic of the fortress on the table of the apartment they had commandeered for the mission. The owners were fed a story about fumigation. Spiders. They'd be out for two days. The temporary HQ was a four-story mustard-colored building directly across the river from the cliff. Their vantage point was from the top floor. "The Emperor's Tower is the most prominent structure in the complex, but it has very steep stairs and small rooms. It was used for a museum, so it is unlikely they are there. The Lower Castle Barracks was used by the monks as a working area. There are living quarters upstairs."

"And where is that?" McQueen asked.

"Here," Gustav pointed to a rectangular building on the plat. "And this is Fuchs Tower." He pointed down to the schematic, then out the window up at the fortress. "You see it right there." The squatted round turret hung at the cliff's edge. "The only point of entry is a short wall around the right of the tower."

McQueen surveyed the tower with the night vision binoculars. "I can't tell because of the foliage at the top, but it looks like there might be a window on that wall."

"Bars," Gustav said. "It is covered with thick metal bars." He pointed back down at the layout of the fortress. "Right here. You will enter over this wall here. Turn right then turn to your immediate left. The barracks will be right in front of you."

The fortress had been lit up at night before it was mysteriously closed to the public. Now it sat ominously in the dark illuminated only by the evening's half-moon. The conventional way up was by cable car. That's how the tourist had gained access to the fortress, but the car stayed locked at the top and only came down with an armed escort. There was a covered walkway, but that, too, was secured. This made the conventional means of reconnoitering impossible.

Although it was hardly late, the cobblestone streets of Kufstein were already almost deserted. The only sign of life was the music coming from the Auracher Löchl, the six hundred-year-old restaurant up the alleyway behind the riverfront hotels that sat at the foot of the mighty fortress. McQueen tried to block everything out except for the climb on the short trip across the river. Agent Barton pulled to the side of the road just past the bridge. McQueen concealed himself in the back seat. Once Barton had thoroughly scanned the area, she gave him the green light to get out.

"McQueen," she said, "please be careful."

McQueen looked at her for a moment. "I'm touched, Barton."

He exited the back seat of the BMW and sprinted down the steps and onto a paved bike path beside the river. He had already scoped out his entry point. He stood at the base of the cliff and looked up. It was intimidatingly high. The rock jutted out approximately four stories up. Tricky. Rubbing his hands together he took a deep breath then began his ascent.

Gustav nervously worked a sucker from one side of his mouth to another and peered through night vision binoculars, his elbows resting on the table of the balcony. McQueen was at about ten meters when Barton arrived back.

"How's he doing?" she asked nervously.

"*He* is doing fine," Gustav answered. "Me? Not so good."

Barton took a seat beside him and picked up her night vision binoculars. "I hope to God he knows what he's doing."

The wind was blowing a bit more than McQueen had anticipated. He hugged the face of the cliff until another gust passed. After he was sure it was gone he continued his climb. As a climber you're told not to look down, but after the first ten meters you're either too petrified to continue or the length of the fall doesn't matter to you. McQueen had neither the inclination nor the time to be scared. His mind was on the top, not the bottom. It was also on every grasp, every foothold. He would often try two or three possibilities before deciding on the best one. The wind whipped across his body. The Inn River snaked out of sight behind him and the Kaiser Mountains loomed in the distance. When he would feel the terror creeping into his mind he would fight to push back. If he freaked out and froze and could go neither up nor down he would surely die. Nobody was coming to rescue him.

There were bigger things than his fears to consider. The answer to who was behind the recent kidnappings—including Gerber's—and, possibly, a clue as to their next move awaited him beyond the walls of the fortress. And the only way to it was straight up.

At about twelve meters the cliff began to jut out. This would be the most difficult part of the climb. Each grip had to be solid. For a time, he would almost feel like he was hanging upside down. Like a bat. He chose the next crevice carefully. Then the left foot. Left hand. Right foot. His legs strained. Right hand. He was hanging at the bellybutton of the big gut of a jut-out. Left foot. He thought he had solid rock, but the rock broke free and dropped to the parking lot below. McQueen lost his balance and his right foot lost its grip. Vivian Barton gasped and grabbed Gustav's arm. McQueen's feet dangled like worms on a hook, clawing desperately to find solid footing. But they were too far away from the cliff.

"Come on, Sterling," Gustav growled, staring into the binoculars and working his sucker from one side of his mouth to the other.

McQueen gave up on getting his footing. He mustered all the upper-body strength he had and slowly pulled himself up over the gut of the cliff. He felt the searing pain of the rocks dragging across his bruised stomach. Right hand. Left hand. He pulled his body weight with each burn of his arm muscles. At first he got a knee in place, then the other. He crawled over the top of the jut-out and continued the steep climb. He pushed through each movement, each grasp, each foothold. The wind whipped through his hair and whistled through holes in the rock. He found his rhythm and made good time until about sixty meters. McQueen stopped. His breathing became rapid and shallow. It's a body's involuntary reaction to stress and fear. Once it starts it's almost unavoidable. One's hands begin to sweat. Muscles become tense.

"Come on, Sterling," Gustav urged.

"What's wrong?" Barton asked. "Why is he stopping? Is he tired?"

"Doubtful," Gustav said.

"What then?"

Gustav looked over at Barton, then back into the binoculars. "He has climber's panic."

A wave of sheer terror washed over McQueen. He was shaking

and his sense of awareness was reduced to what amounted to tunnel vision. His peripheral vision was gone. He couldn't move. He was frozen on the side of that mountain. His mind was telling him he was going to fall. He looked down to the point where he started and it looked so small. Would he die right there? If he didn't regain control soon he knew he would. The absurdity that he was clinging to the side of cliff with just his bare hands consumed his awareness. The reality of that only served to feed the panic. The wind whipping across his body almost blew him from the surface. He tried to take a step down but instantly recognized that wasn't an option. He could move neither up nor down. Fatigue would surely set in and he would simply lose his grip and fall. Death screamed in his ears. Sweat fell from his nose onto his lips. He closed his eyes and breathed deeply. His stomach tightened. He felt as if he were being peeled off the face of the cliff.

"Oh my God!" Barton exclaimed as McQueen's left arm dropped from the rock and hung back across his body.

"It is all right," Gustav said. "He is doing exactly what he is supposed to do."

"What do you mean?"

"He is stretching."

After a moment, McQueen wiped his left hand on his pants and grasped the rock with it allowing his right arm to fall to his side, breathing deeply as he stretched. He began to slowly regain his awareness. His confidence began to return and he felt a rush of adrenaline. He reached his hand up, found a suitable crevice, and began to ascend again.

"That is one tough customer," Gustav said. He nervously moved what was left of the sucker from one side of his mouth to the other.

"Come on, McQueen." Barton urged in a whisper. "You can do it."

He got to approximately 80 meters and glanced up the face of the rock. He could see the top. He dug his left foot into the next crevice lifting his right to find another toehold and pushed his 180-pound frame up the cliff. But the rock his left foot found was fragmented and it gave way under his weight. McQueen's body lunged downward. He grasped the cliff with both hands.

"Oh my God!" Barton screamed.

# Chapter Twenty-Seven

Rock, dust, and debris bounced off the face of the cliff on its way to the bottom. McQueen hung by both hands in the moonlight, his feet flailing about, scrambling to find a solid piece of rock. He looked down past his chest to his legs trying desperately to find a crevice. His arms burned under the immense pressure. He scrambled his feet hoping one would find its mark. Just before he thought his arms would give out, his right foot found a solid split in the rock. Once he pushed his body upward it was a simple matter of finding a crevice for his left.

The rush of adrenaline from the near-fall energized his whole body. He almost effortlessly glided up the mountain the final ten meters which put him on a ledge at the base of the massive 20-foot fortress walls.

"He is up. He is up," Gustav repeated in an almost sing-song manner. "Up, up, up." He turned to Barton and gave her a high five then quickly returned his eyes to the night vision binoculars.

McQueen pulled himself up the right side of the base of Fuchs Tower holding onto vegetation. He had spotted the brown metal downspout on the right side of the wall from across the river. He figured that might be his best mode up the wall, but another downspout on the left side, hidden from view from the ground, was his best option. He climbed like an ape and lifted himself to the top of the fortress wall. He then threw himself over it like a gymnast, landing feet first on the gravel about a meter-and-a-half below the top of the wall.

"You better get into position," Gustav said.

Barton grabbed the key fob off the table and headed out the door.

It was imperative that his reconnaissance went undetected if McQueen was going to find out what they were planning next. He deduced the upper floors of the Lower Castle Barracks would be used for lodging, since that's what the monks had used it for. The bottom floor would be used for operations. That's what he would do were he utilizing the fortress.

He prowled to the right. An iron gate covered a large hole cut out of the rock. He turned left. Directly in front of him was the Lower Castle Barracks. He spied to see which windows were lit. He trotted lightly on the gravel and planted himself up against the end of the barracks. He eased around the corner and down to the first lit window. The bottom of the window was about waist high. He crouched and waddled up to it. The window was slightly ajar to allow in the summer night breeze. Four men sat around a table playing cards. The room had two windows and was made entirely of wood with wide-planked floors, wood walls, and exposed beams. Automatic weapons hung from hooks on the walls alongside several monks' frocks.

McQueen lowered his head below the window sill then proceeded to the third window. Looking inside, he found a room half the size of the first. This one was lined with equipment: computers, servers, television monitors, and the like. The window was closed, so he could hear little of what was going on. The only similarity to the last was the wood and the automatic weapons that hung from hooks.

He passed a medieval-looking door then came to a fourth window. It was dark. At the next lit window he could hear talking albeit muffled. He eased his eyes above the window sill. This room was wood like the others, but the motif was decidedly more elegant. At the right side of the room hung a pendant light fixture. It shone a pale light over a beautiful mahogany nineteenth-century partners' desk with a gilded tooled leather top and cross-banded surround. Lining the walls at spaced intervals were stacked map chests of solid oak with cast brass pulls and label holders. On the floor in front of the partners' desk lay a wool Persian Bijar tribal hand-knotted oriental rug with colors of rust, blue, green, ivory, and navy. A large flag hung on the wall behind the desk. McQueen had never seen one like it before. It had a red background and what looked like the Nazi iron cross turned sideways in black. Between the two top terminals of the cross was what appeared to be a backwards apostrophe.

Sitting at the desk was a man. He was fit and fiftyish with thick black hair and a full black mustache that covered his entire top lip. His nostrils were perpetually flared. His heavy eyebrows framed angry eyes that almost seemed to shoot lightning bolts from them. He was talking to a rather atrocious-looking skinny man with greasy hair and a complexion the color of a napkin. McQueen retrieved an earbud from his rucksack and a device that worked similar to a stethoscope. He gently placed it on the window.

"—if that is agreeable to you," the skinny man finished saying in German.

"Whatever it takes to get the information we need," the man behind the desk responded. "We have cleaned up the mess the professor made. We just want to make sure there are no more loose ends. You know how I detest loose ends."

"Ja, mein Herr. He has proven to be quite resistant so far," the skinny man said, picking the dirt from beneath his fingernails, "but he will tell us what we want to know. It is just a matter of time."

The man with the lightning eyes slapped the desk and the little man jumped. "We do not have time!" His face was red with rage. "The operation is upon us! Do you understand?"

"I understand, mein Herr."

"Find out who he told, if he told. Do it now!" The man went back to reading papers on his desk. The slight man rose and excused himself silently.

McQueen burned the image of the flag that hung behind the apparent leader of this operation into his brain. He then scampered around the corner hoping to see where the little man was going. He watched him make the steep climb up the cobblestone path then pass under a rock archway. McQueen tiptoed behind. He passed through another archway, this one part of the base of the Upper Castle Barracks. McQueen stopped in the shadows of a doorway and watched. The man came to a fork in the path and took the left fork. McQueen almost followed, but stopped. Just ahead on the right up considerable stone steps was a sentry. He followed the man with his eyes until he disappeared at the bottom of the hill.

McQueen had enough intel to make it worth the trip. Going inside the Lower Castle Barracks and snooping around on the outside chance of learning more was pressing his luck. Gerber was there. That was for sure. As for the other hostages, the complex was too big to explore alone. There were catacombs of tunnels and dungeons. Plenty of places to hide prisoners. But there was something much bigger brewing. The thick-haired man was obviously in charge. McQueen could attempt to take him now, but the building was full of hostiles. He'd never make it out in one piece. They needed this guy alive if they ever hoped to find out what was planned. It was time to regroup.

Retracing his steps, McQueen ran back down the cobblestone path, then around the Lower Castle Barracks. He stopped to map out his exit. And he better hurry. Someone was coming. Two of them by the sound of their boot steps on the gravel. He could hear them talking. Their steps turned from gravel to cobblestones. They were passing through the archway at the Upper Castle Barracks where McQueen had just been. If they were headed for the door on that side of the Lower Castle Barracks he had some time. If they continued down the hill and turned left they would walk right into him. He'd be a sitting duck. He looked around and analyzed his options. They were limited.

McQueen scrambled up the small grassy hill outside the barracks and over to a short stone wall. The wall was covered on top with grass. Just beyond the wall was ninety dizzying meters straight down to the pavement. He needed more time to plot his exit. The voices were louder. They weren't stopping at the barracks. Their footsteps were getting closer. He hopped up on the grassy top and peered over the edge. Closer they came. McQueen steadied himself against the wind. He could not be caught. That would compromise the entire mission. There was no place to hide. They were just around the corner. Twenty yards and closing. If they turned left they would spot him immediately. Ten yards away. Now he had no choice. They made the turn at the end of the Lower Castle Barracks. McQueen bent his knees, swallowed hard, and jumped.

It was a perfect swan dive. McQueen pulled the cord of his rucksack immediately. The black canopy unfolded above him and made the gentle sound of someone ruffling a bed sheet. He glided along over the Inn River then turned left behind the fortress over a residential area. He saw Barton's headlights just in front of the rendezvous point which lit up a large vacant lot. McQueen guided himself just over the car and touched down running until he came to a stop. The black parachute floated softly to the ground behind him. Barton was already on the scene quickly folding up the chute with her arms. McQueen removed the rucksack from his back and helped her finish the job, both cramming the equipment into the trunk and leaving within seconds of his touchdown.

"Nice landing," Barton said. "Anything interesting going on up there?"

"Oh, yeah," McQueen answered. "And Gustav ain't gonna like it."

"What do you mean?"

"That tight bastard owes me fifty bucks."

# Chapter Twenty-Eight

McQueen trotted down the steps of their temporary headquarters, located across the river from the fortress, and out into the pre-dawn Austrian morning for a jog. The shadowy figure he caught out of the corner of his eye closed on him fast. The move was instinctual. Before he could even get a good look, his hands were doing what they were trained to do. He had begun to throw a punch to the face of the figure when he heard someone whisper, "It's me." He caught a familiar scent.

"Alena?"

"Hello, Sterling," the soft British accent greeted.

He tried to keep his voice down. "What the hell are you doing here?"

"I came bearing gifts." Alena Sharabi moved in closer so she didn't have to raise her voice.

"What kind of gifts?" McQueen asked.

"Information."

"How'd you find me?"

"Your partner or girlfriend or whatever she is."

"Barton?"

"I'm jealous." She was so close McQueen could feel her breath on his lips.

"How'd you find Barton?"

"When she was watching me back in the hotel room in Frankfurt. I locked onto her mobile signal. You think she's cuter than me?"

"What kind of information do you have?"

"These people that keep turning up dead. I know what ties them together."

"I'm listening," McQueen said.

"They were all members of something called the Chopin Cultural Center."

"Is that a place?"

"More like a society," she said. "They would go to concerts together, meet at each other's homes and discuss Chopin, things like that."

"Doesn't sound like the kind of activity that would get you killed."

"No, it doesn't, does it?"

"Is it a front for something?"

"Could be. I would think they had more in common than Polish composers, but you're asking the wrong girl."

"Well, you found out this much."

"And that's all we needed to know. If they're not Islamic terrorists, then we really don't care what they are. We were just making sure they weren't a threat to Egypt. They're your problem. Our work is done."

"That's it?"

She smiled, "That's it."

"Thanks for the tip." McQueen turned to leave.

Alena grabbed his arm and pulled him close. "Not even one kiss in exchange for all my troubles? I came such a long way."

McQueen looked into her eyes for a long moment. She did smell delicious. He kissed her passionately then turned and jogged off into the night.

She tasted her own lips and watched his image disappear.

●

MCQUEEN POURED HIMSELF a cup of hot coffee and looked out the window. The morning sun was rising over the mountains. Gustav and Barton studied the piece of paper McQueen had placed on the table.

"I have never seen this flag before," Gustav said.

Barton looked at the image McQueen had sketched on the paper. "It looks like the iron cross set on its side."

"Yeah, that's what it looks like to me too." McQueen finished stirring sweetener and cream into his coffee and took a sip walking over to the table. "You're sure there are no Neo-Nazis using that symbol?" he asked Gustav.

"Not that I am aware of, but, as you know, the swastika is outlawed in Austria and Germany. The Nazis these days are very clever in their symbolism. I will gladly check, but I have followed that movement very closely. I have never seen anything like this symbol."

"And that apostrophe at the top," Barton said, "what could that mean?"

"We need someone who can decipher this thing," McQueen said.

"I will work on it." Gustav snapped a picture with his phone then called the NATO Intelligence Fusion Centre in London.

"Listen, McQueen," Barton said, watching Gustav leave the room.

McQueen sensed what was coming and tried to head it off. "Barton, you don't have to apologize."

Her face was drenched in disbelief. "Apologize?"

"Yeah, I know you think you almost got me killed on the way to Zurich, but I really think—"

"Almost got you killed? I didn't almost get you killed."

"That's what I was saying—"

"You're a piece of work, you know that?"

"Funny," McQueen said, "that's what they said about you."

"*Who* said that about me?"

"It doesn't matter. I just thought you felt bad about exposing me on the train and that's why you told Bragg."

"I told Bragg because he debriefed me. I told him everything that happened, just as I'm required to do. I also told him you were a sexist male chauvinist dinosaur."

"Really?" McQueen smiled. "What did he say?"

"He said he wished he had ten more dinosaurs just like you."

"They will work on it," Gustav said, walking back into the room.

"OK, I've got to get busy planning this operation for tonight. Orders from NAIT were delivered this morning. Waiting for me when I returned from my jog."

"Jog," Gustav said. "You are making me tired."

"Which reminds me," McQueen said. He turned to Barton. "Let me see your phone."

She looked at him curiously then pulled it from her pocket and handed it to him. He looked down at it and walked across the room.

"You know how to use one of those?" she asked.

McQueen opened the door to the balcony, took a step out, then threw the phone as far as he could. It landed with a splash in the middle of the chilly Inn River.

"What the hell are you doing?" she yelled.

"Had a visit from Alena Sharabi this morning. Take a guess how she found us."

Barton didn't say a word.

"This time it was friendlies. Next time we might not be so lucky."

"What did she want?" Gustav asked.

"She came to tell me that Schneider, Hensel, and Amstutz were all members of something called the Chopin Cultural Center."

"CCC," Gustav said.

"Exactly. At least that little riddle is solved. The bigger question is, what is it?"

"Probably something more than a music appreciation group," Gustav said.

"A front for this Edda Society maybe?" Barton said.

"That'd be my guess," McQueen said, "but we'll have to worry about that later. We don't have much time to work out the logistics for tonight's mission. Gustav, I'll need your help in that area. After that, you'll have plenty of time to rest."

"Thank God," he said.

"What about me?" Barton asked.

"You're coming with us tonight," McQueen said.

Suddenly McQueen had made up for ditching her phone. "We got a name for this operation yet?" she asked.

"Yeah," McQueen said. "Barbican."

# Chapter Twenty-Nine

The snipers wound quietly up Mitterndorfer Strasse just outside Kufstein in a nondescript van. They rode in silence—four marksmen, four spotters—each alone in their thoughts in the darkness. Someone would die tonight. In their line of work it was easy to become detached from it. Better said, it was essential. Killing is such a personal thing unless you're a half mile or more away, but, to these professionals, those on the other end of their scopes were targets, nothing more.

The van turned off Mitterndorfer Strasse and took a less-traveled single-lane path that led to a rustic rental home on the side of the Kaiser Mountains. The mountain range loomed over the small town like a watchful guardian. The vantage point from the front porch gave them a clear view of Kufstein fortress. The driver cut the engine and the lights. The men disembarked under the moonlight, gathered their equipment, and quietly began to prepare for the job at hand.

The schematic of the fortress showed a redoubt on the south side of the complex. There were gravel paths leading north and northwest from the southernmost tip. That tip was the planned insertion point. McQueen had asked for a bird to scope out the sentries. He saw a guard himself at the northwest corner of the redoubt when he breached the fortress. Sat recon showed there were three more. One was on the east side between the redoubt and the Emperor's Tower. Another was at the southern tip where they planned to drop. Yet another was a few yards away from the south sentry on the west side.

McQueen consulted the layout of the fortress and determined from where he saw the skinny man heading the night before that Gerber was probably being held in a place called Rock-Cut Passage. This was a tunnel built in the 16th century. It was used during both world wars as a shelter. Vivian Barton was assigned the task of finding Gerber.

The rest of the team would clear the Lower Castle Barracks. McQueen would try to take the ringleader alive.

Four sniper positions were set up on the porch. The snipers unslung their 52-pound back packs, each holding a Barrett M107A1 .50 caliber rifle system. That included the disassembled rifle, sound suppressor, optics, and night vision/thermal hybrid. Each sniper knelt over the case and began withdrawing components to assemble the six-foot weapon. They quietly unfolded the bipods and stood the lower receiver on the porch floor. With one stroke, they withdrew the upper receiver with enough momentum that allowed the barrel to slide into battery position. They grasped the barrel key, pulling against its 70-pound tensioned springs, and worked the barrel key until it was firmly seated in the barrel slot.

The sentries stood watch over Kufstein fortress. The sun had disappeared behind the mountains an hour before. One guard glanced at his watch. It was a little before ten, two long hours until their relief showed up.

The snipers tossed the upper receiver out over the lower receiver trusting the barrel would guide the upper and lower perfectly together. Then a quick grasp of the charging handle with the right hand pulled back the bolt carrier. They lowered the upper receiver and replaced the rear lock and midlock pins. After they rotated the lock ring on the suppressor to the lock position the .50 caliber rifle was good to go.

They checked their magazines to make sure they had ample ammo. If all went according to plan they would need only one round each. They took the front of the magazines, inserted them into the magazine wells, then rocked the rear of the magazines into place until they clicked. They attached the Leupold 14-power scopes. Mounted on the scope was a BORS, the Barrett Optical Ranging System. The snipers used the BORS to determine the barometric pressure, temperature, and angle of elevation or depression. The shooter could simply turn the scope's elevation knob to the distance to the target and the shot should be on the mark. That is if there was no wind. They then attached the HISS-XLR hybrid scopes in front of the Leupold to give them a clear view of the target at night.

The Sikorsky stealth helicopter hummed along with Sterling

McQueen, Vivian Barton, Pierre Bujot, and Victoria Carrington in its belly. They communicated through headsets and mics riding mostly in silence until McQueen turned to Barton. Her hair was pulled back in a ponytail.

"I almost didn't recognize you without your glasses," he said.

She smiled, "Funny thing. Turns out I don't need them anymore."

There were three major objectives in the mission. The first was to bring the leader in alive. If there was an operation in the works, then they needed to interrogate him. The second was to rescue Gerber. The third was to secure the release of the other hostages, if there were other hostages there. Gerber's well-being had taken a back seat given the new intel about a planned operation. McQueen figured he'd find the leader right where he left him the night before.

From the reconnaissance, the number of hostiles was estimated at between thirteen and sixteen. It all depended on how many might have already bedded down for the night when McQueen was able to observe their movements the prior evening. They would clear their areas, perform their tasks, then rendezvous just outside the boss's office at the Lower Castle Barracks.

The spotters were busy setting up to the left of each shooter. This was not going to be easy for them tonight. It's hard enough calling the wind in daytime. Trying to find something blowing or moving all along the distance to the target was nearly impossible. At 1,000 meters, a five-mile-per-hour cross wind will blow a .50 cal bullet off by as much as 63 inches. And there can be four or more different wind directions and speeds on long shots. Shooting from a mountain across open air leaves little to read making tracking the vapor trail all the more important.

Colonel Bragg had personally briefed General Bushing on the intelligence gathered by McQueen. There was no doubt that Franz Gerber was being held in the fortress. The assumption was that all of the other surviving hostages were there too. It was determined that an aerial assault was the only option. NAIT agents would be dispatched under the cover of darkness. The only non-NAIT agent on the mission would be Vivian Barton. No time to waste. It was clear those inside the fortress were planning an attack soon. If they wanted to get ahead of it they had to take the senior commander alive. After careful coordination with Austrian authorities, Operation Barbican was given the green light.

The spotters used their laser range finders to confirm the SAT distance to the targets. From hillside to Target One was 1,157 meters, about seven-tenths of a mile. The other three targets were within 50 meters of the first. They would be shooting into a slight headwind of five miles-per-hour if that's the only wind they encountered on the way to the target. Elevation at the sniper site was roughly 300 feet higher than the target elevation. The BORS gauged the angle cosine. The snipers turned their elevation knobs to their specific targets then studied and doped the other three targets. Each man was to fire until his target was down. The team leader may redirect him to engage any target sill remaining.

Their scopes doubled as cameras and Colonel Bragg could see everything on his large monitors. The Battle Room back in Brussels was a bee hive of activity. A tech was assigned to each camera. The operational team in the field couldn't hear the techs, but their job was to keep the colonel apprised of anything he needed to know. The sniper team leader sat with Bragg. He checked in with his team.

"This is Command, Team One. Sound off."

Softly, each sniper gave his number.

"One."

"Two."

"Three."

"Four."

"Outstanding. Two, your target is moving slightly," the sniper commander observed. "Be prepared to lead him if necessary."

"Roger."

"We are approximately two minutes out," the leader announced.

The scene inside the fortress was eerily tranquil. The man with the thick black hair and mustache sat at his desk writing notes on the day's activities. Several men relaxed in the rec room. The communications team kept tabs on news reports and monitored radio communications from law enforcement.

McQueen looked at his watch. Thirty seconds until ten o'clock.

The Sikorsky would be in position in forty seconds. Twenty seconds until ten. The sniper team leader in the command post watched the monitors of the four sentries. Fifteen seconds. Colonel Bragg chewed on his unlit cigar and watched the monitors. The snipers' scope cameras showed the sentries. The bottom-mounted cameras on the chopper showed the fortress illuminated in green from different angles. Victoria Carrington readied her gloved hands around the rope. Ten seconds. The snipers took deep breaths then exhaled.

"Wait for my command," the team leader instructed.

The organ music was loud and abrupt. Although they had heard it each and every night for months at the exact same time the sentries still flinched. Once they had settled back into their stances the sniper team leader back at the command post gave the countdown.

"Four...Three...Two."

On the unspoken beat of one, the snipers all fired simultaneously.

It's an interesting thing about a shot nearly three-quarters of a mile away. Most people don't realize it, but it takes time for the bullet to reach its destination. Traveling at about 2,750 feet per second, that's about 1.62 seconds to the target. One-point-six-two seconds. That's how long it took the round to make its way from the barrel of the Barrett on the hillside of the Kaiser Mountains to the targets at Kufstein fortress.

The bullets left vapor trails as they cut through the night air. One-point-six-two seconds of anticipation from the sniper team. In their minds they counted. Mississippi one. The first sniper's bullet hit its victim on the bridge of the nose taking out the back of his head at the base. The second caught its victim in the back of the head leaving a gaping hole in his throat. The third hit just about ear level and exploded the skull like a watermelon. The fourth missed the man's skull by a mere centimeter. That sentry had the good fortune of turning his head just as the bullet left the barrel. "Hit." Three spotters said the word simultaneously. "Miss," the fourth spotter said calmly. The sentry saw his comrades drop and started to walk.

"Give four a little help," the sniper team leader said.

"I got it," four said.

The other men knew exactly how he felt. They held their fire.

Four's target took another step forward. The second round hit the gravel right behind him. The other snipers turned their weapons on him. The sentry turned and was reaching for his mic switch. Sniper four calmly squeezed off a third round. The sentry caught it like a football, center chest.

"Hit," the fourth spotter said.

The sound of the suppressed shots echoed off the mountains, but the boom was absorbed inside the town by the overwhelming sound of the organ. The Heroes' Organ. How appropriate.

# Chapter Thirty

The sniper commander looked to Bragg. "Four confirmed kills, sir."

"Roger." Bragg turned his attention to McQueen's team.

"Chopper's in position," one of the techs said.

"NAIT team. Go!" Bragg ordered.

Agent Carrington was out of the chopper fast-roping toward the ground. After three meters space, McQueen followed, then Bujot, then Barton. They hit the ground, shed their gloves, drew their suppressed weapons, and went to work. McQueen recognized the organ music immediately—Chopin's Revolutionary Étude—a stirring piece almost certainly chosen to rally the fortress occupants to the coming operation.

Agent Barton would head to Rock-Cut Passage to locate Gerber. Carrington and Bujot were in charge of taking out the remaining men, including the organist, once the raid was complete. For now, that organ provided them cover, but that cover was limited. Revolutionary Étude would not last much more than three minutes. Time was of the essence.

Victoria Carrington led the team single-file from the insertion point down the stone steps. Barton peeled off and headed down the path to the right toward Rock-Cut Passage. The rest ran straight down the gravel path through the archway at the base of the Upper Barracks and onto the cobblestone path.

The footwork of the monk playing the Heroes' Organ was breathtaking. Revolutionary Étude is one of the most difficult organ pieces in the world to play. A guard stood and watched in stunned amazement.

Down the steep hill McQueen's team went to the Lower Castle Barracks. Carrington took the metal steps leading to the top floor elevation. Almost immediately she encountered the first hostile. The man had just drawn his sidearm and was beginning to take aim when her silencer popped and he was dropped in his tracks.

Colonel Bragg watched via the body cam.

"One hostile neutralized," a tech said. "Carrington."

Bragg's eyes darted from screen to screen.

Pierre Bujot killed a man on the backside of the barracks who appeared to be out for a stroll.

"One hostile neutralized," another tech announced. "Bujot."

Bujot hoped the man he just killed wasn't outside because he heard something. That might mean another hostile was lying in wait. He backtracked the dead man's steps to a door on the bottom floor on the other side of the barracks. No one else was there. He joined McQueen back around on the east side underneath where Carrington had entered the top floor. Through hand signals McQueen instructed Bujot to enter the bottom floor hallway, turn left, and go all the way to the end. That would place him at the rec room where the men would either be playing cards or watching TV. Their automatic weapons would be just a step away, so he would have to act fast. McQueen would take the next room, which was the communications center.

McQueen opened the door to the barracks bringing in the loudness of the organ music with him. The music went back to being moderately loud again when he shut the door. The mustachioed man stopped what he was doing momentarily and looked at the door. He then went back to his work.

McQueen and Bujot hurried to their positions. Carrington cleared the upstairs sleeping area encountering three more hostiles on the second floor.

The leader continued writing. He was one of the few in the complex who actually enjoyed the nightly organ music. McQueen and Bujot stood by their respective doors while McQueen counted down silently with his free hand. Three, two, one. They casually opened their doors and systematically killed anything that moved. Bujot took out four in rapid succession: two at the card table, one watching television, the other standing by the window. The pop from his silencer was muffled by the organ music. No one even had a chance to cry out. He peeked behind the door to make sure no one else was hiding.

"Three more hostiles down. Bujot," a tech said.

McQueen neutralized three. Two with headphones on, one without. All three simply slumped over in their seats. McQueen scanned the entire room to make sure he got everybody.

"Three hostiles down," another tech said. "McQueen."

The organist in a monk's robe played like he was playing for his life. His feet moved adroitly across the pedals. His hands complemented the bass line with stabs of organ music that sounded like a war. The killing was almost surreal with the sound of the stirring organ music as a backdrop like a scene from a Quentin Tarantino film. The boss, just next door, turned another page and continued to write while humming along softly to the music.

Barton used her flashlight to search the dank chamber of Rock-Cut Passage. She dared not call out for Gerber for fear someone might be close by, but with the lights off and no sign of movement it was unlikely anyone was in the vicinity. It was only after she had settled into some sense of security that her light hit his image. Her torch made the scene all the more grisly. There in a bare rock room with only a table filled with instruments of torture, the blood still on them, sat Professor Gerber. His hands were tied behind his back. He wore no shirt and his torso was cut, burned, and bruised. His head slumped to one side. Below it a pool of blood. Barton eased closer and saw the single shot to the temple. It was a formality, but she had to know for sure. She placed a finger on his neck in a futile search of a pulse.

"Gerber's dead," Barton announced to the command center.

It was as she turned to join the others that she saw him. She let out an involuntary yelp, but her earpiece with microphone had already been ripped from her ear. Her body cam was disconnected. Her video screen in the Battle Room went dark.

"Barton," Bragg's voice called.

McQueen wanted to ask what was the matter but he couldn't risk being heard.

"Barton's camera's offline," Bragg said. "She's not responding."

*Dammit*, McQueen thought to himself. He slipped down the hall and out the door.

"Barton," he whispered into his microphone. No response. They were running out of time. The organ music would end soon. Then their element of surprise would be gone. The last thing McQueen needed was to divert from the plan. He thought for a second, looking back over his shoulder, then made his decision. The boss would keep as long as the music played. If he decided to leave the office Carrington and Bujot were there to nab him.

Up the cobblestone path McQueen ran toward the left fork he'd seen the skinny man take the night before.

"We have sixteen hostiles down," he announced for the benefit of Bragg and those monitoring the situation at command. "The prize has not been secured yet."

"Roger that," Bragg said, watching McQueen's monitor. "You heard that the hostage is dead."

"Roger," McQueen said.

"Don't go looking for her if it risks the operation," Bragg ordered.

McQueen pulled his torch from his belt and cautiously entered Rock-Cut Passage. Aside from the light he was casting, it was pitch black. The tunnel turned to the right a few feet in. The wet sand crunched beneath his feet. He could feel his heart pumping in his ears. A dead end, then a right, a quick left, another quick left, then a right. He shined his light on the puddle of water in the dirt. He sensed the urgency of the clock. The cover of the organ would only last a little longer. He could hardly hear it in the distance.

"Remember the objective," Bragg said.

For a second McQueen thought he heard something, but he couldn't tell what. He quickly moved in the direction of the sound. A drop of water splashed into an accumulated pool and echoed against the stone walls. Each step into the sand echoed no matter how much he tried to keep his footsteps silent. After a long straightaway the tunnel turned right, then two quick lefts, and right like before. A set of rock steps lay in front of him. He could see a glow up ahead and the same noise. This time it was a bit clearer. He couldn't be sure, but it sounded like the muffled sounds of somebody struggling. He eased up the steps just as he'd been trained—quietly and with his firearm ready to kill.

"You see, darling? I told you they would come for you."

Meinhard Metzger held Agent Barton's back close to his weak

frame. His left hand covered her mouth. His right pointed a pistol at the base of her skull. His skeletal head was level with hers on her right shoulder. Her eyes were large and apologetic. McQueen glanced over at the body still tied to the chair. Although he couldn't clearly see the face he didn't need a retina scan to know it was Franz Gerber.

"Drop the weapon. Now!" McQueen ordered.

Metzger laughed as if McQueen had told an off-color joke. "I am assuming you and your team have already neutralized everyone else."

A tech looked up at Bragg who was glued to McQueen's body cam. "Sir, the organ music is going to stop—"

The sign of Bragg's outstretched palm silenced the young man.

"You would like to put me on trial for some unknown, trumped-up charges," Metzger said to McQueen. "It is typical of capitalists controlled by the Jews. If you so much as move a muscle I am going to splatter this young lady's brains all over this room. Now, listen to me very carefully. You are going to drop *your* weapon. If you are so foolish as to choose—"

That gaping hole of a mouth of his, that purple tongue that danced around his purple lips, and the crooked teeth made such a tempting target. The bullet struck the back of his throat just as he opened wide to enunciate what McQueen assumed to be the word 'not.' Crimson splattered on the wall behind him so quickly he never got a chance to close his eyes. He fell backwards, his mouth and eyes forever frozen ridiculously wide open like some awkwardly candid photograph.

"Son of a bitch," Bragg whispered.

Barton fell to the ground. "You should've left me!"

"Don't think it wasn't tempting," McQueen said and bolted back down the same tunnel he entered.

"Bastard," Barton muttered. She pulled herself to her feet and glanced once more at the dead body of Professor Gerber. Then she took in the grotesque image of Meinhard Metzger. She knelt down, retrieved her gun from the floor, and hurried out after McQueen.

"Make that seventeen hostiles down," McQueen announced to the Battle Room. "Heading for the prize."

He rejoined the other two just outside the office. He knew the organ piece was near the end. He gently turned the knob ever so slightly.

The door appeared to be unlocked. He had his Sig at the ready, but before entering the room he had a thought. Instead of bursting in not knowing where in the room the target would be or even if he was there, McQueen decided on an odd plan. He simply knocked. A short official knock one would make if coming to see the leader.

"Kommen," the man said gruffly. The organ music still played the soundtrack to this macabre little saga.

The techs all looked up at Bragg in surprise. Bragg watched the screen.

McQueen looked at the Frenchman who turned down the corners of his mouth, raised an eyebrow, and shrugged his wide shoulders as only the French can do as if to say, 'What the hell.' McQueen turned the knob and walked in with his gun drawn.

Carrington and Bujot saw him safely inside the room then left to find the organist. From the schematic they'd studied they knew exactly where to go. It was probably twenty meters from their location. The Civic Tower.

The leader had become so accustomed to dismissing the presence of other human beings that he didn't even bother looking up from the paper on which he was writing when McQueen came in.

The guard in the Civic Tower who had been standing there watching the monk playing the organ saw Bujot and Carrington enter out of the corner of his eye. He swung around to engage. He had his gun halfway drawn when Carrington's throwing knife caught him in the throat. She couldn't risk interrupting the music with a suppressor shot and putting McQueen in danger. The monk continued to play, completely oblivious to the life that was just taken not three yards behind him.

McQueen made no sudden moves but casually walked up to the partners' desk. By the time the man gave him the courtesy of acknowledging him he did a double take and was looking up into the barrel of a gun.

Bragg's monitor was looking down the barrel into the stupefied eyes of the ringleader like some video game. The colonel smiled to himself and pulled the stub of an unlit cigar from his mouth.

"Damn, I love that boy's style."

The end of the raid was as anticlimactic as the beginning had been dramatic. The leader simply laid his pen upon the desk and slowly raised his hands in the air in an ignominious gesture of surrender as the organ music reached a crescendo and theatrically concluded. It was like the ending to a gruesome silent movie.

# Chapter Thirty-One

The spotlights that illuminated the fortress shone through small waves of mist from a light fog that moved through the area. It was close to midnight and the first time the fortress had been lit in months. It was crawling with law enforcement that came from all over Austria. The entire town of Kufstein was awake with the news that some Nazi organization with designs on taking over the government—perhaps the world—had been operating in their midsts, undetected, for months. Television news trucks had arrived with reporters filing live reports against the backdrop of the fortress. Police cordoned off the base of it only allowing credentialed law enforcement on the cable car and up to the scene of the crime.

"His name is Karl Luxemburg," Vivian Barton told McQueen. "He's a community organizer. Agitator is more like it. No criminal record to speak of. Just some arrests involving protests."

"What kinds of protests?" McQueen asked.

"Anti-capitalist, workers' rights, that kind of thing."

"Hitler took over the German Workers' Party. Looks like their tactics haven't changed much. Any surviving hostages?"

"Yes," Barton said. "All the missing hostages are accounted for. The monks weren't so lucky. They spared only one. The organist. There appear to be human remains in what was the main outdoor cooking area back when this was occupied by Bavarian royalty. We can only assume that all of the monks were murdered and burned."

McQueen shook his head. "What kind of human filth does something like that?"

Franz Gerber's remains inside a body bag rolled by on a stretcher. Gustav followed behind in unqualified sadness. They watched while the gurney was loaded onto the inclined railcar for the trip to the bottom.

McQueen laid a gentle hand on his friend's shoulder. "It's not your fault," he consoled. "It's not *our* fault. We did everything we could do."

"If it makes any difference," Barton said, "he was cold when I reached him. That means they killed him long before we ever began our raid."

Gustav looked up at them with a forced smile, his eyes glistening with tears. "I do not know how I will tell his wife and son," he said softly. "They trusted me to take care of him."

The remaining hostages were found chained to walls in the Upper Castle Barracks. Medical personnel tended to them on the scene then loaded the ones unable to walk under their own power on gurneys and took them to waiting ambulances at the bottom of the fortress. A handful of unaccounted for hostiles were handcuffed and escorted to police vans.

McQueen walked back into Luxemburg's office in the Lower Castle Barracks and stood silently staring at the flag hanging on the wall above his desk. The red background. The black iron cross turned on its side. The backwards apostrophe between the two top terminals.

"London came up with nothing."

McQueen turned to see Gustav entering the room pointing at the flag.

"Nothing?"

"They have nothing in their data base about such a symbol. No known group is using it."

"It has to be Nazi. That pig who killed Gerber was spitting venom about capitalists controlled by Jews."

A uniformed officer from the Austrian Federal Police stepped inside the room. "Herr McQueen, they are ready for you."

The crime scene investigation was winding down. The throng of media clamored to get a picture of Karl Luxemburg as he was brought down in the cable car in leg shackles. McQueen boarded the Austrian prisoner transport van from the rear. Luxemburg was loaded into the van and seated on the bench seat opposite him. His leg shackles were chained to a lock on the floor. His hands were cuffed in front of him with chains linking the cuffs with the shackles. They both were separated from the driver's compartment by a steel cage. An officer of the Austrian police closed the door and took his place in the passenger's seat. The gray van wore a thin red stripe down the side. No windows. Below the red stripe was a larger blue stripe with the word 'POLIZEI' emblazoned in large white letters. The driver started the engine, hit the blue light atop the van, and pulled out of Kufstein with a four-car police escort to Vienna.

It seemed everyone wanted their pound of flesh from Karl Luxemburg. The city of Kufstein and the state of Tyrol wanted him tried in Innsbruck. The Austrian federal government wanted him tried in the capital of Vienna. Luxemburg being a German citizen, the Germans were pushing for extradition through diplomatic channels to try him on sedition and treason charges. For the moment, the Austrian federal government had won that fight. This was a NAIT operation and even though Austria was not a member nation of NATO, they made a practice of cooperating, especially on an issue as sensitive as a Nazi plot. McQueen was the designated point man by order of General Bushing. He would see to it that Luxemburg got to Vienna and was processed. He would be allowed to question him further once the formalities were taken care of and Luxemburg's lawyer was present.

Luxemburg would await arraignment in Vienna. Federal prosecutors were already beginning the process of compiling the evidence and filing the charges. First degree murder: fifteen counts, including the murder of fourteen monks and Franz Gerber. That count may rise if they could pin any of the hostage killings on him. Kidnapping: multiple counts covering Gerber, the monks, and the rescued hostages. Torture: at least one count for the torturing of Gerber and perhaps more if forensic evidence proved the monks were tortured before they were killed and burned. Treason and conspiracy to overthrow the government would be harder to prove without knowledge of the full plot.

They rode in silence for most of the nearly four hours to Vienna. McQueen looked out the windshield at the darkness trying to piece together the complex puzzle he had been handed. He attempted to crawl inside the head of Karl Luxemburg and found an uncomfortable similarity. Both men were driven by an enormous sense of duty, the kind of duty that leads one to commit unimaginable acts in the name of it.

Luxemburg's duty was to his own twisted cause. McQueen's loyalty was to his own country and its security. He had been asked to do some unsavory things in the name of duty and he had done them without questioning. Politicians had decided policy. Intelligence agencies had decided courses of action. He had done the dirty work. Were they really the good guys? No country, like no man, is truly all good. It's a matter of degree. It's a matter of the end result. McQueen thought how rationalizing that sounded, the end justifying the means and all that. He reckoned Karl Luxemburg was probably having the very same thoughts as he sat across from him. Man can rationalize a lot if he truly believes he's right. Much ugliness can be committed if one is dedicated to a cause. McQueen's cause was freedom and protection of his country. Was his cause so entirely different from Luxemburg's? Did Luxemburg have someone whispering reassurance in *his* ear that some folks just needed killing?

"Du bist sehr stolz auf dich selbst," Luxemburg finally said.

McQueen looked at him in disgust. "If you're going to talk to me, then speak English, you son-of-a-bitch."

Luxemburg stared at him for a moment. "You are very proud of yourself," he repeated in his thick German accent. His eyes observed McQueen with the compassion of an executioner. His head bobbled a bit to the bumps in the road.

McQueen glared back at him. His comment didn't deserve a response.

Luxemburg smiled confidently. "You have no idea what you are involved in."

McQueen looked at him for an instant then turned his attention to the road through the front windshield.

"You can ignore me if you like," Luxemburg continued, "but you will not be able to ignore the inevitable. Your days are numbered. The wheels are already in motion. You cannot stop it."

McQueen looked back at his smug face. "It's going to be hard to run a revolution from a jail cell."

Luxemburg laughed. His laugh seemed incongruous with his predicament, chained to a seat in the back of a police van on his way to face charges that would lock him away forever. "The world's best manifestos have been written from jail."

"The revolution is over," McQueen answered deridingly.

Luxemburg's eyes turned to rage then quickly melted to indifference. "Du Narr," he said under his breath.

"No, *you're* the fool," McQueen shot back.

Luxemburg looked surprised that he understood what he'd said.

"The problem with you," explained Luxemburg, "is you do not understand that the greedy Jews rule the world by proxy. What is the worldly religion of the Jew? Huckstering. What is his worldly God? Money. Emancipation from huckstering and money, from practical, real Judaism, would be the self-emancipation of our time. But the Jews have emancipated themselves because the Christians have become Jews. They employ fools like you to fight and die for them. You are merely a puppet. Your Congress. Your White House. Hollywood. Wall Street. They are all owned by Zionist capitalists. In the final analysis, the emancipation of the Jews is the emancipation of mankind from Judaism."

McQueen wanted to beat the hell out of him right then and there but thought better of it. Allowing Luxemburg to drone on might offer a glimpse into what sort of evil he had planned.

Luxemburg continued, "Anyone who criticizes the Jew is made to pay. Do you know what percentage the Jewish population is in America?" He didn't wait for an answer. "Two." His chains rattled as he held up his thumb and index finger. "Two percent, but they control every major studio in Hollywood. You think that is just by happenstance? Who do you think controls your Federal Reserve? Jews. Who do you think controls your banks and your investment houses on Wall Street? Jews. Your government is scared to death of the Jews, scared to even criticize them. They have a blind allegiance to Israel, and most could not tell you why. There was once a British Member of Parliament by the name of Tom Dalyell. You ever heard of him? No. He said, 'A Jewish cabal have taken over the government in the United States and formed an unholy alliance with fundamentalist

Christians.' He was exactly right. You are so naive it is sickening." He went silent for a moment, then his eyes were once again animated. "If you are so ready to die, do you really know what you are dying *for*?"

"I know what I'm *not* dying for," McQueen responded sardonically. "I'm not dying for a bunch of murderers and thugs and people who believe their bloodline makes them superior."

Luxemburg scoffed. "Then you *are* a fool. I am not dying for a bloodline. I am dying for a cause that is bigger than me. A cause that is more important than me, that has ramifications for all mankind. We are liberating the world from the grip that has enslaved it. Capitalism. You are a slave and you do not even know it. You are a slave to your contentment. Although your every move is dictated by someone else you are a happy slave."

"And *you* are a slave to your hatred, to your nutty conspiracy theories, to your paranoia, to your dreams of a German utopia," McQueen fired back.

"You in America do not know what it means to suffer. You are soft. Prosperity has made you weak. Weak for the pickings of the capitalist Jews." He gave McQueen a disgusted look. "They control your news, your money, your entertainment, and you do not complain as long as you have plenty of it all. You do not even know you are a prisoner, and they keep getting richer and stronger and you keep getting more dependent and weaker. You are *owned* by the Jews and the sad part is you do not even care. You sicken me." He turned his head to the side as if the conversation was over.

McQueen paused a moment before choosing his words carefully. "You wanna talk about sick? You just killed fourteen monks and a wonderfully decent college professor. What unspeakable crimes did *they* commit?"

Luxemburg's eyes were filled with rage. "Do you not understand? These people are meaningless compared to the cause. Remember," he tapped his temple with his finger, "two percent of your population and they run everything. The world cannot be turned over to the Jews. They will destroy it as they have everything else they have ever touched down through history. The goal is perfection. Utopia. The goal of all species is perfection. The animal world strives for it. Why should we not?"

"Because we're not animals. We're humans. We work our problems out. We use violence as a last resort."

"You denigrate violence as something to be rejected when we all know that in the end nothing can be achieved without violence. The Jews have only come to power because they are liars and connivers and they are cunning and they have tricked the Americans into believing that they are the chosen ones." He laughed. "I thought the *Christians* were the chosen ones according to your Bible. The fact is, no one chooses a people. The people choose themselves. This is our calling, that we shall become the Templars of this Grail, gird the sword round our loins for its sake and stake our lives joyfully in the last holy war which will be followed by the thousand-year reign of freedom." Luxemburg's voice became low, his tone portentous. "The time of reckoning is upon us, and the world will be made right again."

His words hung in the air.

"We're coming up on Josefstadt," the driver informed McQueen, shattering the ominous mood.

Josefstadt was the prison adjacent to the court where Luxemburg would be processed. It was called the gray house because of the gray clothing the prisoners wore. Luxemburg's fame had attracted a throng of reporters, protesters, and curiosity seekers who all gathered in an early morning mist in front of the prison. Police had set up barricades along the front sidewalk leading to the building. Media personnel jockeyed for position to get the best camera angles. The van pulled up in front of Josefstadt.

"You cannot stop the inevitable," Luxemburg said.

"Shut up," McQueen said.

The passenger guard unlocked the back door of the van. He unlocked Luxemburg from the van then locked his handcuffs and leg shackles together. Just before Luxemburg stepped out into the media circus he muttered, "Die Revolution lebt." He exited the vehicle with McQueen's hand firmly grasping his left arm.

The crowd was in a feeding frenzy. Photographers snapped picture after picture. Video cameras crowded in for the best shot. Reporters screamed questions which Luxemburg ignored. Protesters screamed slogans of anger. He smiled confidently at the crowd. The polizei struggled to keep the throng at bay. McQueen calmly blocked everything out. His mind was focused on getting the prisoner the few steps to the front of the building where they would find calm once again behind the large glass doors. Luxemburg would be processed, then McQueen could get down to the questioning.

Luxemburg had something planned. He just had to find out what. Luxemburg's attorney would most certainly advise his client not to answer, not to incriminate himself. McQueen had to appeal to his ego. It was gargantuan. He could bait him with false assumptions about the plot, flush him out in the open by insulting him with a feeble plan. He could glean some morsel of information that might uncover what Luxemburg and his henchmen were up to.

Almost casually out of the crowd came the gun. It was as though everything shifted into slow motion including McQueen's own reactions. The outstretched hand was just before firing when McQueen first saw it. He screamed at the police to get the gun when the first shot rang out and then another. The assailant turned the weapon to his own temple and pulled the trigger. The officer closest to the gunman at the barricade was already going for the gun, grabbing the gunman's arm as the third shot fired harmlessly into the air. Two cops were all over him, one wresting the gun from his hand and the other tackling the man as he fell backwards. Both officers' knees came crashing down on the man's chest. They used their hands to pin his arms to the ground.

The crowd was in full panic. Those closest to the epicenter reflexively threw themselves in the opposite direction and as far from harm's way as possible. Trained cameramen ignored their natural tendencies for survival and kept their electronic eyes glued on the action. More police followed their instincts toward the commotion and hovered around the gunman ready to offer assistance.

McQueen, who had lunged forward toward the gunman, jerked his head back to his prisoner. If there was one thing McQueen knew very well it was death. Karl Luxemburg had the smell of it all over him. His shirt on the left side of his chest was stained in crimson and the stain grew larger. The smug smile had been forever erased from his lips.

McQueen pushed through the crowd of officers that surrounded the gunman. People were yelling, some were crying, some cowered on the sidewalk in fear. Even through the contorted screams of pain and agony McQueen recognized the face. From the dossier he remembered it completely. Far now from the innocent smile of the young man posing with his family on a snow-covered summit the face was still unmistakable. The face of the man who had just killed Karl Luxemburg belonged to Erich Gerber.

# Chapter Thirty-Two

Karl Luxemburg was dead, but how far up in the Edda Society was he? From the looks of the Kufstein operation, he was running the show. That was the presumption. What about all of the members? McQueen consoled himself with the likelihood that Luxemburg would never have talked even had he lived. These individuals might never be caught, which meant the movement was not really dead depending on how motivated the members were without their Führer.

McQueen felt extreme sorrow for Erich Gerber. His father was dragged into the whole affair against his will then tortured and killed for his work. His son, so distraught over his father's death, was willing to avenge him then take his own life unable to live with the unspeakable crime he committed. It was all so tragic.

And what of poor Gustav? Had he left the good professor alone, Gerber would be teaching his classes and enjoying his family instead of lying in the morgue. No man should die so violently, especially a man so gentle and so caring. Were it not for Gustav, Gerber's son would have his life back, and his mother would not have lost the two most precious people in her world all in one day.

But then Karl Luxemburg would never have been found out. There would have been more hostages, more families destroyed. Whatever unthinkable diabolical event he was planning would have transpired and doubtless more people would have died. The Gerbers were collateral damage. That's the term those in McQueen's line of work used to blunt the pain and rationalize the suffering.

Gustav drove over to Lisa Gerber's home to console her as best he could and to apologize the best he knew how. McQueen contemplated questioning Erich Gerber, but to what end? The Viennese police said he was like a zombie, not saying anything to anyone. Why should he?

Everyone looked like a cop to him. The cops had allowed his father to be killed. Perhaps a judge or jury would take pity on him, consider his circumstances, give him a lenient sentence. Maybe by then the urge to take his own life would pass and he and his dear mother could begin to pick up the pieces and make sense of it all. Would they draw any solace in knowing Franz Gerber had died a hero? What if there were a ceremony of some sort, a proclamation and a plaque to hang on the wall? Would that help? Would it be any consolation if the chancellor of Germany passed along the heartfelt thanks and condolences from a grateful nation?

McQueen heard the outer door of the temporary office he was using open and Gustav's voice greet the secretary assigned to him. He dreaded to hear Gustav recall the agony Mrs. Gerber was going through and how he felt personally responsible for the whole thing.

"How'd it go?"

"Better than I had anticipated," Gustav said.

"Look, you can't blame yourself. Gerber stumbled upon some very dangerous people."

"Yes, he stumbled upon them at my urging."

"He wanted to find out who was behind the kidnappings just like you. He ultimately led us to them. We couldn't save him, but we saved the other hostages and we stopped whatever horrific plot they were planning. That, too, probably saved untold lives. The man's a hero."

Gustav looked as though he was searching for words. He sat down in the chair opposite McQueen and clasped his hands together. It was a side of Gustav that McQueen had never seen before. The veneer was peeled back. After he gathered his thoughts, Gustav began to speak, "Can I tell you something?" He didn't really need McQueen's permission. "I have a confession to make. I have come to the realization that I have been living in denial. And that denial has hampered my ability to do my job properly. The reason I believed the PLO was behind those kidnappings was because I *wanted* to believe they were behind the kidnappings."

"You can't blame yourself," McQueen said.

"Let me finish. My whole country has been in denial. Not that Nazi Germany ever happened, but that it could ever happen again. No, we wallow in our ugly history so much so that we begin to resent the rest of the world for not having the same burden of guilt. If someone comes to our country from America or from England and makes a Hitler joke we get furious. We call them insensitive. The truth is we do not really think they are insensitive to those who died. The reality is we feel they are insensitive to those of us who go on living. We have to live each day with the knowledge that our people allowed a man of such unspeakable evil to come to power in our country. We like to fool ourselves into believing that he forced his way into power or tricked us, but the real truth—the unspoken truth—is we cheered him on, and for that we can never forgive ourselves."

"Look, Gustav—"

"So we tell ourselves there will never be another Nazi Germany. There will never be another Hitler. We outlaw the Nazi swastika and the 'Heil Hitler' salute. We believe banning such symbols eradicates those who would use them. In fact, our government champions freedom by choosing who can be free. We only serve to breed them under the rocks and in the shadows, hidden from sight. Our government and our culture have become less free and more intolerant in the name of freedom and tolerance." His mouth turned up into a sad smile. "It is ironic, is it not? I may not have known Professor Gerber was walking into another Nazi death camp, but I refused to even consider the possibility. Now I mourn with his widow who not only lost a husband today but a son."

"Don't do this to yourself," McQueen said.

Gustav reached in his pocket and produced his phone. "Look at this." He brought up a video and played it for McQueen. It was a rally outside the peace conference in Vienna. An angry man was shouting into a megaphone.

"If you are complacent, then you are part of the problem," the man told the protesters. "You must safeguard that which you possess, that great feeling of comradeship of being part of something bigger than yourself. If you hold on to this, then there is no force in the world that can take it from you. We will be one people bound together as tightly as we are here today. We must be willing to sacrifice all for the cause. In ourselves lies the destiny of the German-speaking people. We will never realize the full potential of the German-speaking people until Anschluss!" The crowd erupted in cheers. "Anschluss!" he repeated to more cheers. "Anschluss!"

Then seemingly out of nowhere, like a swarm of bees, people dressed head-to-toe in black with black bandanas covering their faces ran in and starting beating the man and those listening to him with clubs. Complete chaos ensued. The brawl spread throughout the crowd and police in riot gear rushed in to gain control of the situation. The video ended.

"Anschluss?" McQueen asked.

"The unification of Germany and Austria," Gustav said. "It happened under Hitler."

"Who is that guy?"

Gustav pocketed the phone. "His name is Bruno Kessler. He is supposedly a member of the Socialist Reich Party."

"Supposedly?"

"No one can say for sure if he is a member. The Socialist Reich Party was the first political party banned by the new federal constitution back in 1952. They are still around, but they are impossible to track. As you would imagine, they do not keep a membership roster."

"This guy been on your radar?"

"Only just recently."

"Why just recently?" McQueen asked.

"He was an active member of the SPD, the Social Democratic Party of Germany. That's a mainstream center-left party. All of a sudden he flips to the opposite side of the political spectrum. He is so new to the movement we do not yet know that much about him."

McQueen rose from his seat and began to pace. "This Kessler character said something that hit a nerve. There're a couple of things Luxemburg said on the ride over today that sounded very similar to Kessler."

"What kinds of things?"

McQueen turned to face him. "Luxemburg said I was so complacent and I was part of the problem. Of course, he was into all this 'the Jews are taking over the world' routine. Kessler used the same guilt tactic. He didn't mention the Jews, but he's out in public in Austria. If they arrest you for carrying a Nazi flag, then no telling what they'll do to you for blaming Jews for everything."

"Yes," Gustav said, "if you are found guilty of downplaying Nazi crimes you can go to jail for twenty-five years."

"Kessler told that crowd they had to be ready to sacrifice everything. Luxemburg asked me what I was willing to die for."

"What did you tell him?"

"I told him that I *wasn't* willing to die for a bunch of murderers like him and his followers. And then he just said in passing, 'I am dying for a cause that is bigger than me.' It was so subtle I didn't really catch it at the time. Not 'I *would* die for a cause that is bigger' but 'I *am* dying for a cause that is bigger.' Then as we were exiting the police van just before he was shot he said to nobody in particular. 'Die Revolution lebt.'"

"The Revolution lives," Gustav said.

"Exactly. It's as if he knew he was going to die, but the cause would live on."

There was a knock on the inside of the open doorway. Gustav and McQueen paused their conversation.

"Excuse me, gentlemen," Agent Barton said. "We've finished our background on Luxemburg. This is a little weird. Luxemburg worked as a criminologist for the state of Bavaria in Germany."

"A criminologist?" McQueen asked. "Sure that wasn't just a backstop?"

"It checks out. We talked to his colleagues. He took early retirement a few months ago," she said, "and it gets stranger. His degree is in philosophy, but he majored in archaeology. Most of his writings recovered from Kufstein are on the history of the fortress and what he found in various digs around the fortress. Everything else he wrote was about supplies needed for the men, guard duty schedules, things like that."

"What?" Gustav said. "What about the operation that was supposed to take place tomorrow?"

"He wrote nothing about that. It's almost as if he was just the caretaker. Nothing on any grand scheme or major operation."

"So this goes above Karl Luxemburg." McQueen scratched the

back of his head. "I wonder if there's a chance Erich Gerber knows any more about Luxemburg other than he killed his father."

"Oh, about Erich Gerber," Barton said.

"What about him?" McQueen asked.

"Seems Erich has been a troubled man for some time."

"Troubled?" McQueen asked. "In what way?"

"He didn't have many friends or associates, but the few we talked to said he was always extremely angry, very negative. He had been that way for some time. With someone killing his father, it's not surprising that he would seek revenge. But it seems father and son had a falling out of sorts years ago. Gerber had tried to reach out to him. He made the effort to stay in touch, but Erich never showed much interest. But you know how a father can be. You never stop loving your child. We learned that Professor Gerber recently hired a private investigator to follow Erich. I got his name and number if you think we need to follow up."

"Interesting," McQueen said. "So Erich's father is murdered. He's estranged from him but suddenly feels obligated to avenge his death?"

"And he tries to take his own life in the process?" Gustav said skeptically.

McQueen said, "Maybe we need to have a chat with him."

"Just got back from seeing him," she said. "He's not talking. He's not eating either."

"I wouldn't have much of an appetite after today," McQueen said.

"It's not really that. This is what I found very interesting. He refuses any meal with meat in it." She raised an eyebrow.

Gustav and McQueen looked at each other.

"I want you to call that private eye. See what Gerber was hiring him for."

Barton dialed the number. She lowered her voice and moved several steps away.

"I have a feeling Gerber knew much more was afoot with his son than just anger management problems," McQueen said.

"Do you think it is even possible?" Gustav asked.

"It is. What do you wanna bet we know where this PI followed Erich Gerber?"

Barton hung up the phone. "He says because of client confidentiality he can't tell us *who* Erich Gerber went to see, but he can tell us *where*," she said.

"Let me guess," McQueen said. "He went to Germany."

"Yep."

"Munich, Cologne, and Frankfurt?"

"You got it," Barton said.

"Ho-lee crap!" McQueen ran both hands through his hair in disbelief. He paced back and forth. "So, that list Gerber had. What was it he wrote on there? Known Associates? It was known associates of his own son! Erich Gerber wasn't avenging his father's death today, he was cleaning up his own mess. He followed his father on his trip to Brussels and he got rid of any loose ends he may have unwittingly untied. That's not some poor, pitiful victim sitting in that jail cell," McQueen said, pointing down the hall. "It's him."

"Him? Him who?" Barton asked, sharing a confused look with Gustav.

"The commodore told me about this hit man for the Edda Society who's so terrifying that he makes sure no one betrays the organization," McQueen said. "They call him the Hangman. That psychotic bastard sitting in jail is the Hangman!"

# Chapter Thirty-Three

Sterling McQueen sat alone at a metal table in a small interrogation room. No one-way mirror. No armed guard. Just a single light hanging overhead that cast a glow out to the edges of the room. The keys clanged at the door, then the hinges squeaked, and it slowly opened. A figure in a gray denim shirt and gray denim pants appeared in the doorway. He was coaxed inside by the nudge of the guard behind him who closed the door and locked it leaving the two of them alone. Erich Gerber, his hands cuffed in front of him and his legs chained together, slowly walked to the only open seat and sat down.

McQueen assessed the prisoner for a time then spoke. "I know everything." McQueen's eyes had the look of a poker player holding one card shy of a royal flush.

Erich Gerber rested his forearms on the table. The chains sounded like jingle bells piling atop the metal. "If you knew everything I would not be sitting here and you would not be sitting there." His German accent was clipped and precise.

"Everybody felt sorry for you because your father had been murdered." A scornful scowl came over McQueen's face. "You were the perfect assassin. The grieving son, out of his mind with rage, shoots his father's killer. Who could blame him? What *jury* could blame him? Probably go easy on you. Hell, as guilt-ridden as these people are over Nazis they may give you a medal. You were just doing what needed to be done. Spare the country the embarrassment of putting another Nazi on trial. And the supposed attempted suicide? Nice touch. You wait until the gun is pulled from your head and then you fire. Did you practice that one?"

Erich Gerber continued to stare at the table. A slight smile formed around the edges of his mouth.

"You think you've beat the system," McQueen said. "A warrant from a judge was issued and the private investigator who tailed you to Germany was ordered to turn over all of his files on your case. *All* of them."

"Am I supposed to be concerned?"

"The files confirm that you met with Holger Hensel in Munich. You met with Katharina Amstutz in Cologne. You met with Richard Schneider in Frankfurt."

"Look, Mister…What did you say your name was?"

"I didn't. The private eye's testimony is enough to link you to all three."

"So I met with some people in Germany. That means nothing."

"The fact that they're all dead means plenty. You killed them."

"And why would I do such a thing?"

"Because you slipped up. Because your father was getting suspicious and these people had been compromised. Because you've devoted your life to the Edda Society." He moved closer across the table. "Because you're the one they call the Hangman. These were all burned assets and you had to eliminate them."

Erich Gerber started to laugh. "This all sounds so sinister. I am what? Some assassin from, what did you call this thing I was devoted to? The what Society?"

"Look, you can play coy with me all you want, but you're going to jail for the rest of your life unless you start cooperating."

Gerber leaned back in his chair, hissing contemptuously.

"There's another shoe that's getting ready to drop," McQueen said. "An operation that's going down. I want to know what it is. I want to know when and where. You tell me and I can talk to the authorities here about a lighter sentence."

Gerber leaned forward again. "I will be out of here before your plane lands in Washington, or wherever you are going back to," he said confidently. "You *are* American, I assume. It is not just the accent. Only Americans are arrogant enough to think that they can bribe anyone into talking."

"You handed your father over to Karl Luxemburg. Who in the hell hands over their own father to be killed?"

"My father was worthless!" The anger bubbled up like an unexpected volcano. "Just like his father before him."

McQueen smiled. "I have you figured out."

"Do you indeed?"

"Your father feared your time in Beirut would make you more loyal to Lebanon than to Germany. He was afraid you'd reject your roots. He drilled national pride into your little skull. Even though you were born in Lebanon, even though you're half Lebanese, he wanted you to love Germany. He wanted you to love it more than he had loved it."

"This is all so amusing," Gerber smiled.

McQueen continued, "He didn't want you to long for your home country as he had because your home country was no longer safe. He didn't want you to grow up and leave him and your mother, so he made sure you were exposed to Germany like no one else had ever been. He made sure you loved it. And the thing is, he had no idea what kind of monster he was creating."

"Monster?" Gerber chuckled. "Listen to yourself. You are an American in Austria doing the work the Austrians or Germans are too impotent to do, at the behest of who? The United Nations? NATO? You no longer have any loyalty to your country. If you did, you would not be here now. You are a hired gun and you call *me* a monster?" He leaned back in his chair with a dismissive wave then leaned forward again. "And if the Austrians who let you in here had any loyalty they would kick you out into the street like the dog you are. If they had any loyalty to their country they would have more pride than to allow some other country to tell them what to do."

"Don't lecture me about loyalty. You had no loyalty to your father."

Gerber's chains clanged as he banged the table. "My father was a traitor!" He said again in a more measured tone, "He was a traitor. God, country, family. Is that not what your military teaches you? I have no god."

"Yeah, well, you have no country either. You seem to think this country of yours is pretty pitiful. What did you call it? Impotent?"

He looked McQueen squarely in the eye. "You do not understand loyalty. I am not German. I am not Austrian. Countries are fleeting. Causes are forever. Germany squandered the family fortune and is now relegated to indentured servitude to the Jews who control the West. Germany was emasculated by weak men who turned power over to women. Women who allowed her to be overrun by religious zealots. I long to be part of the greatest society and the greatest people the world will ever know. But first the vermin must be run from Berlin and executed for what they have done to that great nation. Our war will be followed by the thousand-year reign of freedom."

"Wow," McQueen said sarcastically. "Sounds like an old Hitler newsreel. So, you have no intention of saving yourself by helping me."

"I will be glad to watch you die by firing squad instead."

"Not likely with me in street clothes," he pointed at Gerber, "and you in a four-piece suit."

"Mock me if you please, Mr. McQueen, but I will be free soon. I suggest you catch the next flight back to Washington. You do not want to be around when I am."

●

"AND YOU ARE sure you never slipped during the interrogation?" Gustav asked.

"Positive," McQueen said. "He asked, but I never told him my name. Then he called me Mr. McQueen just before I left. We definitely have a haint somewhere and a damn dangerous one." He massaged a stress ball with his right hand. His feet were propped up on the desk.

"Rather difficult to get in front of these people if they already know our every move," Barton said from the other side of the desk.

"OK, let's go over what we know. Professor Gerber had somehow made the connection that Erich was a member of the Edda Society. How?"

"It is a very good question," Gustav said. "If we knew the answer it might open many doors."

"Surely a seasoned professional hit man like Erich Gerber wasn't sloppy enough to just leave evidence lying around." McQueen swung his feet to the floor and sat up in his chair. "Hey, wait a second. What if the evidence didn't look like evidence?" He picked up the phone on the desk and rang the secretary on duty in the outer office.

"Yes," she answered.

"Ms. Sulzberger, how about call over to the evidence room. See if they found any thumb drives in Erich Gerber's apartment with music on them. I'm looking for one with organ music."

"Yes, Mr. McQueen."

He hung up the phone. "That's got to be the key."

"Why do you think that?" Barton asked.

"That's the only thing that ties all of these people together. Schneider, Amstutz, they both had either audio or sheet music of organ music. Hensel was a graduate of a prestigious music school. Gerber had a copy of the organ music and sent a copy to Schmitt. There's bound to be a code in there somewhere and I think Gerber cracked it."

Gustav stroked his mustache. "Then how does Erich Gerber fit in?"

"Professor Gerber's worried about his son, right? He keeps getting more and more distant. Is he on drugs? Is he involved in some criminal enterprise? Gerber decides to search his apartment. He finds the organ music and immediately he knows his son is involved in the very organization he's just uncovered, the Edda Society."

"How do we know that?" Barton asked.

"Because he sent Professor Schmitt a copy of the organ music to get his opinion on it. Obviously he had already somehow tied the organ music to the kidnappings. You with me?" They both nodded. "So, he hires the private eye to follow his son. The guy comes back with a list of three contacts he made. Gerber doesn't want to let you in on what he's discovered yet, Gustav, because he wants to see if he can extract his son from the whole mess before he has to turn the information over to you. That's why he wouldn't give you the information in Vienna before he left. He waited until he got to Brussels to tell you he had the information because he first wanted to make some stops, talk to the people Erich met with, and see if he could find anything out."

"But wait a minute," Barton said. "He's just discovered a dangerous Nazi cell and he's going to simply walk up to each member and confront them?"

Gustav picked up the theory. "No, not as Franz Gerber, our informant, but as Franz Gerber, the father of Erich Gerber. A Mitläufer."

"A what?" Barton asked.

"A Mitläufer," McQueen said. "It's German for 'fellow traveler,' someone sympathetic to the cause. Professor Gerber was pretending that he was a soldier in arms with his son in the cause. If all he does is confirm each person is a member of the society, then he can just turn that information over to Gustav in Brussels and they can arrest them. But I think he was going for something much bigger. In order to save his son he would have to find out who was pulling the strings. That would be information he could bargain with. I'm guessing he was going to make a deal with you, Gustav. The mastermind behind whatever operation they're planning in exchange for letting his son go free."

"And what if Gustav wouldn't take that deal?" Barton asked.

"You're kidding, right? They'd take that deal." McQueen looked over at Gustav. "You'd take the deal, right?"

"We would take the deal," Gustav said.

"And you think he found out about the operation they were planning?" Barton asked.

McQueen said, "I do. That's why they kidnapped him instead of just killing him. They had to find out what he knew and who he told."

"And once he cracked," she said, "they killed him."

"Naturally. We have to figure out what this big operation is they have planned."

"And how do you propose to do that?" Barton asked.

"The code," McQueen said. "It's bound to be in the organ music. That's how Professor Gerber found out what it was."

"Maybe he used a one-time pad?" Barton guessed.

McQueen shook his head. "Too many players, too spread out. A one-time pad would only get him one clue from one piece of music. No, I think he cracked the entire code. That's why they had to take him. I'm going to need a hotel room with a piano."

"Yeah, good luck," Barton said.

"There's bound to be a suite somewhere in this town with a piano. This is the city of music, for God's sake."

Ms. Sulzberger appeared in the doorway. "They found a few thumb drives with music on them in Erich Gerber's apartment. One of them had organ music on it."

McQueen smiled.

"Shall I have them send it over?" she asked.

"Yes, please."

"Oh and the Steigenberger Hotel Herrenhof has suites," Ms. Sulzberger said. "Sorry. I overheard you. Very nice hotel. I think they have a piano in one of them."

"Great!" McQueen said. "See if we can book it for the night." He looked at his watch and grabbed his coat.

"You are leaving?" Gustav said.

"Got an appointment. You gonna be here when I get back?"

"Early morning tomorrow. President Hofsteiner has assigned me to the security detail for Heinrich Müller at the peace conference."

"What about you, Barton?"

"I'm running on fumes after that all-nighter at the fortress. I'm getting some shut-eye."

"Where are you going?" Gustav asked McQueen.

"I gotta see a lady about a flag."

# Chapter Thirty-Four

McQueen climbed the steps of the University of Vienna and entered the hallowed halls of a public institution of higher learning that had been around since 1365. He had an appointment with Professor Magdalena Pfeiffer, Austria's foremost expert in the discipline of political science. She was a handsome woman with long gray hair streaked in white, years past retirement age. McQueen let himself into the dimly lit classroom. The sideways cross with its backwards apostrophe was illuminated on a screen at the front of the room. The very one McQueen had seen hanging on Karl Luxemburg's wall at Kufstein fortress. Professor Pfeiffer studied it intently.

"I've thought a lot about that flag since I first saw it," McQueen said.

"As have I since you first contacted me about it," she said in her educated German accent, not taking her eyes off the image.

"What does it mean?" McQueen asked.

She clicked her remote and the image of a black X with a white background was on the screen. "This is the Southern Nationalist flag in the United States," she said. "Very similar to the flag you found at the fortress. You see this Southern Nationalist flag is obviously inspired by the stars and bars of the Confederate flag. But then I started to think that it did not quite make sense. Why would a Neo-Nazi group from Germany or Austria use a derivative of the Confederate flag? Same thing for the Ku Klux Klan." She clicked to show the Klan emblem. "They use a cross with an apostrophe in the middle similar to the mark on the flag you found. But why use something so American?" She clicked back to the flag found in the fortress, lingered on the image a moment longer, then turned to him. "I have a theory, but before

I tell you what it is I need for you to tell me more about this Karl Luxemburg."

"A nasty Nazi. Not much else to tell."

"A Nazi you say. What makes you think so?"

McQueen laughed. "You're kidding, right?"

"I do not joke about such things. You concluded he was a Nazi. Why?"

"It was obvious from the way he spoke."

"Such as?"

"The vitriol he had toward Jews."

"What did he say about Jews?"

"You know, the same old stuff you hear Nazis say about Jews. How they control the world. How they were controlling me."

"Can you be more specific?"

"He called them hucksters."

"Hucksters?"

"Yes. He said their god was money."

"Interesting," she said. "Tell me if any of this sounds familiar. 'What is the worldly religion of the Jew? Huckstering. What is his worldly God? Money. The emancipation of the Jew is the emancipation of mankind from Judaism.'"

"That's it exactly. How did you know?"

"Because it is from a fairly well-known paper called 'On the Jewish Question.'"

"By Hitler?" McQueen asked.

Professor Pfeiffer smiled and turned back toward the flag. "By Karl Marx."

"Marx? Are you sure?"

"Quite."

"But I thought Marx was a Jew."

"Ethnically, ancestrally, but his father converted to Lutheranism. Marx himself was baptized into the Lutheran church, but neither he nor his father was very religious. His father was a man of the Enlightenment. Karl Marx himself was an atheist."

"So you're telling me Luxemburg wasn't a Nazi? He was a communist?"

244

"Yes. And like Marx he was also born a Jew. Isaac Deutsher, Leon Trosky's biographer, coined a term to describe people like Luxemburg. Non-Jewish Jew. Deutsher once tested God by eating non-kosher food at the grave of a holy person on Yom Kippur. He saw that nothing happened to him, so he became an atheist."

"So you think Luxemburg was a non-Jewish Jew who embraced communism."

"I do. You must understand that communism requires you to reject Judaism and all other religions. Not only that, you reject any notion of country. You are an internationalist. Communists are capable of severing all ties to anything but the Marxist movement. The philosophy Luxemburg was quoting you was most definitely Marxist. Marx built on the work of Gracchus Babeuf. Are you familiar with Babeuf?"

"I'm afraid not."

"François-Noël Babeuf, or Gracchus Babeuf, was a political agitator during the French Revolution. He advocated for a concept called equality of results or equality of outcome."

"Communism."

"Essentially, but the term was not yet widely used. Equality of results was in direct competition with another concept called equality of opportunity. Both were in response to the class system of the royal society. Advocates for equality of opportunity wanted the government to remove the shackles from the common folk that prevented upward mobility. The great British Admiral Jacky Fisher once said, 'We fight God when our social system dooms the brilliant clever child of a poor man to the same level as his father.' In other words, Admiral Fisher believed government had a moral duty to ensure everyone had the opportunity to be all they could be. Babeuf and his followers, on the other hand, believed that government should make all things equal for everyone. He and his followers staged a coup in 1796. Babeuf was beheaded. The failed coup became known as the Conspiracy of the Equals. What else did Luxemburg tell you?"

"I'm trying to remember. He justified violence. Said something about being the Templars of the Grail or something."

Pfeiffer smiled. "'We all know that in the end nothing can be achieved without violence,'" she quoted.

"Yes," McQueen said. "That's it."

"'We shall become the Templars of this Grail, gird the sword round our loins for its sake and stake our lives joyfully in the last holy war which will be followed by the thousand-year reign of freedom.'"

"Yes, that's it exactly. Erich Gerber used the same words about the thousand-year reign."

"Friedrich Engels," Pfeiffer said.

"Engels?"

"Karl Marx's partner in the communist cause."

"Hold on. I'm confused. This sounds just like the Nazis. Aren't fascism and communism at polar opposites of the political spectrum?"

"Quite the contrary," she said. "They're two wings of the same bird. They both share in common control of industry and autocratic rule. Hitler, Mao, Lenin, Stalin, Mussolini. The people these men ruled over cared not about the semantics of political science. Their lives were completely dominated by their government."

"But if fascism and communism are so similar," McQueen asked, "why are they so vehemently opposed to one another?"

"Excellent question." Pfeiffer took a seat at the table. "Down through the ages most major conflicts have been between factions that were actually very close together. It is what Freud called the narcissism of small differences. The theory is that communities, or in this case movements, in close proximity engage in constant conflict. Catholics and Protestants fight over who is the better Christian. The Shias and Sunnis fight over who is the better Muslim. If you dig deeper you will learn that the fight is usually over control. The fascists and the communists are fighting over control. Control over you and me. Most of us would rather be left alone. Fascists and communists are obsessed with controlling everyone else. These fascists and communists have been fighting one another since the 19th century. That is when modern communism became organized. Of course, the brutal Bolshevik Revolution gave communism its bad name. Take a look at this."

She turned to the screen and brought up another image. It was a red circle with 'Antifaschistische' rounding the top in white and 'Aktion' rounding the bottom. In the middle were two waving flags, one black, one red.

"The Anitfa logo," he said.

"Yes it is," she said. "What you Americans call 'An-TEE-fuh' and we in Europe call 'An-tee-FAH.' It is short for Antifascists. This particular logo, however, is from 1932 Germany."

"You're kidding me."

"Not at all." She clicked and brought up the current Antifa logo. It was identical. "They use the traditional communist black and red colors. A black flag and a red flag." She clicked to reveal a flag with a solid red background for the top half, a solid black background for the bottom half, and 'FSLN' in white letters. "The Sandinistas," she said. Click. "The National Liberation Army of Columbia. Communists. Same flag, different lettering." Click. "FAR in Guatemala. Communist. Same flag, different lettering." Click. "The PVP in Uruguay. Communists. Same flag, different lettering." Click. "The MIR. Communists in Chile. You see, Antifa is just another communist group. If you are against the anti-fascists that must make you a fascist. Clever marketing."

"Unbelievable. What about Luxemburg's flag?"

She brought it back up on the screen. "This is very interesting. The colors fit. Red background, black lettering. It stumped me for a time. It looked for the world like a Nazi iron cross laid on its side."

"That's exactly what I thought," McQueen said. "But the backwards apostrophe."

"Yes, that is what I focused on. It is not an apostrophe. It is called a grave accent," she said.

"A what?"

"A grave accent. It is used in many different languages. Haitian, Creole, Italian, Mohawk, Portuguese, Vietnamese. Lots of languages. Then it hit me. That is not an iron cross on its side. It is an 'X.' An 'X' with the grave accent between the top two terminals is Chinese."

"Chinese? What does it mean?"

She clicked to the next slide to show the large Chinese symbol. "Justice."

"Justice?"

"Yes, social justice, peace and justice, fight for justice. Justice is an important word with the communists. You will find it all through their writings and literature. They define social justice as the distribution of wealth and privilege. Capitalists believe wealth is not distributed, it is earned."

"This is incredible," McQueen said. "And we were led to believe that Luxemburg and his cell were Nazis."

"I believe that was intentional. It is a typical Antifa tactic. They want everyone to believe the Nazis are the real threat. To be honest with you, the Nazis are not that smart. There is not a group on earth that has a bigger public relations problem than the Nazis, yet they never change. They still march with swastikas where they can legally do it. They still do the silly Hitler salute. It is the Antifas you really need to worry about. They are crafty enough to disguise their communist roots. And they have, as Lenin was reported to have called them, plenty of useful idiots doing their bidding."

"Useful idiots," McQueen almost said to himself. He felt like just that. He had fallen for the Nazi bait. It was so easy to do. Nazis were so repugnant, so vile, such easy scapegoats. He caught himself. "Surely you're not saying we don't have to worry about the Nazis."

"No, I am not saying that at all," Professor Pfeiffer said. "What I am telling you is the Nazi Party has been marginalized. They still live in this dreamworld of a 1940s-era Hitler utopia. They cannot part with the symbolism of that time, thus they remain exposed for what they are. No one really takes them seriously. Their agenda is not being advanced. The Marxists, on the other hand, position themselves as the anti-Nazis. They equate themselves to the heroes of World War II who vanquished the fascist scourge. They actually learned a great deal from the Nazis. You have to create a common enemy. For the Nazis it was the Jews. For the Marxists it is the Nazis. They have remade themselves into modern-day liberators when their goals and aspirations are just as sinister as the Nazis."

"Is that possible?" McQueen asked.

"Mr. McQueen, please do not misunderstand what I am trying to tell you. Nazism, especially to my people, is the most horrible nightmare imaginable. But the fact is, the Nazis killed far fewer people than the communists. Best estimates are the Nazis killed roughly eleven million non-combatants. The genocide of communism is easily ten times that amount. And the death toll from communism still rises, while Nazism as a government entity is dead and has been for many, many years."

"So you believe communism is far more dangerous."

"Is that not obvious? I can name for you several communist countries. Can you name for me one Nazi country? And these communist countries still imprison, still terrorize, and still murder their own citizens to this day. They are still very much in the business of subversive expansion."

McQueen walked around the table looking at the image of Karl Luxemburg's flag on the screen. The pieces of the puzzle started to fall into place in his mind. "These hostages taken by this group. These billionaires liquidating their assets. This wasn't a money grab to fund terrorism. It was an all-out assault on capitalists and capitalism."

"It would appear so," Professor Pfeiffer said. "They were targeting some of the richest people in the world, apparently. This was forced redistribution of wealth done not by a government but by individuals."

"And we can only assume that some of these so-called charities these billionaires were forced to give to are run by these Marxists."

"That would be a pretty good bet," she said. "When communists talk about redistribution it usually means redistribution to them."

"So we didn't cut off the head of the snake when we captured Karl Luxemburg," McQueen said. "And whatever was going to happen is still going to happen. Then what about this Edda Society?"

"It is obviously a decoy," Pfeiffer said.

"A decoy?"

"Yes. You indicated when you contacted me that your Agent Wagner believed the Edda Society was a myth. He was correct. These Antifa people exploited that myth."

McQueen said, "We were supposed to uncover the Edda Society to give credence to this notion that the Nazis were on the rise again?"

"Exactly." She shuffled through some papers on the table. "You asked me to research something called the Chopin Cultural Center."

"Yes, the people who were murdered were all part of it," McQueen said.

"This is what kept me searching for the truth on that flag. This group has its origins in America. They were part of a list I uncovered."

"A list?" McQueen asked.

"Yes. President Truman tasked his attorney general in 1948 with compiling a list of communist front groups in the United States. One of those listed was the Chopin Cultural Center."

"We thought it was a front for the Edda Society," McQueen said. "The Edda Society was actually a front for the Chopin Cultural Center."

"Yes, and what ties this German incarnation of the group together is they are not only experts in music, they are all vegetarians," she said.

*And so is Erich Gerber,* McQueen thought. Erich Gerber was killing fellow Marxists. The Hangman was cleaning up his own mess. How could a kid brought up in such a nurturing environment turn out to be such a monster? He looked at the professor. "Do you know anything about a guy named Bruno Kessler?"

"He was active in the Social Democratic Party of Germany," Pfeiffer said.

"And then he switched sides," McQueen said.

She nodded. "To the Socialist Reich Party. It appears Herr Kessler has been playing the role of agitator."

"Agitator?"

"Yes, it is a familiar Antifa tactic. Kessler's job was to work up the Nazis so the Antifa people looked like the heroes. You hear someone spouting off like Adolf Hitler to an adoring crowd then people appear on the scene and beat them senseless. The public tends to rally behind a group like that."

"To build sympathy for their cause," McQueen said.

"Exactly. They define the battle lines. You are either with the Nazis or you join Antifa to fight the Nazis. They leave you no other option. This Antifa movement has allowed the Marxists to advance their agenda far beyond what would ordinarily be possible simply because they prey on the fears of politicians who believe there is nothing worse than being labeled a Nazi sympathizer. There is certainly something much worse than being labeled a Nazi sympathizer, Mr. McQueen. What is worse is becoming a useful idiot for the Marxists. What these politicians should fear most is a movement that long ago vowed to bring down the West from within without firing a shot. From what you have uncovered, it appears they are doing just that."

# Chapter Thirty-Five

McQueen checked into the Steigenberger Hotel consumed with the notion of a coded message. The very fact that Professor Gerber had tracked down three of the members indicated he had come across some kind of information. If the puzzle was in those notes McQueen was determined to find it.

He found the black lacquer baby grand piano in the suite just as Ms. Sulzberger had said. He listened to the music that each of the Chopin Cultural Center members had listened to. A piece by Chopin was the trigger. The odd pieces of music always followed a piece by Chopin. He pulled out the sheet music from Schneider's apartment. He poured himself a cup of coffee and sat down at the piano. Playing the piece gave him no sense of a code. He moved forward from various keys on the keyboard starting with middle C just below the 'N' in the STEINWAY & SONS logo and worked his way up and then back down the keyboard again. No pattern was evident. Another cup of coffee. He tried skipping keys in different intervals—two, three, four, and so forth—and got nothing. He took a break to think, pacing back and forth clasping the bridge of his nose with his index finger and thumb.

He played the piece on the piano again in the hopes that something in the music would hit him or stir him. There was nothing. He then had the notion that, perhaps, the messages were in Latin. Another cup of coffee. He reworked each experiment he'd tried before in the new language. Nothing. Then he tried Greek. Nothing. Then German. He banged the keys of the piano. His exhaustion was winning the battle against the caffeine.

He took another break and collapsed on the sofa in a defeated heap wondering how long he would torture himself with this puzzle. Maybe it was never a code to begin with, he fretted. Perhaps Gerber had discovered the truth by other means. If that was the case, this had all been a colossal waste of time. He'd never find out what was happening having squandered precious hours on some incredible presupposition that an assortment of Antifas were clever enough to hide a message in a song. But they were clever enough to fool everyone into thinking they were Islamic terrorists and then Nazis.

Just as night was turning to day McQueen drifted off into a deep sleep. He dreamt of piano keys and musical clefs. His mind drifted back to his code-breaking training. The instructor slowly paced between the classroom desks observing the work of his students. Raw recruits feverishly worked the problem in front of them. McQueen wrote letter after letter as if it were being dictated to him. He quietly turned his paper over. The rest of the class groaned. The instructor walked to his desk and turned the paper over. GENERAL DONOVAN IS CONSIDERED THE FATHER OF MODERN AMERICAN INTELLIGENCE GATHERING, McQueen had written. The instructor smiled.

"The next code was actually intercepted from the Soviet Union in 1986," the instructor said.

The students shuffled their papers to the next problem.

The instructor looked at his stopwatch. "Go."

The students began poring over the complex code. Almost immediately, McQueen began writing. The instructor looked at his stopwatch. Others began writing almost a minute into the exercise. Just before two minutes had clicked over, McQueen turned his paper over. The instructor clicked the stopwatch. The class groaned again.

Musical notes danced in his head. Images of Mozart and Bach at their pianos floated by. He could see the notes rising from the instruments like smoke from a fire. Kings applauded. The masters took bows.

And then the images started playing in his mind in reverse. The great composers backed up to their seats and sat down. The kings seemed to be unapplauding. The masters' fingers bounced unnaturally across their keyboards. Musical notes were sucked back into the pianos. The images grew faster and faster and faster. The instructor back in class mouthed a slow-motion 'No!' He took McQueen's paper and ripped it into shreds and threw the remains into the air. They drifted to the ground as notes. When they hit they exploded. The students in the classroom frantically dashed from their desks for cover. The room shook. Then an even louder concussion. Pieces of wall exploded. McQueen looked around. His classmates were all in military camouflage. One was screaming into a field radio for help. The others scrambled to evade incoming mortar fire. It was bedlam.

McQueen looked over in horror. His instructor was screaming at him, but the words were muffled. He tried to read his slow moving lips. "You...got...the...code...wrong." *What*, McQueen thought. Impossible. He knew he had deciphered it correctly. Again the instructor screamed in slow motion, "You...got...the...code—" A mortar shell hit and blew him to bits. Then images started flashing past his eyes backwards. Images from his current mission. Gustav talking to him but walking in reverse. Colonel Bragg giving him instructions. The operation in Kufstein. Then the man in Madrid. McQueen clawed at the lamp cord but it was moving further and further away from him. He scrambled harder and harder to reach it, but he couldn't. The man retrieved his gun from the floor. He lifted it slowly and pointed it at McQueen. Nowhere to run. No way to hide. McQueen tried to scream, but no words came from his mouth. The man pulled the trigger. McQueen heard the loud bang of the gun and braced himself for the impact. He closed his eyes as tight as he could and screamed.

And then he was awake. He blinked his eyes to make sure. The morning sun began to shine slivers of light through the half-opened blinds onto the edge of the baby grand. He popped upright on the sofa. It hit him.

He almost leapt from the sofa and back to the keyboard. He picked out the notes, one by one, and wrote a corresponding letter on the notepad. The letters were gibberish at first, but then he began to see recognizable words. His heart pounded with excitement. It was like a 3D stereogram he had seen at a novelty shop once. The kind of picture you have to stare at for minutes until the hidden 3D image comes into focus. He had been staring at this one for hours and it was right there all along. The human brain is conditioned to see the usual and sometimes misses the obvious. And like that 3D image that finally comes into focus, the code was clear and detailed and it was marvelous.

This particular musical code was brilliant in its simplicity. It started at the high A note on the keyboard and worked its way *backwards*, not forwards. Whole notes signaled the beginning and end of sentences. Quarter notes were used for the individual letters. Half notes were used to separate words. The words were in German. Yes, it was ingenious. Entire songs could be written with short words or phrases sprinkled here and there. One had only to look for the whole notes as the brackets around the messages and ignore the rest. The music might sound a bit odd for a measure or two, but the rest of it would be built around the message so that nothing really sounded out of place. He read the deciphered message.

*Schneider Amstutz Hensel to coordinate Berlin abductions. Hensel has access as graduate. Prepare extraction team. Coordinate with Hensel.*

The two hostages in Berlin had been abducted leaving a concert, McQueen remembered. Hensel had apparently used his access to the music school to give the kidnappers inside information. McQueen scrambled for the latest piece of sheet music and placed it on the piano stand. Using his newly discovered decoder, he found the whole notes then decoded each note between them. It was a tedious task of making sure the note was a high or middle or low note. When he was done he had a message. It was the message transmitted the night before the raid on the fortress at Kufstein. He translated from German to English.

*Project Mazdak on schedule. Explosive transported to site.*

An explosive has been transported? Where? When is the operation? The message didn't say. And what was the significance of the word Mazdak? He fished in his pocket for Professor Pfeiffer's phone number and dialed it.

"Professor, this is Sterling McQueen. I apologize for bothering you again, but I came across a word in a deciphered code and I was hoping you could tell me what it means."

"I would be glad to help," she said.

"The word is Mazdak. M-A-Z-D-A-K."

"Mazdak was a Persian Zoroastrian priest back in the fifth century. Are you familiar with the Zoroastrians?"

"I'm afraid not."

"The Zoroastrians followed the teachings of Zoroaster, an ancient prophet from around 1000 BC. He was also known as Zarathustra."

"Like Richard Strauss's Zarathustra?" McQueen asked.

"Yes, Strauss wrote *Also sprach Zarathustra*, Thus Spoke Zarathustra, the piece that became better known as the theme for the movie 2001: A Space Odyssey. Mazdak went against Zoroastrian teachings with the philosophy of free love, communal possessions, and redistribution of wealth. Very radical notions for his time."

"So, he was basically the Abbie Hoffman of the day."

"You could say that," she said. "It is one of the earliest examples of communism. But the Mazdakites were not peaceful flower children. This redistribution of wealth and sharing of possessions came by force. He converted the gullible King Kobad who demanded a miracle of Mazdak before he would join his religion and was fooled by a fire that spoke to him. The speaking fire was actually one of Mazdak's men hidden behind the altar. Once he had the blessing of the king, Mazdak was able to do as he pleased. The rich became poor, the poor became rich. Women were stolen from their husbands and shared with everyone in the cult."

"What happened to them?"

"That's still debated. Some say Kobad's son had them all killed when he ascended to the throne. Jewish tradition says Mazdak was defeated by the Jews in the year 495. The Mazdakites were never fully wiped out. Some historians claim they melded with the more radical elements of Shia Islam."

"Pretty clever," McQueen said. "If the name of the operation were ever exposed, then people would assume it was an Islamic terrorist plot."

"Probably. Something else you might find interesting as it pertains to the Chopin Cultural Center we were talking about last night. Mazdak was also a huge advocate of vegetarianism."

"That would certainly fit," McQueen said.

"It is said that to kill a rich man was sanctioned by Mazdak, but to kill even a lowly insect was a punishable crime."

"It's amazing how much this communist leader sounded like Hitler."

"The narcissism of small differences," she said.

"Thanks so much for the information."

"My pleasure, Mr. McQueen. Auf Wiedersehen."

McQueen decoded the message that was sent the day prior. *Stand by for activation,* the message said, but there were no details about the operation itself. He went back in chronological order deciphering the messages. There were several references to hostages and the various cities in which they were kidnapped. Then a message made his heart stop.

*Project Mazdak scheduled for two August exactly at eleven.*

The second of August. Today! McQueen looked at his watch. It was ten forty-five. *Think,* he told himself. What was the significance of Mazdak? Then it hit him. That had to be it. It all fit. He grabbed his jacket and bolted from the room.

# Chapter Thirty-Six

Dignitaries and their guests mingled and chatted in the back of the great hall. A small ensemble was seated to one side performing Le quattro stagione, The Four Seasons, Concerto No. 1 in E Major, La primavera, or The Spring, by Antonio Vivaldi. Just a little more than a block away, McQueen ran out onto Herrengasse and turned left past the umbrellaed tables in front of the hotel. He ran the full city block dodging pedestrians and horse-drawn carriages until he reached the cobblestone roundabout at Michaelerplatz. The protesters were thick, ringed by riot police. McQueen pushed his way through until he came to the entrance of Hofburg Palace.

"I need to talk to whoever's in charge of security for the peace conference," he told one of the guards who kept the mob at bay.

"Who are you?" the man insisted over the crowd noise.

There was no way McQueen could tell him. He didn't carry any official ID. He looked past the man at the delegates who were filing by. "I have urgent business. I need to talk to your chief of security."

"Is there a problem?"

"Yes, there's a problem. Look, I'm an American. I've been working with the BND. I—" He looked up to see Gustav walking just inside with the German delegation. "Gustav!" he waved frantically.

It took him a moment to catch his eye. Gustav hurried over to the entrance.

"We have to talk," McQueen said.

Gustav looked at the guard then flashed his BND credentials. "He is with me."

McQueen bypassed the metal detectors. "Where's the peace conference?"

"Festival Hall," Gustav said.

"Take me there."

Gustav started walking. "What is going on?"

McQueen hurried their pace. "There's a plot to assassinate the Israeli prime minister. He's getting an award today, isn't he?"

"Yes."

"At eleven," McQueen said.

"Yes. President Kaiser is giving the award. How did you know?"

"I cracked the code. It said Project Mazdak is today at eleven."

"Mazdak?"

"Long story, but the name is what lets me know it's a plot to kill the Israeli prime minister. Project Mazdak is about pitting the Muslims against the Jews. What do you think would happen in the Middle East if Muslim terrorists were successful in killing the Israeli prime minister? All of these kidnappings and killings and blaming them on Muslims has been leading up to this moment. They've already planted in everyone's minds that Muslims are kidnapping and killing Jews. Then they kill the Israeli prime minister? All hell breaks loose."

"This is incredible," Gustav said, "if it is true."

"It's true."

"What more do you have to go on?"

"Just the decoded message," McQueen admitted.

"We cannot go shutting down the peace conference on such unsubstantiated evidence."

"You're right." McQueen looked down at his watch. "It's ten 'til now. We don't have much time."

Gustav asked, "Have you checked in with the colonel?"

"And tell him what? That I've uncovered some conspiracy to assassinate the Israeli prime minister in some organ music?"

"He might believe you."

"Yeah and he also might tell me to stand down. You said President Kaiser is giving the award?"

"Yes."

"Then it all makes sense."

"What makes sense?" Gustav asked.

"I know who the haint is."

"Who?"

They rounded the corner to the hallway that led to Festival Hall.

"Let me worry about that," McQueen said. "You're BND. You can't be a part of this. Plausible deniability and all that."

"Sterling, what are you up to?"

They stopped in front of the huge doors that were guarded by plainclothes officers from the Austrian Federal Police. They could hear the music from the ensemble even before the door opened. Gustav showed his identification and they entered the great hall through the middle of three large wooden doors.

Festsaal, or Festival Hall, was the largest hall at the Hofburg at almost 11,000 square feet. It was originally built as a throne room but never used as one. It served primarily as a concert hall. Six gigantic chandeliers hung on either side of three ceiling paintings by Alois Hans Schramm which glorified the Habsburg Monarchy.

At the front of the venue was a red carpeted stage large enough for a small orchestra. Two large marble columns at the rear of the stage framed a red curtain covering a wall with the logo of the United Nations in the center. Below it was a lectern and a thin black microphone. They squeezed through the crowd toward the front of the room. Security officers were stationed all around.

McQueen spotted Leopold Hofsteiner, head of the BND. He quickly turned his back toward him and faced Gustav. "I need to see what's behind that curtain."

"Sterling," Gustav scolded.

McQueen disappeared into the sea of humanity.

The lights flickered and everyone moved toward their seats.

Just a few miles away a SWAT team assembled at the end of a residential street. Soldiers and plainclothes officers quietly signaled one another. Elite Cobras were dressed head to toe in black. The plexiglass visors on their helmets were in the up position. Armed with Steyr AUGs and a battering ram they led the small contingent down the street.

The seats at Festival Hall filled from the rear all the way to the front. After the guests had been seated, Heinrich Müller, the president of the German Bundestag, took to the stage.

Ten fifty-five. Gustav stood near the front and off to the side. He unwrapped a sucker and stuck it in his mouth.

Colonel Bragg's helicopter skimmed just above the trees. The landscape blurred beneath it.

"Has McQueen checked in?" Bragg said into his headset.

"No, sir," the officer back at the Battle Room responded.

Bragg exhaled and looked out the window. "Let me know as soon as you hear from him. Understood?"

"Understood, sir."

The audience ended their conversations as Müller approached the podium and they politely applauded upon recognizing him. He returned a grateful smile, removed his watch, laid it on the podium, then announced with great fanfare, "Ladies and gentlemen, I present the president of the Federal Republic of Germany, President Sebastian Kaiser!"

The hall erupted into applause and the assemblage stood and turned its attention toward the rear of the hall. President Kaiser walked the center aisle. He smiled and waved amiably to the crowd.

McQueen looked around in the dark storage area backstage. Folded tables and chairs were stacked neatly. He spotted a black tablecloth. He grabbed it and scanned the room.

Once President Kaiser had taken his seat, Müller began his second introduction.

"Ladies and gentlemen, I present the prime minister of the state of Israel, Prime Minister Shamay Mizrahi!" The same reception greeted the Israeli prime minister who waved politely— minus the grin—and took his seat. When the standing ovation was over, Müller began the introduction for the Peace Award.

McQueen spotted what he was looking for. A plastic receptacle that held silverware. He grabbed a knife and cut the black tablecloth then ripped it the rest of the way.

The SWAT team rounded a corner. Alarmed residents peered wide-eyed through windows and cracked doors. The unit proceeded silently up the street.

"Your Majesties, Your Royal Highnesses, Heads of State, Heads of Government, Excellencies, distinguished guests, ladies and gentlemen," Müller began. "The strength of nations is too often judged by their use of might. History is filled with stories of nations that conquered other nations, but to what end? To enslave their people or, worse, to wipe them out completely. These are not stories to be glorified. The Roman Empire, the Ottoman Empire, the Han Dynasty, yes, even the Habsburg Dynasty that gave us this opulent palace, all built on brute force. This was in a less civilized world, a world which only appreciated the utter domination of one civilization over another. I say to you here and now the days of utter domination by *any* civilization are over!"

The audience applauded enthusiastically. Gustav looked at his watch. Three minutes until eleven.

"There is a new measure by which we judge the strength of nations. That is by their level of restraint. It is easy to use your power to bully the other nations of your region. The more laudable act is to use your power to de-escalate a crisis. That is why we honor the state of Israel today with this special peace citation. They have shown remarkable restraint in the face of the latest Middle East crisis and have chosen not to escalate an already difficult situation. We applaud them. Once again, I give you President Sebastian Kaiser and Prime Minister Shamay Mizrahi!"

Müller finished his introduction to thunderous applause, but before the president and prime minister could even rise from the seats McQueen emerged from behind the large curtain behind the podium, his face covered from the top of his nose down by a makeshift black bandana. He pulled Müller to him, his Sig pointed at the base of the man's skull.

The security teams for both world leaders sprang into action as their training had taught them. Their job was to get their charges out of harm's way, which is exactly what they did with great haste. The audience screamed as Kaiser and Mizrahi were whisked from the room. All the better as far as McQueen was concerned.

The remainder of the guests at the Hofburg watched on in horror. McQueen pulled the figure of Müller up to the microphone. "I swear to you I'll kill him if you don't back off!"

The armed men who had crept up the first couple of steps of the dais hesitated then looked at one another and slowly backed down. Gustav looked over at Hofsteiner. His eyes were glued to Sterling McQueen.

"I'm not a terrorist," McQueen continued. "I didn't come here to terrorize. I came here to expose a plot. This man's a murderer," he announced to those present as well as the worldwide television audience that had joined the drama in progress. An audible gasp was heard in the great hall. "He's behind the recent kidnappings that have been blamed on Muslim terrorists."

Müller managed a nervous but condescending laugh. "Nonsense!"

"He was behind the conspiracy with Karl Luxemburg as well as Luxemburg's murder yesterday. And he came here today to kill President Kaiser and Prime Minister Mizrahi and ascend to the presidency of Germany."

"This is preposterous!" Müller shouted indignantly.

McQueen grabbed Müller's wristwatch from the podium and shoved it in front of his face. Müller looked nervously down at the second hand.

"He planned to carry out this assassination at exactly eleven. That's fifty seconds from right now. He denies it. Well, then, we'll all wait here together to see who's right."

The crowd exchanged puzzled looks. All wait together? What in the world could he mean?

"He's a lunatic!" Müller cried out defiantly. Sweat was thick on his brow. His eyes darted from side to side taking inventory of the police presence in the room.

"Forty seconds!" McQueen shouted.

Müller's mouth was dry. His breath was short. He tried to force a confident smile.

"Thirty seconds," McQueen announced calmly.

"Is no one going to do anything?" Müller shouted.

"What's wrong, Heinrich? If you have nothing to hide, what's the rush?"

The SWAT team came to a stop on the sidewalk. The Cobras parted and allowed the soldier with the battering ram to the front.

"Twenty seconds."

"Kill him!" Müller shouted.

"Tell them the truth!" McQueen screamed.

"Somebody do something!" Müller was sobbing.

"Tell them the truth!"

The team leader held his free hand high and looked over his soldiers to make sure everyone was in place. He dropped his hand and the soldiers moved rapidly up the walkway toward the stone house.

Müller made one final plea. "Help me! Please!"

McQueen paused an agonizing moment. "Ten!"

Müller could hardly get the words out. "Yes! Yes! He is right! Everything he has said is true! Please!"

The crowd gasped in collective shock. Less than five seconds remained. McQueen snatched Müller away from the lectern and ran with him like an awkwardly heavy rag doll. McQueen counted in his head. Three...two...one. He threw Müller and himself to the floor just as his internal clock ticked to zero. The Sig clattered across the floor.

The battering ram knocked the front door of the house off its hinges. The soldiers stormed into the residence with guns drawn fanning out through every room.

The explosion splintered the lectern into a million pieces and propelled the two bodies across the stage. They slid to a stop at the edge. The crowd was shrieking, but McQueen could barely make it out. He wasn't quite sure if he was still conscious. Smoke was thick in the air. Bits and pieces of the podium rained down upon his back. Humans scrambled over other humans clawing themselves away from the blast site as quickly as possible.

The smoke began to lift itself toward the ceiling of the great hall. McQueen heard shouts through the muffled pumping of his own heart. He looked around to take inventory of the situation. Most everyone had pushed themselves away from the blast site. The crowd had bottle-necked at the three massive doors at the rear of the hall. Those closest to McQueen kept shoving forward, looking over their shoulders with screams of terror.

Police—the ones who hadn't been knocked off their feet—hurried in McQueen's direction. Gustav pushed ahead of them. McQueen sat up. Debris fell from his back, the black bandana now almost entirely soot gray. He looked over at the pathetic figure of Müller lying in the fetal position sobbing a few feet away, and, for a glint of a moment, he actually felt sorry for him. Then Müller turned over on his back to reveal McQueen's gun in his hand. He pushed himself to a sitting position with his free arm. McQueen knew there would be no negotiation. Once Müller stood upright he took more careful aim and that's when McQueen heard the gunshots. Two of them in rapid succession.

McQueen flinched when he saw the smoke leave the muzzle of his own gun. Then he watched Müller clutch his shooting arm with his free hand and fall to his knees in agony. The Sig dropped harmlessly to the floor. The first shot had hit him just above the elbow as he pulled the trigger. Müller's bullet lodged into the floor of the stage just beyond McQueen's left shoulder. In the echo of the great hall McQueen couldn't quite decipher from which direction the bullet had come. His Sig was now lying on the stage in front of him.

"She is with us!" Gustav shouted, hoisting his identification in the air for the rest of the security team to see.

McQueen did a double take and smiled.

Slowly walking up the steps of the stage with her gun still drawn was Vivian Barton.

Two officers rushed to Müller's side to assess his wound.

"I'm losing count," Barton said with a sly smile offering McQueen a hand. "Are we even now or do you owe me one?"

The polizei wrested Müller from the ground and the rubble, his tears cutting paths through the caked-on dust on his face. He was handcuffed and led away, his legs buckling beneath him.

McQueen retrieved his gun from the stage and holstered it. He was reminded of what Alexander the Great once said: An army of sheep led by a lion is better than an army of lions led by a sheep. Heinrich Müller had disguised himself as a lion, but he was nothing more than a pitiful weeping little lamb.

"The colonel has ordered us to the gray house," Gustav said. "Says it is urgent."

"Josefstadt?" McQueen asked through the dirty bandana.

"Yes."

"What's up?"

"They have arrested the ringleader of the Chopin Cultural Center."

# Chapter Thirty-Seven

Müller's chief of security would be arrested for planting the bomb and conspiracy to commit murder—two counts—as well as treason. Richard Schneider was apparently not working alone inside the German Ministry of Foreign Affairs. The deputy foreign minister would also be arrested on conspiracy and treason charges and multiple counts of kidnapping and murder, if the charges could be made to stick. Various other minor players would be arrested in the weeks to come, but it was doubtful if everyone involved was apprehended or ever would be. The planners of this conspiracy were too careful to keep the pieces separated from the whole. Heinrich Müller himself would be tried for multiple counts of murder, kidnapping, conspiracy, treason, and various other crimes against the state.

Nothing, however, would compare to the shock back at the gray house. The team was escorted to an observation room where Colonel Bragg was waiting at a table. The room had a full window view of the interrogation room. Black curtains covered the window.

"We'll talk about your little off-road experience in a bit," Bragg said to McQueen around his unlit cigar. "First, I thought you'd all like to see this. It took us some time to piece all this together. There's a long history in communist conspiracies to compartmentalize. Dating back to the early 1800s, they developed a practice of establishing small communities of 3 to 12 members, totally unknown to each other, and each adopting a code name for themselves."

"A cell," Gustav said.

"Yes, exactly," Bragg said. "One of the cells instrumental in Project Mazdak was the Chopin Cultural Center, but there have been dozens, probably hundreds, of others. Innocuous names like the Citizens Protective League and the Committee for Peace and Brotherhood

Festival. Few if any of the groups know the full picture. Apparently Luxemburg was in charge of the operation in Kufstein, but it's impossible to know how far up the food chain he was. Given what we found out at the fortress, it appears he was little more than a glorified warden. But we now know who was involved in the Chopin Cultural Center."

"And how do you know?" Gustav asked.

"Hofsteiner," Bragg said.

"My boss at BND? Leopold Hofsteiner?"

"Yes. Hofsteiner apparently became suspicious of Heinrich Müller. We gave him a dye tracer. Hofsteiner and I agreed to the disinformation he would feed Müller and then we just waited for it to surface."

"And it did, obviously," Barton said.

"And it did," Bragg said. "You were that dye tracer, McQueen. On the train to Zurich."

"The one that almost got me killed in Basel?"

"Yes. Hofsteiner let Müller know you would be on that train. No one else knew but the three of us."

"And that's why you had the BND agent shadow me," McQueen said.

"Actually, that was Hofsteiner's idea," Bragg said. "Frankly, I didn't think you'd need it. When Agent Jäger killed that guy we knew Müller was the haint, but we still didn't have the full picture of the plot. When you went incommunicado I figured you'd cracked the code. We knew wherever Müller was that's where whatever they were up to was going down. That's when I sent Barton to the Hofburg."

McQueen looked at her and she took a head bow with a smile.

"You probably thought you'd have a hard time convincing me Müller was the guy," Bragg continued, "so you started ad libbing, as you're prone to do." He pointed a thumb at Gustav. "I knew this one would follow you anywhere, so Hofsteiner sent orders through the intelligence services on the ground at Hofburg to give you a wide berth. And Agent Barton here was there to pull you out of the fire."

"Yeah, well, I appreciate that," McQueen said, "but a solid body shot would've been preferable."

"That was on my order," Bragg said. "Top brass wanted him alive. I suspect they need a trophy after all we've been through."

"And the rest of the Chopin Cultural Center ring?" McQueen asked.

"We raided Müller's office in Berlin. Got a copy of his phone records. He wasn't a member of the ring, but he was conspiring with them to pull off this assassination. As for the Chopin ring, we think we've located all of 'em. About a dozen all told. BND and Austrian Federal Police are rounding up the rest as we speak."

"You have the leader here?" Gustav asked.

"Yes," Bragg said, "and I think you'll find this particularly interesting." He nodded to the officer by the window and he pulled the curtain.

Sitting at the interrogation table chained to the top and looking around distastefully was the last person any of them ever expected to see sitting there.

"I do not believe it," Gustav said.

"Oh my God," McQueen said.

Vivian Barton brought her hand up to her closed mouth and shook her head.

Gustav said, "That little bitch."

The angry expression on the ringleader's face masked the beauty Gustav Wagner had witnessed on several occasions before. The leader of the Chopin Cultural Center Marxist cell was Lisa Gerber.

"I do not think I can even comprehend this," Gustav said softly.

Bragg said, "Well, y'all were wondering how an upper middle-class German like Erich Gerber can be radicalized. There sits your answer."

"What's her story?" McQueen asked. "What would drive a woman to participate in her own husband's torture and murder?"

"Professor Gerber got too curious for his own good," Bragg said. "He was so concerned about his son's erratic behavior that he had him tailed. Once he started interviewing the people Erich met with he ran the risk of exposing the entire ring. Erich was dispatched to clean it up."

"Did Gerber know about his wife's involvement?" Barton asked.

"No, poor bastard," Bragg said. "She was operating the ring right under his nose. She's the one who composed all the organ codes that were coming out of Kufstein."

Gustav's mind flashed back to his first meeting with Professor

Gerber. "Do you play?" he had asked the professor after seeing the baby grand piano in the parlor. "My wife," Gerber had said. "A woman of many talents." Many talents indeed.

"That's why he was such easy pickings in Brussels," Bragg continued. "Aside from Gustav and his team, Lisa Gerber was the only one who knew where he was staying. She gave him up to Luxemburg and his men."

"What kind of person would do that?" Barton asked.

"Someone who's totally committed to the cause," Bragg said. "Her father was killed by a suicide bomber. We have pretty good intel now on who that suicide bomber was."

"Who?" Barton asked.

Bragg took the unlit cigar from his mouth. "Her father."

"Wait a minute," McQueen said. "He was an Islamic terrorist?"

"That's something the general public isn't aware of," Bragg said. "Most of the suicide bombers in Lebanon have been secular. Groups like the Lebanese Communist Party. She was literally born to do this."

"A sleeper?" Gustav asked.

Bragg nodded. "Both she and her father were followers of the teachings of Mahdi 'Amel who was leader of the Marxist movement in Lebanon until his assassination in 1987. He was a professor at the Lebanese University in Beirut, the same university she worked for and the same place she met her husband. Seems unlikely she just showed up out of the blue. In all probability she was assigned to Gerber, maybe because his father had been a member of the party but turned them in to the Americans. They ultimately killed him along with all the other people on that train. Maybe they thought they could turn Franz Gerber because his father had been a member. Maybe they just wanted to keep an eye on him if they foresaw that Gerber would be utilized by Western intelligence because of his unique expertise."

"Unbelievable," McQueen said.

"Believe it," Bragg said, "it's something normal people have a hard time getting their minds around, but it's as old as the Soviet Union. If you thought Marxist zealots died with the fall of the Berlin Wall, take a look through that window."

Barton said, "It's hard to fathom that someone could be so

committed to a cause, so brainwashed, that they would sacrifice their whole family for it."

"And there's something else we all have to understand." He pointed with his cigar to the pitiful image of Lisa Gerber dressed in prison gray on the other side of the glass. "There are more out there just like her." He plopped the cigar back in his mouth. "A lot more. Evil doesn't grow in a vacuum. Its seeds are planted. Its leaves are carefully tended. It grows tall and strong through years of nurturing. You're looking at the patient gardener."

●

STERLING MCQUEEN PULLED the Mercedes into the garage. He decided he'd come back and retrieve his luggage after he'd had a chance to relax. He walked up the dock toward his boat. Ransy called after him. He recognized the voice and turned to greet the almost out of breath young man who trotted up behind him.

"Mr. McQueen, this came for you special delivery yesterday morning."

"Thank you, Ransy." McQueen took the small package wrapped in plain brown paper with international postage markings. "Everything go OK with the boat while I was gone?"

"Yes, sir. I cleaned the deck real good. Polished the chrome just like you taught me. Me and the Cap'n changed the oil in both engines. She's runnin' great."

"Fantastic." They continued to walk. "I'll pay you Friday. Just get me your hours. I also owe you a boat ride. When's your next day off?"

"Tuesday!"

"Tuesday it is. Meet me at the boat at eight a.m. Oh, and bring your fishing pole."

"Yes, sir!" Ransy said then scampered off to tell his boss.

McQueen continued onto his boat, unlocked the door to the main salon, and stepped down into the awaiting luxury. Locking the door behind him, he placed the package on the coffee table and fixed himself a brandy. After a slow sip, he reached for the package and gingerly began to cut through the taped seams with a Christofle letter opener that he picked up on a trip to Paris. The first glimpse inside the paper revealed a book. It was a copy of *A Perfect Spy* by John Le Carré. He opened the book to the title page and found a notecard-sized envelope. He lifted the envelope from the page and immediately noticed the signature of the author. He opened the envelope with the letter opener and removed the note card. "Something for your collection," the note read. "Gustav."

McQueen turned to the copyright page. First British edition. Another envelope, this one standard-size. McQueen opened it and emptied its contents. A twenty, a twenty, and a ten. Fifty American dollars.

CPSIA information can be obtained
at www.ICGtesting.com
Printed in the USA
BVHW03*2101130618
518946BV00006B/67/P